WAYWORN LOVERS

Praise for Gun Brooke's Fiction

Fierce Overture

"Gun Brooke creates memorable characters, and Noelle and Helena are no exception. Each woman is 'more than meets the eye' as each exhibits depth, fears, and longings. And the sexual tension between them is real, hot, and raw."—*Just About Write*

Coffee Sonata

"In *Coffee Sonata*, the lives of these four women become intertwined. In forming friendships and love, closets and disabilities are discussed, along with differences in age and backgrounds. Love and friendship are areas filled with complexity and nuances. Brooke takes her time to savor the complexities while her main characters savor their excellent cups of coffee. If you enjoy a good love story, a great setting, and wonderful characters, look for *Coffee Sonata* at your favorite gay and lesbian bookstore."—*Family & Friends Magazine*

Sheridan's Fate

"Sheridan's fire and Lark's warm embers are enough to make this book sizzle. Brooke, however, has gone beyond the wonderful emotional explorations of these characters to tell the story of those who, for various reasons, become differently-abled. Whether it is a bullet, an illness, or a problem at birth, many women and men find themselves in Sheridan's situation. Her courage and Lark's gentleness and determination send this romance into a 'must read.'"—*Just About Write*

Course of Action

"Brooke's words capture the intensity of their growing relationship. Her prose throughout the book is breathtaking and heart-stopping. Where have you been hiding, Gun Brooke? I, for one, would like to see more romances from this author."—*Independent Gay Writer*

September Canvas

"In this character-driven story, trust is earned and secrets are uncovered. Deanna and Faythe are fully fleshed out and prove to the reader each has much depth, talent, wit and problem-solving abilities. *September Canvas* is a good read with a thoroughly satisfying conclusion."
—*Just About Write*

Soul Unique

"This is the first book that Gun Brooke has written in a first person perspective, and that was 100% the correct choice. She avoids the pitfalls of trying to tell a story about living with an autism spectrum disorder that she's never experienced, instead making it the story of someone who falls in love with a person living with Asperger's. ...*Soul Unique* is her best. It was an ambitious project that turned out beautifully. I highly recommend it."—*The Lesbian Review*

Thorns of the Past

"What I really liked from the offset is that Brooke steered clear of the typical butch PI with femme damsel in distress trope. Both main characters are what I would call ordinary women—they both wear suits for work, they both dress down in sweatpants and sweatshirts in the evening. As a result, I instantly found it a lot easier to relate, and connect with both. Each of their pasts hold dreadful memories and pain, and the passages where they opened up to each other about those events were very moving."—*Rainbow Reviews*

The Supreme Constellations Series

"*Protector of the Realm* has it all; sabotage, corruption, erotic love and exhilarating space fights. Gun Brooke's second novel is forceful with a winning combination of solid characters and a brilliant plot. The book exemplifies her growth as inventive storyteller and is sure to garner multiple awards in the coming year."—*Just About Write*

Visit us at www.boldstrokesbooks.com

By the Author

Romances:
Course of Action
Coffee Sonata
Sheridan's Fate
September Canvas
Fierce Overture
Speed Demons
The Blush Factor
Soul Unique
A Reluctant Enterprise
Piece of Cake
Thorns of the Past
Wayworn Lovers

Supreme Constellations Series:
Protector of the Realm
Rebel's Quest
Warrior's Valor
Pirate's Fortune

Exodus Series:
Advance
Pathfinder
Escape
Arrival

Novella Anthology:
Change Horizons

WAYWORN LOVERS

by
Gun Brooke

2018

WAYWORN LOVERS

ISBN 13: 978-1-62639-995-2

This Trade Paperback Original Is Published By
Bold Strokes Books, Inc.
P.O. Box 249
Valley Falls, NY 12185

First Edition: June 2018

CREDITS
Editor: Shelley Thrasher
Production Design: Susan Ramundo
Cover Design By Sheri (hindsightgraphics@gmail.com)
Cover Art By Gun Brooke

Acknowledgments

I'm not alone in finishing this novel. There are lots of people working in the wings and/or encouraging me. My wingmen are some awesome people, let me tell you.

Len Barot, my publisher and the boss at Bold Strokes Books, is relentless in the best of ways when it comes to keeping her company the best possible for writers and readers. Shelley Thrasher, my beloved editor, knows my work through and through. An author in her own right, she is nothing short of amazing. Sandy Lowe, the go-to person at BSB, must be the most charming and caring person ever. Always lovely and professional, not to mention patient. I want also to mention Ruth Sternglantz, Cindy Cresap, and Sheri, plus all the other people who work in the wings at BSB to help produce our books.

Privately, I must acknowledge Sam, Laura, Georgi, and Eden, my first readers who pick up on things that my brain happily skipped, forgot, or disregarded. Thank you for the save, my friends.

Every writer needs to recharge their batteries, physically and emotionally, to be able to work. I have some terrific people in my inner circle that helped with that, whether they realized it or not. Elon, my soulmate, you do more than anyone else when it comes to my battery. Sounding board, cook, driver, grocery-shopping partner, and last but not least, the love of my life…you are just awesome. My children and grandchildren, my son-in-law, my brother, my sister-in-law…the inner circle is pretty big.

My friend Soli deserves her own paragraph. I can't imagine there being anyone else so encouraging and interested in the craft of writing as her. Plus, she is fun, warm, and very loyal, and you can imagine why I love and appreciate her very, very much.

And then there are the most important people of all—you, my readers. Thank you for buying my books, for the support, and for many, many lovely emails over the years. I love hearing from you and try to respond within a few days.

Dedication

For Soli
You are such a great, encouraging friend.

For Birgitta
The best neighbor in the world whose career in music is
amazing and added to my inspiration to write this story.

PROLOGUE

G iselle knew she had made a mistake as soon as she sat down at the table. Across from her, Mary Nelson, the woman Giselle had had a crush on when they were eighteen, sat smiling as she raised her glass.

"Glad you could join me, Giselle. I heard you rarely come into town, so I take this as a compliment." She winked at Giselle and sipped from whatever strange green cocktail she was having.

"I work a lot," Giselle managed to say as a waiter approached them. "Some mineral water, please."

"Ah, come on. Mineral water here at *La Mer Turquoise*? You've got to have some of their famous red wine at least." Mary crinkled her nose and turned to the waiter. "A glass of the house red for my, um, friend." She giggled and shook her head as if Giselle were a child who simply didn't know any better.

Giselle wasn't thrilled that Mary had ordered her something she didn't want but decided to let it slide. Perhaps Mary was nervous too. Granted, she didn't appear ill at ease, but she might just be able to hide it better. Giselle's palms felt damp, and her pulse had to be at least a hundred beats per minute.

The waiter returned with her glass and some more water. "I hope you'll like it, ma'am." One lingering look at Giselle and then he was hurrying to another table.

"You still got it, Gissy." Mary winked at her. "Any ideas what you'd like as a starter? Want to share some calamari?"

Giselle wouldn't, but since Mary had her heart set on it, she didn't want to be the perpetual downer. "Fine. Why not? And what do you mean by I 'still got it'?" She honestly had no clue.

"Aw, come on," Mary said and giggled. "You were turning all the boys' heads twenty years ago. Little did they know you were a lesbian. And neither did I, for that matter. When I moved back to East Quay three months ago, I was floored when I heard you came out." Laughing, Mary patted Giselle's hand.

Giselle wanted to pull her hand free, but anything that could escalate into a scene would harm her sense of inner stability. "You were braver than I was," she murmured. "You were always out."

"I was, wasn't I?" Laughing even louder now, Mary looked pleased. "I always did go my own way. That's what took me to New York, LA, and then back to East Quay. I heard this town has managed to produce some of the world's most talented musicians right now. Including you!"

Giselle cringed. "I'm hardly a household name," she said, waving her hand dismissively. "I'm very much behind the scenes."

"Which is a shame." Tilting her head, Mary winked. "I mean, you are the one writing the music and the lyrics. Without you, the vocalists couldn't perform."

The altogether-too-familiar buzz began to echo in Giselle's head as she noticed how some people at the closest tables began turning their heads in her direction. She tried to convince herself that everyone around them was watching the stunningly beautiful Mary, but that attempt didn't slow Giselle's pounding heart. "Please," she murmured. "I prefer to work like that, and I'm not fond of too much attention."

Clearly Mary thought she was playing it coy, because she gave a loud laugh that drew even more attention from the other patrons. "Oh, no. Don't give me that. Of course, you should demand credit where it's due. You're a genius. I know some people in the music industry, and they sing your praises, no pun intended. That's partly why I looked you up, you know. I had to see for myself how the shy girl from school could have changed so fundamentally. I mean, you were mostly homeschooled as well, which added to your mystery."

"I really haven't changed, Mary." Palms damp now, Giselle experienced the all-too-familiar tunnel vision that often preceded a full-blown panic attack. Anxiety rose like hot bile inside her, and she gripped the napkin on her lap. "I honestly am the same person."

"Aw, come on. I find it hard to see how someone who's written songs for the most famous names in the industry both here and in Europe could be cut from the same cloth as little, scrawny Giselle from twenty-some years ago." Mary tilted her head and scrutinized Giselle. "Are you all right though? You look pale."

"I'm fine. I just need to visit the restroom." Giselle stood but moved too fast, and her chair fell backward, hitting the hardwood floor with a resounding clatter. Flinching, Giselle knew it was too late for breathing into her ever-present paper bag in the restroom now. She gasped for air, and the familiar excruciating pain erupted in her chest. She was certain she'd faint.

"Giselle!" Mary was suddenly by her side and grabbed her arm. "What's wrong?"

"Must…get out of here…have to go home." Sounding husky and barely getting the words out, Giselle tried to feel her way toward the exit. Instead, she misjudged her position and bumped into an unknown woman, who gave a startled yelp.

"Hey! Watch where you're going, lady." A male voice rose above the noise in Giselle's head.

Giselle took several, rapid steps backward and stumbled into something that fell to the floor with a loud bang. Small, bitter cold projectiles hit Giselle, and the last remnant of calmness in her mind suggested they were ice cubes. Frigid water splashed against her thin blouse.

Standing there unable to move, Giselle was now hyperventilating and whimpering. Hands, which she surmised belonged to Mary, nudged her toward the exit.

"Let's go, Giselle. You need some air."

It should be reassuring to recognize Mary's voice, but instead, Giselle withdrew.

"Easy. You're having some sort of panic attack or something."

"Must go home." Giselle tried to free herself, but Mary kept a firm grip of her left arm as they exited the restaurant.

"I'll take you, okay? You're not doing too well."

Giselle blinked several times, trying to clear her vision. The pity in Mary's voice coincided with the expression on her face.

"No. Just leave me alone. I should have…known better. I'll go to my car and….and just wait it out. It'll pass. It always does."

Giselle freed herself, but then the male voice from the restaurant sounded again.

"I have called an ambulance," he said, apparently calmer now. "She clearly needs help."

"No ambulance," Giselle pleaded. Now when her vision was back, she could tell people had gathered around her on the sidewalk, and the restaurant patrons were staring at her through the window.

"Just sit here," Mary said, pushing her down onto a bench. "It's a great idea to have a doctor examine you."

Fury and fear battled inside Giselle, and she locked them all out of her mind and withdrew again. Her shell seemed to become increasingly impenetrable with time. This was her worst episode yet, and she would make sure she didn't have any more, even if that meant retreating into her house or garden.

She would never subject herself to this type of humiliation again. Never.

CHAPTER ONE

Tierney stepped off the bus and retrieved her large backpack from its belly. Hoisting it, she looked around, pleased with the lovely scenery and picturesque main street. East Quay had looked awesome on the map on her cellphone, and so far, it didn't disappoint.

Gazing around, Tierney found a message board with tourist information and began walking over to it. The trees on either side of Main Street were almost in bloom. Small green leaves flickered in the faint breeze, bathing the street in a green light.

Tierney ran her fingertip against the first notes, humming. Clearly the inhabitants of East Quay posted everything from missing pets and garage sales to temp jobs on this message board, much like people did in similar towns all over the US. Aware she had only eighty-some dollars left in her wallet, she had to find something fast. She didn't need money for accommodations, as she had her lightweight tent and her brilliant find in a thrift store in Stowe, Vermont—a high-end sleeping bag. It would keep her warm even if the temperature dropped below zero. Granted, she hadn't tested it in such extreme weather, but the review in a hiking magazine she had read at a library claimed that was true. It was still only September, and a persistent Indian summer had made it a moot point so far.

Pulling off a few tabs asking for someone to walk dogs and trim hedges, as well as one wanting someone to paint a garden shed, Tierney couldn't help but overhear two women talking. The one to the left—curvy, middle-aged, and with jet-black hair—shook her head.

"I was walking Timo along past her place last week. Speaking of Timo, I'm still trying to find a decent dog walker." The dark-haired woman shrugged. "Like that's going to happen in this town. Anyway, I saw her standing there, just outside the door, tearing up a note. I swear she was trembling."

"Really," replied the other woman, a brunette in her thirties. "Well, can you blame her? She hasn't left that place by herself in ages. Losing Frances must be a blow. Should we offer to grocery-shop for her?"

The first woman raised her head as if warding off such an idea. "I wouldn't stick my head into her garden, let alone her house. She doesn't know how to accept true human kindness. Remember how she tore poor old Mrs. Craig to pieces for suggesting she needed a gardener and perhaps some of those happy pills?" Shrugging, the woman snickered, a thoroughly unpleasant sound. "I mean, the nerve. She may be pseudo-famous, but that doesn't give her the right."

"Excuse me?" Tierney interrupted the two women before they ripped the woman they were talking about to pieces. "Did you say you need a dog walker?"

"Yes?" Looking suspiciously at Tierney, the dark-haired woman placed a hand on her hip. "And who might you be? I've never seen you around East Quay."

"My name is Tierney Edwards, and I just arrived in town." She put on her best winning smile that usually did the trick. The women before her appeared to relax marginally. Good. Time to reel them in with a well-thought-out lie. "I'm checking out colleges and have to do it on my own, since my parents can't afford to take time off from work to drive me." Donning a pensive look that she had rehearsed in the bathroom mirror many times, she allowed her voice to mimic her expression. "I just didn't realize how expensive even backpacking is. Got to earn some cash whenever I can. I'm very reliable." Tierney knew she looked several years younger than her twenty-seven. Adding how innocent she could appear if need be, she usually could fool people. Her old social worker at the CPS had often stated that Tierney could manipulate anyone to give her the key to their safe after knowing her only fifteen minutes.

"I'm Leanne Walters," the dark-haired woman said, looking quite taken in by Tierney's story. "You poor girl. Kudos for still trying for an education. If I can help with that by letting you walk Timo, that would be a win-win situation, wouldn't it?"

"It sure would!" Tierney didn't have to fake the relief streaming through her. She had a foot in the door now. "If you know of anyone else needing help around the house or other chores, could you please let me know?"

Leanne exchanged furtive glances with her friend. "What do you say, Daphne? This could be a way to help Ms. Bonnaire without her knowing we're behind it." If she hadn't looked entirely gleeful, and if Tierney hadn't listened in on the tacky conversation from before, she would have assumed the two women were really looking out for a friend.

"You know of someone?" Tierney blinked, making sure she appeared unassuming.

"Yes. We do, actually. A woman living on the outskirts of East Quay, in the countryside. She just lost her housekeeper/gardener and might be looking for a replacement." Daphne nodded, as if to emphasize how important this information was.

"Surely I'd need references to land that type of job?" Tierney thought the two women might be naive to think they could spring her on someone who appeared unlikely to accept a new employee.

"I know!" Leanne clapped her hands, making Tierney suck her lower lip in between her teeth and bite down in order not to let loose the loud guffaw that was threatening to spoil everything. "Why don't you just say that Frances recommends you? Before Ms. Bonnaire has time to check your credentials with Frances, who's on her way to Europe as far as I know, you will have made yourself indispensable."

Tierney wondered if Ms. Bonnaire had any serious problems, since these women were jumping through hoops to get her a new housekeeper. Hoisting her backpack, Tierney tried to rid herself of the fatigue she'd struggled with the last few weeks. Hardly eating anything would do that to you.

"Ms. Bonnaire is very withdrawn and rarely ventures out of her house, let alone her property. She has an amazing park-like garden." Leanne, the more soft-spoken of the two women, pulled out a small notepad and a pen from her purse. "Now, here's my phone number and address, and, oh, let me write down Giselle Bonnaire's. If you can walk

Timo for an hour Mondays and Thursdays? My daughter takes him the other days during the week."

"Sure. I charge fifteen dollars an hour, no matter what service I provide. As for dogs, I don't have any formal training, but they are my favorite people." Tierney blasted off another broad, toothy smile. "Especially big dogs. What kind of dog is Timo, by the way?"

"An American cocker spaniel," Leanne said, and her features softened. "He's quite headstrong but walks well on a leash."

Thank God. "Sounds great. Today's Tuesday. I'll call you Wednesday evening to set up a time for the first walk."

"I hope you realize I will have my husband run your name for any potential priors. He's the chief of police in East Quay." Leanne looked apologetic. "I just can't take any risks with my baby."

Tierney knew there was nothing to find—at least not in this state. Her only run-ins with the police had taken place in Chicago more than ten years ago and were in sealed juvenile records. "Absolutely." She nodded eagerly. "I totally understand."

"If you prove trustworthy with Leanne's dog, I might need you to babysit my two-year-old in a few weeks." Daphne didn't offer Tierney a business card but merely looked at her as if she might turn into a tentacle-swinging alien at any given time. Odd that neither of them thought twice about giving her this Bonnaire woman's name and address. Was she really that good at putting on her best face, or were these small-town women that gullible? Or, worse, did they enjoy making trouble for Giselle Bonnaire—and if that was the case, why?

Either way, Tierney couldn't afford to let the opportunity of a steady income pass her by, and she *was* harmless, even if Daphne and Leanne couldn't possibly know that fact.

"Thanks." Tierney always carried handwritten notes with her cellphone number in the breast pocket of her army-surplus jacket, and now she handed one to each woman. "Just call me if you need something done."

"Thank you, dear." Leanne tucked the note into her purse. "Talk to you Wednesday, then."

Tierney nodded and fastened the buckle of her backpack. A quick map search on her phone showed the location of Giselle Bonnaire's home and gave the walking distance as one hour and ten minutes.

At one time that would have seemed very far, but these days it was nothing. Placing the earbuds to her phone in her ears, Tierney pulled up her favorite playlist. She'd illegally downloaded the music off the internet at a library in Detroit, and now she referred to this playlist as her marching music. With the upbeat songs in her ear, she could appreciate walking for more than an hour.

As she strode along the picturesque streets of East Quay, the beat of the music urging her forward, she was already imagining scenarios that might unfold at Bonnaire's house. She had to pick her best approach, and if successful, she might have weeks of a real salary, perhaps even somewhere to stay. Giving herself pep talks was another of her habits.

But though Tierney was a major fan of the art of visualization, she wasn't prepared for someone like Giselle Bonnaire.

CHAPTER TWO

Giselle closed the lid over the keys of her Steinberg grand piano. She loved the instrument her father had given her when she graduated from Juilliard. Nowadays she could barely remember when she had lived in an apartment with three other students. Granted, the apartment had been located close to the school, so she didn't have to suffer the crowd in the subway, but living there and being out on her own had given her a certain freedom.

She stood and walked into her bright white-and-yellow kitchen. Her former housekeeper, Frances, had claimed it was one of the most nauseatingly cheery kitchens she'd ever seen. Giselle missed Frances and her matter-of-fact humor. The utterly maternal way Frances acted toward her had somehow worked for Giselle in a manner she never would have expected. Frances was extremely loyal and equally protective of her. Now on her way to stay with her recently widowed sister in London, Frances might be gone a long time. Perhaps she would even decide to stay in Europe.

Pushing such depressing thoughts away, Giselle ran the water, filled the electric kettle, and started it. She was a coffee person, but the caffeine might trigger an anxiety attack that she normally could avoid. She indulged in one small cup in the morning, usually, but any more than that later in the day set her up for failure.

Something curled around her legs, and she looked down at the duo sitting there. Her dog, a black retriever mix named Charley, and her red-and-white cat, Mister, looked up at her with equally pleading eyes.

"You're joking. You two work in pairs now?"

Charley gave a sound that sounded almost like a purr, while Mister managed to produce what could only be described as a growl.

"Seriously?" Giselle opened a container where a divider kept the dog and cat snacks separate. With both of her furry friends sitting at attention, she gave them a piece each, which disappeared in half a second. "Good Lord. You're voracious creatures. Eating me out of house and home." The last sentence reminded her that it was time to buy new pet food.

Normally Frances would take care of that task while grocery shopping, but now Giselle had to figure out how to do it. Perhaps she could call the pet store and find out if they delivered? Eventually she would need groceries as well, and she was pretty sure the local whole-food store didn't do that.

Groaning, she poured herself a tall glass of strawberry iced tea. She truly hated to be so dependent on her housekeeper, but she couldn't figure out how to fix her dilemma. The mere idea of getting into the car and driving to the center of East Quay, or worse, the mall just south of town, made her nauseous. When she needed a break from her work, she sometimes took the car and drove into the countryside, stopping at favorite places but never leaving the vehicle. Sometimes other cars would be parked at the beautiful sites, and then she would return home, angry at herself and dismayed at the disappointment coursing through her. Why couldn't she function like everybody else?

Sighing, she picked up her cup of Earl Grey, walked out onto the front steps, and sat down. She blew on the hot beverage she was cupping and then carefully sipped it. Her garden was looking nice, and she loved spending time reading in her hammock when she wasn't working in her music study. She felt safe venturing only as far as her white picket fence, afraid another attack would hit.

Once, Frances had persuaded her to ride along with her to an outdoor coffee place. It was uncrowded and provided plenty of space between tables. The outing went quite well to begin with, until a busload of senior citizens flooded the shop and loud chatter filled the entire place. Frances had taken one look at Giselle, no doubt spotting the complete panic written across her face, and dragged her off to the car like a rag doll.

After that, Giselle had flat-out refused to go anywhere where people might gather, whether it was one person or a hundred. Nothing Frances could say would make her risk having the panic that felt like death claim her. No matter what anyone said, Giselle was sure it was entirely possible to die from such fear.

Something moved to the left, behind her fence. A person was walking along the gravel road leading from the main road to her property. As the figure neared, Giselle saw it was a young woman dressed in khaki pants and what looked like an army-surplus jacket, carrying a large backpack and a messenger bag. She stopped at Giselle's gate, pulled off the backpack, and placed it on the ground. Spotting Giselle, she waved and smiled broadly.

"Good afternoon, ma'am. My name is Tierney Edwards. I'm looking for Giselle Bonnaire," she called out.

Giselle gripped her mug harder. "Why?"

"I'm here to inquire about a job." The woman, Tierney, didn't attempt to open the gate, which helped Giselle relax, if only marginally.

"Nobody is hiring here. I'm sorry." Giselle stood on shaky legs but remained on the steps, curious about Tierney. "Who sent you?"

Tierney looked hesitant. "I heard from an acquaintance of yours in East Quay that your housekeeper had to leave." Tierney then told Giselle a story about visiting colleges and needing to earn some extra cash. "Are you Ms. Bonnaire?" Tierney placed her hands on the gate but kept her distance.

"I am. And as I said, I don't need to hire anyone."

"That lawn and those flowerbeds beg to differ. I'm good with my hands. Gardens and pets are my specialty, but I can take care of a house too, if need be."

As if on cue, Mister and Charley came from the back of the house, no doubt after hearing a strange voice. Charley rushed over to the gate and rose on her hind legs to greet the newcomer with a wagging tail.

"Traitor," Giselle muttered. Mister stayed by Giselle's side, looking regal where he sat, regarding the fool of a dog with whom he only deigned to cooperate when something was in it for him. Like treats.

"Hi, girl. What's your name?" Tierney scratched Charley's head and under her chin. "Oh, here's a tag. Ah. Charley. That your name, pretty girl? Charley?"

Charley now wagged her tail as if it was attached by a hinge to her body and gave a muted woof as if to confirm her name.

"Such a pretty girl." Tierney massaged Charley's ears with both hands. "Good girl."

"Charley, come here." Annoyed, Giselle called her dog over, which under the best circumstances worked fifty percent of the time. This wasn't one of the better attempts. Charley turned her head over her shoulder and glanced at her, grinned with her tongue lolling out between her teeth, and then returned her attention to her new friend.

"No." Tierney took a step back. "Return to your mom. Go back."

Charley's tail dropped so fast, Giselle felt the corners of her mouth threaten to turn up. Charley tried her charm by barking and wagging her tail again, but Tierney pointed at Giselle and said, "Go back to your mom" as she took another step back. Charley sat down and looked between the two women, clearly confused now. "Call her again," Tierney said.

Giselle wanted most of all to go back into the house and leave her dog to socialize in her absence, but as that seemed beyond childish, she raised her voice. "Charley. Come here!" She added more of the same stern tone that Tierney had used, and to her amazement, Charley slowly turned around and walked back to her as if she expected to be scolded.

"Now tell her to sit and then praise her. Maybe give her a treat if you have one. Or a toy." Tierney remained a few steps from the gate.

Now Giselle was reluctantly interested. "Charley. Sit." She snapped her fingers as she spoke the last word, which usually worked. Charley sat down with a thud, wagging her tail again.

"Good girl." Having spotted Charley's favorite ball within reach, Giselle took it and gave it to the easily forgiving dog. "That's a good girl."

Charley bounced around with her ball near the flowerbeds, while Giselle got on her feet and slowly approached the gate. "You do know your way around dogs." She stopped two yards away from it. "A Jack-of-all-trades?"

"Pretty much." Tierney remained where she was. "You sure you don't need some help with that rascal as well as the garden? I charge fifteen dollars an hour. If you offer room and board, then I charge half."

Giselle gaped. She hadn't offered this woman anything! "Who referred you to me?"

"Actually, two rather chatty women in town set me up. One of them hired me to walk a dog, and the other one mentioned something about babysitting a kid once her friend's chief-of-police husband checks my nonexistent priors." Tierney looked unwaveringly into Giselle's eyes. "They told me you'd lost your housekeeper and said you'd give me a job if I said Frances sent me. I'd never dream of telling such a blatant lie."

"Dear God." Giselle had to put her mug down or she might shatter it. She was furious at the women Tierney was talking about. They were clearly up to their old tricks, sticking their noses where they didn't belong. "I'm sorry you walked all the way here for nothing."

Of course, Charley had to return for a repeat performance. She sat down between them, looking happily from Giselle to Tierney and back again. She barked and then tossed herself onto her back and waved all four paws in the air.

"Retrievers. They're such clowns, it's unbelievable." Tierney laughed.

It was such contagious laughter, a sound like nothing Giselle had ever heard before…and something she wished she could have replicated at the piano. She smiled reluctantly.

"They sure are. I'm pretty sure I got the silliest one in the litter, as she was the only one left out of nine puppies." Giselle shook her head.

"Can't you give me a try? Please? It's not like you have to let me stay in the house. I have a tent. I can camp in your backyard or in the woods over there." Tierney pointed toward the small forest behind Giselle's house. "I'm sure you could use me to do something."

Giselle meant to turn Tierney down once and for all. She opened her mouth and intended to begin her next sentence with "Sorry," but instead she heard herself say, "Can you make a decent plain omelet?"

Tierney shot her a blinding smile. "Sure. I saw the movie with Meryl Streep about that chef. I'm not through Julia Child's entire cookbook, but when I get a chance, I try a new recipe. The French omelets were the first one I tried."

Nothing Tierney had just said made sense, but she looked so cute when she talked about Meryl Streep and some cookbook, and she might at least stick around to help Giselle stock up on enough food for her to be all right for a while. If Leanne Walters's police husband was going to check her record out, that would be an adequate safety measure.

"You don't have to use your tent." Giselle pointed to the left of her house. "Up there is a guesthouse. You can stay there for a few nights. Then you have to find something else. This is just temporary."

"All right! Thank you!" Tierney carefully extended her hand. "This is awesome."

Pulling herself together, Giselle took Tierney's hand for a few seconds. "Good. I hope you have a driver's license?"

"I do."

"Good." Walking back toward the house, Giselle called over her shoulder. "The key to the guesthouse is under the flowerpot by the door. Once you finish putting your things away, you can make us some omelets."

"Sure. No problem."

Giselle reached her front door and stood there watching while Tierney hoisted her backpack and entered through the gate. A beeping noise next to her showed that the alarm worked, and Giselle punched in her code to mute it. All the entrances to her property were connected to the alarm system. Was letting a perfect stranger inside the alarm's perimeter an even bigger mistake than she feared?

CHAPTER THREE

Tierney found it odd that Ms. Bonnaire merely left her to her own devices. She walked along the long flagstone path to the guesthouse that lay nestled against a large group of maples. As her new employer, well, of a sort anyway, had said, the key to the house, which was bigger than the last apartment Tierney had stayed in, was hidden under a flowerpot. She unlocked the blue door and stepped inside. Gawking, she forced herself to close her mouth. This had to be the cutest, most Goldilocks-inspired house she'd ever seen. Who was she kidding? She'd never even come close to seeing something like this cottage in real life.

With pine floors covered in pink and white rugs, white furniture, and geraniums in the windows, it was beyond adorable. Tierney picked the bigger of the two bedrooms that boasted a queen-size bed with a lilac quilt as a bedspread. Opening the two closed doors outside the bedrooms, she found a family-style bathroom. An antique five-feet-long hip bath, something she recognized from historical movies, looked inviting. The small washer-dryer set was even more enticing. She hadn't had time to wash her clothes in a couple of weeks, and with this setup she could at least start out with clean stuff when Ms. Bonnaire didn't want her there anymore.

As she went back for her backpack and pulled out her dirty clothes, she focused on the woman up in the big house. Giselle Bonnaire wasn't beautiful in the classic sense of the word, but she sure was striking. Her white-blond hair reached her collarbones, and she was wearing it pulled back from her face with a blue hairband. Dressed in light khaki pants and a white golf shirt, she looked like a thoroughly preppy woman.

Her frame was slender, and if it hadn't been for wiry, defined muscles in her arms, she would have seemed frail. Tierney guessed Giselle was in her late thirties. Piercing blue eyes seemed to scrutinize the person she was talking to and had made it impossible for Tierney to pull her usual happy-go-lucky routine. What had worked effortlessly on the two women in town wouldn't go down well with Ms. Bonnaire. Of that Tierney was certain.

After changing from her dusty pants into her last clean pair of jeans and donning a white T-shirt, Tierney pulled her sneakers back on. She checked the washing machine to make sure it was set to the correct cycle, locked the door to the guesthouse behind her, pocketed the key, and headed back toward the main residence.

The garden was indeed like a small park. A vast lawn stretched between maples, birch trees, and copper beeches. Flowerbeds with perennials ran along the paths in front of the house. Now, as the sun was out, the golden light rendered the garden a fairy-tale ambiance, much like the guesthouse had.

After Tierney knocked on the front door, she opened it and stepped inside. She was going to have to find her own way around Ms. Bonnaire's home, and her most pressing concern was to make some French omelets. At one point, she had to search for the elusive woman, and her curiosity spiked when she thought of why she was nowhere to be seen. Was she hiding?

The kitchen turned out to be located to the left of the front door. It was meticulously kept, which suggested that either Ms. Bonnaire was a neat-freak or she didn't cook. Tierney rummaged through the fridge and decided on the latter. She found eggs, milk, vegetables, but no meat. The freezer contained four microwave-ready meals and some ice cream. The bottom shelf contained a few packages of frozen pet food. It certainly looked like the dog and the cat ate better than their owner.

Tierney started the coffee brewer and used a lemon to make a fresh jug of water, which she placed in the fridge. After she cracked two eggs, she added water, salt, and pepper, poured them into a skillet, and barely stirred the mixture as it cooked. Soon she had two omelets and a salad ready and went to look for Ms. Bonnaire. She passed the foyer and entered a large living room. Rectangular, it held a dining area over by the window and a sofa group in the inner part of the room. A fireplace made from flat stones created an ambiance of formality. Did Ms. Bonnaire have a separate TV room? She didn't see an entertainment center in this one. No doubt this was the posh room meant for entertaining. It looked pristine to a fault. Did her temporary employer do much, if any, socializing?

Walking farther into the room, she spotted a closed door at the other end at the far-left side. Only when she neared it did she hear faint piano music. Was Ms. Bonnaire in there listening to music, or perhaps playing? She didn't recognize the melody, but it was beautiful. She knocked on the door and waited for a response. Not hearing anything, she was just about to knock again when the door opened. Ms. Bonnaire stood there, her expression even more reserved, no, downright haughty, than before.

"Lunch is ready, Ms. Bonnaire. Where would you like me to serve it?" Tierney folded her hands behind her, a habit since her childhood whenever she felt uneasy. Not a smart idea to let anyone see her fidget.

"For heaven's sake, call me Giselle. And the kitchen is fine. You will eat too, yes?" Giselle strode past Tierney and headed for the kitchen.

"Sure. I made plenty." She was starving. Tierney hadn't eaten anything but very cheap cheeseburgers in the last week. If she didn't come across a hamburger within the foreseeable future, that would be fine with her.

The kitchen had a nice breakfast nook, and the windows boasted yellow curtains. The sunny atmosphere they gave the room contrasted with its owner's sullen expression. Or perhaps not sullen but more like darkness tinged with frustration. Tierney was blessed, or cursed, with a powerful radar for other people's emotional states, and Giselle sent out her exasperation on full volume.

"You're a musician?" Tierney asked as she carried the food over to the table, wanting to break the silence.

"Yes." Giselle sat down and served herself some of the omelet and the salad. "This looks nice."

"I hope you like it." Tierney wanted Giselle to elaborate about the music, but her employer seemed interested only in the food. Tierney ate in silence for a few minutes, but then she couldn't stand her own curiosity. "Concert pianist?"

Giselle flinched. "God. No. Composer." She gripped her utensils harder.

"Oh. That's fantastic. What genre?"

"Different ones."

Tierney leaned forward, curious now. "Please. I love music. Always have. What genres? Pretty please? I'm dying to know if I've heard any of your compositions."

"Fine." Giselle scowled, clearly thinking Tierney was a nuisance. "Soundtracks for films. Musical numbers. Occasional pop songs. A few jazz or blues pieces." She shrugged.

Tierney knew she was staring, but she couldn't help herself. "For whom?" she asked, then realized that this question was too intrusive. It sounded like she doubted the truth in Giselle's words. "Sorry. Now I'm being too forward."

"Oh, well." Giselle waved her hand dismissively. "Noelle Laurent. The Maddox movies. Right now, I'm working on several pieces for Chicory Ariose's new album. Those are the best known ones. I've worked with some local choirs and jazz orchestras as well." She still spoke matter-of-factly, as if she were recounting her grocery list.

"That's impressive. Do you enjoy composing?" Tierney had forgotten about her food, but now she scooped up some of the fluffy omelet.

"I do." Giselle put her fork down and shifted her gaze to the bay window. "Music is such a savior, honestly." She looked out toward the garden for several moments.

"I agree. I've used music as a pick-me-up ever since I was a little kid." Tierney wasn't sure why she felt she could tell Giselle that. Normally, she kept such things, no matter how trivial, to herself. If someone needed to know something personal about her, she had no qualms about making it up. She was an excellent liar.

"Most people can claim that. The look in your eyes suggests that it means more to you than just a way to meditate." Tierney's noncommittal response clearly didn't impress Giselle.

"All right." Tierney held her fork tight enough to make a permanent indentation in her hand. "I'm an orphan. Someone left me in a hospital bathroom when I was a few months old. Growing up in the system made music my number-one escape."

"Tierney." Giselle closed her eyes briefly. "I'm sorry I pried."

"Hey. I started the prying, so no big deal." Wanting Giselle to relax again, she donned her broad smile. "So, music it is. The more the better."

"What kind?" Giselle returned her blue gaze to Tierney.

"Most kinds, though I have a tough time stomaching too much accordion." Tierney smirked.

"I'm like that too," Giselle said, now smiling faintly. "Though I find the concertina quite charming when played by a virtuoso."

"What's a concertina?" Tierney ate the last of her salad and reached for her glass of water.

"A small, hexagonal accordion that has a very special tone. I think it reminds me of my childhood, as its tone is quite happy. My grandfather played it." Frowning now, as if she'd caught herself saying something personal and regretting it, Giselle stabbed a piece of lettuce with her fork.

"Do you play any instruments other than the piano?" Tierney hoped to distract Giselle, which was baffling. Why did she care if Giselle was in a bad mood? Sooner, rather than later, she would be on her way. She just had to make some money first. Once she reached Boston, she hoped to find something that lasted a little longer. Sure, East Quay was nice, unless you counted Leanne and Daphne, who had strange ideas about how you helped someone.

"Not at the same level, but I can play the guitar and the violin fairly well. And you?" Giselle asked. "Play any instruments?"

Surprised that Giselle really wanted to know anything about her, Tierney blinked. "Piano, very amateurish. Guitar, very badly, if you mean the classic way. I prefer to play it percussion style."

Giselle's eyebrows did a detour toward her hairline. "Percussion style?"

"Yes. Slapping on the front and on the strings."

Giselle looked reluctantly intrigued. "Perhaps you can show me. I mean, before you leave."

"Sure. If you don't mind me beating the shit out of your guitar." Tierney smiled broadly, and she could sense the expression being genuine rather than her manipulative grin, which she normally used.

"I doubt you would damage an instrument. At least if you truly love music as you say you do." Giselle stood and placed her empty dish in the dishwasher. "I'm going to return to work. When you've dealt with the dishes, I need you to drive to town and buy enough food for Charley and Mister for three months."

"And how do I pay for it?" Tierney also rose and began straightening up after them.

"I have an account there. If you give the owner my name, he'll give you exactly what I need."

Tierney hesitated. "You know, I'm not exactly known around here. They have no reason to trust me. For all they know, I could be scamming them for pet food." She shrugged awkwardly. "Perhaps you want to tag along? I'm sure it'll be a quick trip."

Giselle pressed her lips together until they paled. "Not an option. I've got to work. They have my cell-phone number. I dislike being interrupted, but if there's a problem, they can call me, and I'll verify that you're working for me, if only temporarily."

"All right. Thanks. I won't be making any money dog-walking in East Quay if they think I'm a thief." Tierney placed the rest of the dirty dishes in the dishwasher and stood, pushing her hands into her jeans pockets. Why had Giselle gone gray and fidgety when Tierney had asked if she wanted to join her?

"Good. Car keys are in that cabinet, marked Jeep." Giselle pointed at a small, white metal cabinet. "It's an automatic."

"Okay, though I'm quite good at driving a stick shift."

Nodding, Giselle walked toward the hallway. "I trust you, Tierney."

A pleasant buzz erupted at the sound of her name from Giselle's lips. Her alto voice was stark and cropped, but the way she spoke her name, pronouncing it properly, was…well, strange, somehow. Some people called her Tinny, while others dared to pronounce it Timmy and, worst of all, Turney. Some kids she'd shared a foster home with had heard their foster dad say that to her and kept changing it to Turkey. "I do have a license, and it's up to date." This was true. She'd managed to renew it during a very brief return to her home state. It had taken her quite the finagling to have it delivered to her last address since she had to keep watch over the new tenant's mailbox to get it.

"Well, then." Giselle merely turned and returned to her music room.

After taking care of the kitchen, Tierney removed the keys to the Jeep and walked to the garage south of the main house. She saw what looked like a brand-new, forest-green metallic Jeep sitting there looking spotless. After she climbed behind the wheel, she started the car with ease and drove down the driveway. The gate went up automatically, but she spotted a remote on the visor that she surmised would open the gate from the outside.

Driving into town took only twenty minutes. Walking from East Quay to Giselle's place had taken Tierney two and a half hours with her large backpack and tent. Humming to the radio, she let her strong voice fill the car along with Noelle Laurent, who was singing her latest hit song. Tierney had admired the charismatic and beautiful singer for a decade, and when Noelle had begun singing her own material, Tierney would have done just about anything to be able to do that. She had several notebooks filled with her own song lyrics. She was good with words but found it hard to come up with original and catchy melodies to accompany them.

The pet-food store was located on the outskirts of East Quay, close to the new mall. She didn't see many cars in the parking lot and hoped to complete her errand quickly. She grabbed a shopping cart and pushed it through the doors. The place was huge. She'd been to many pet stores, but this was one of the biggest, perhaps *the* biggest. As she looked around for someone who could assist her, she didn't pay attention to where she was going. She bumped her cart against someone else's and winced.

"I'm so sorry," Tierney said in a gush. "I should watch where I'm going."

"I would say the same, but that would be wishful thinking," the woman holding onto the other shopping cart said, sounding amused. "No harm done." She was blond, curvaceous, and wore very dark sunglasses. And held a white cane. Shit.

"Vivian?" a younger voice said, and a tall, dark-haired woman dressed in black jeans and a blue chambray shirt appeared. "You okay, sweetheart?" She placed her arm around the middle-aged woman's waist and kissed her on the temple.

"I'm fine. This young woman apologized profusely."

"Only right," Tierney said. "I was too busy looking for a staff member. Glad I didn't actually hit you, ma'am."

"Oh, good Lord. Do call me Vivian." The blond woman smiled warmly. "I think Mike was doing the same thing. Did you find someone, darling?" She turned to the other woman, who had to be this Mike.

Wait…Vivian? Mike? Tierney's mind whirled. As in Mike Stone and Vivian Harding? For a few seconds, Tierney contemplated pretending she hadn't recognized either of them, but perhaps this thing of being up front with Giselle was becoming a habit. "I'm Tierney. I admire your music, Vivian, Mike, and listen to it often." She almost added that their music was very good to take one's mind off having to sleep outdoors, barely sheltered from the rain.

"Ah. That's wonderful." Vivian nodded regally. "Now, if you and Mike could scare up a staff member so I can buy the special food the vet recommended for my boys, I'd be happy to sing for you."

Mike snorted. "You'll get us in trouble if you teach those parrots over there to sing one of your arias." Turning to Tierney, she motioned for her to come along. "Leave the cart with Vivian. I thought I heard someone in the back."

Still stunned, Tierney followed Mike to the back of the store, where they finally found a stocky, thin-haired man hauling large sacks of dog food from the fork lift. Mike asked for a special brand of food, which he quickly guided her to.

"And you, miss?" the man said politely, looking curiously at her. He had clearly known who Mike was but now regarded Tierney as if she was a rare entity.

"I'm currently employed by Giselle Bonnaire, and she asked me to pick up three months' worth of food for her cat and dog. And charge it to her account."

The manager's eyebrows slanted down toward the bridge of his nose as he gave her an apprehensive look. "How would I know you're who you say you are? Normally Frances shops for Ms. Bonnaire."

"Frances is in Europe. I'm filling in for a while." A long while, Tierney hoped. "You can call Ms. Bonnaire and double check. She said you have her cellphone number." This wasn't going well. Tierney could feel a major déjà vu from her teens. Back then, if something was amiss in any way, the foster kid got the blame. The one without parents, without a real home to call her own, and the one who had every reason to shoplift or steal something from someone at any given time had to be guilty.

"I most certainly will." The man pulled out his phone and scrolled down with a short, stubby index finger.

"Something wrong? You're pale." Mike showed up with a shopping cart and two large sacks of dog food.

"He's just checking so I don't rip him off. Or my employer," Tierney said, trying to sound casual and facetious. "You know. I'm new at my job, and he's got to make a living."

"Well, so do you, I would imagine." Mike remained where she was.

A rhythmic clicking sound approached from an aisle to their left, and then Vivian came into view. "I couldn't help but hear the entire exchange, Tierney. I understand he needs to check, but he didn't have to sound so condescending and downright suspicious." Vivian clearly wasn't impressed. "We know Giselle very well, and though I'm surprised Frances isn't with her, I'm glad she found someone to help her in the meantime."

"I didn't hear that part. Here he comes now. All smiles."

Thank God. Tierney saw the man hurry toward them, looking benevolent and service-minded now. Well, perhaps he was just a gruff sort of man who always sounded brusque when he talked to his customers.

It took the manager ten minutes to stack the large amount of dog and cat food, kitty litter, and treats in her shopping cart. As she signed for the purchase, he offered to help her load it into the car. Perhaps it was his way of smoothing things over, but Mike, who had waited with Vivian until Tierney was done, interrupted.

"I can help you, Tierney. No problem."

"Thanks. I appreciate it." Tierney was strong, but it would go easier with Mike's help. "I'll help you with yours."

"Brilliant!" Mike grinned at her as they left the store.

After placing their pet supplies in the respective cars, Vivian tugged Mike's sleeve. "Give Tierney our card, darling." She turned to Tierney. "Just in case you need something. We're coming to Giselle's on Sunday to listen to some of her work. It'll be nice to get to know you better, dear."

Tierney clutched the card. "I'd like to get to know you too, but I won't be there on Sunday. I'm a very temporary employee. Just for a day or two." Furious at how her throat constricted, Tierney forced one of her broad and blinding smiles onto her lips. "After this job, I intend to try to find more dogs to walk in East Quay for as long as possible. Perhaps your dogs need walking?" She refused to sound pitiful and injected as much cheer in her voice as humanly possible.

"A day or two?" Mike gaped. "But what will Giselle do after you move on? You can't quit after two days."

"I think you misunderstand," Vivian said quietly. "If I'm not mistaken, it's Giselle who's set the time—the far-too-short a time—for Tierney's services."

"What—oh." Mike tapped her chin with her fingertips. "Go figure. Stubborn as hell."

"As stubborn as she is ingenious." Vivian extended her hand to Tierney and shook it in her usual firm way. "Don't tell Giselle about this conversation. I plan to call her later today, and I'll make sure she realizes how much she needs you. You're young, much younger than Frances, but my radar tells me you're a good person. I'm rarely wrong."

"She truly isn't." Mike shrugged. "So just hang in there and, in the meantime, try to make yourself indispensable. That is, if you truly want to stay on as Giselle's assistant?"

"I do," Tierney said quickly. "But I'm more like her housekeeper."

"Nonsense," Vivian said. "You're replacing Frances, and she was her assistant."

"All right." Tierney could smile easier now. "Thanks to the both of you. I'm so glad I ran into you."

"Literally, as it were," Vivian said brightly. "So, if all goes well, we'll see you Sunday." She waved and climbed into the passenger seat. "I think I'll let you drive this time, darling," she said to Mike, who groaned at what must be a very old private joke between them.

"Ha-ha. You kill me, Harding." Mike rounded the car and waved at Tierney before she took the driver's seat.

Tierney did the same, and on the way back to Giselle's place, she asked unnamed deities to let Vivian be successful. She truly didn't want to be on the road again, but that wasn't the most important part. Something about Giselle made Tierney want to really assist her in a meaningful way by training Giselle's retriever to be a good, reliable kind of service dog. An emotional-support dog. Something told Tierney that Giselle needed exactly that.

CHAPTER FOUR

Giselle let her hands hover above the piano keys and listened for the Jeep to return. For all she knew, Tierney could have taken her car and kept driving. She sighed and wrote some notes on the music sheet. Tierney didn't seem the type to scam someone, at least not by stealing a car. The pet-store manager had called half an hour ago, making sure what Tierney was buying was correct. Giselle had found his condescending tone infuriating and firmly told the man to charge it as usual.

It was odd how Tierney seemed to switch between complete authenticity and that weird, bright smile she'd faked a few times. Thinking back, she realized it had happened when Tierney had tensed up. How could Giselle read this stranger like that? She was usually clueless and awkward in social settings, the very few she ended up in. Normally, her only visitors were clients for whom she composed. Some of them had become friends, but she could still slip into her role, feeling safe in her home and secure in knowing she was good at what she did. Social settings outside the house? Thinking back, Giselle knew very well when that had last happened. The restaurant catastrophe, when she had agreed to go on a date, of sorts, with Mary. Humiliation, still making her feel so raw, so exposed, even after several years, coursed through her. Slamming her fisted hands on the piano keys, she was glad the disharmonious tones broke her out of the downward spiral that would only lead to an anxiety attack.

Giselle kept trying several melodies, attempting to capture the feeling of regret Chicory Ariose had requested. She had written six of the ten songs, which was a major deal since the all-female group normally improvised their special brand of music. These songs would eventually have words, which was another rarity for the group. They had collaborated with Noelle Laurent, the brightest star on the US music sky, a few times, and those songs had also had lyrics, all of them written by Noelle. Giselle didn't know who would write the lyrics for these new melodies, but she hoped they would pick up on the nuances. She was known for subtle changes within her music, and not all people detected them.

Humming the current melody, Giselle attempted to change the key, but it didn't do very much for the song. She hadn't wanted to go the usual route and write a sad melody in minor, but now she changed the chords that way, and the sound made her straighten her back. Perhaps this was supposed to be in a minor key, as clichéd as that would appear. Playing the two versions of the chorus over and over, Giselle was so caught up in her work, she barely glimpsed a car pass on the road.

Eventually, she stopped playing and glanced out the window. The Jeep was back. Getting up, she debated whether to go find Tierney and make sure she'd bought the right food for her pets. Would that be micromanaging? Inwardly rolling her eyes at her indecisiveness and for debating if she should go wherever she wanted in her own house, she stepped out and headed for the kitchen.

It was empty. She could hear sounds from the mudroom where she kept the dog food and had installed a dog shower. Poking her head through the door, she saw Tierney hauling the heavy sacks with a stubborn—and impressive—tenacity. She walked in. "I could have helped you. The bags are very heavy."

Tierney flinched and looked over her shoulder. Her long, red hair was damp at her temples, which made it curly, and she looked so damn attractive, Giselle just stared.

"I'm nearly done. Just have to stack this one—oh, okay." Tierney grinned at Giselle when she grabbed one end of the last dog-food sack and helped her swing it up on top of the pile. "That'll keep your darlings fed for months." Tierney walked over to the stainless-steel sink and washed her hands.

"The store manager was helpful then?" Giselle stood where she was, thinking she could wash her hands in her private bathroom upstairs.

"Only after your call. That and how Vivian and Mike nailed him with their best glares. I don't think I look enough the part of your housekeeper, or assistant, for the guy to take what I said at face value." She jutted her hip out and crinkled her nose as she smiled. "Can't say I blame him."

"Vivian and Mike? You ran into them at the pet store?" Giselle was certain she'd heard wrong.

"I sure did. They were getting some special food for their dogs."

"I see." Giselle really didn't. How could Tierney already be on a first-name basis with two of the most famous daughters of East Quay? "All right. You can consider yourself off the clock until it's time for dinner. If you get bored, you can walk Charley."

"I'm not easily bored, but a walk would be great. I'll hop right to it. By the way, would you like to join us? You can see how I train Charley to walk nicely on the leash and other useful things."

Tierney stepped closer to Giselle, smelling sweet and fresh, with undertones of clean sweat. The combination was heady, and Giselle truly wanted to take a few steps back, but she didn't, as that would have seemed too obvious...and too curious.

"I can observe this activity within the grounds of my property," Giselle said darkly. "I prefer it that way."

"Sure thing. I'll just walk her to wear her out a bit. She'll listen better when she's not all jazzed up."

Tierney didn't seem to think it strange that Giselle didn't want to leave her home, even to go on a walk out here where nobody ever came unannounced. Well, except this odd young woman.

"Fine. Come get me when you return. I'll finish up some things in the music room in the meantime."

Annoyed with herself for explaining herself to Tierney, someone she paid to take care of her kitchen, her pets, and general things around the house, Giselle frowned as she stalked back to the music room. She really wanted to watch from the kitchen window when Tierney and her dog went on their exercise walk, but that was a ridiculous thought.

Giselle had to force herself not to hammer at the piano keys as she played the last chorus. Her grand piano was priceless to her, such a beautiful-sounding instrument, and wonderful to look at as well. She couldn't let herself be so frustrated that she attacked what she sometimes thought of as her one true love. Caressing the keys, she tried again, and this time the melody for the chorus sounded right. In fact, it sounded so good, *felt so good*, she lost herself in the work, inspired by the beauty of the tones ringing out in the soundproofed room.

Time flew before she heard a gentle knock on the door. Having written down the last of the revised chorus on her music sheet, Giselle flinched and looked up. Tierney wouldn't be able to hear her say "come in," so she rose and opened the door. "What time is it?" she asked, knowing she sounded annoyed. But her tone didn't seem to faze Tierney.

"Ten past five. Want to come out into the garden to see what Charley learned while we were out?" She grinned—an authentic smile, Giselle noted—and motioned in the direction of the front door.

"You were out for two hours?" Had Charley ever had a walk that long? The poor dog must be exhausted.

"It's lovely outside, and you have some great paths around here. I didn't meet a single person, so I could walk Charley off-leash." Tierney strolled ahead of Giselle out through the front door, and there sat Charley with her tail wagging up a storm, as usual. But she was sitting. Not jumping, frolicking, or chasing Mister until he ran up the closest maple.

"Here's your mom, Charley. Remember what we talked about?" Tierney was addressing the retriever as if she were a human. "Lie down." Charley lay down, looking attentively at Tierney. Sure enough, Tierney produced a very small snack from a pouch attached to her belt. "Good girl. Now, sit up." Charley complied. New treat.

"She'll grow fat," Giselle said acerbically. "Retrievers put on weight easily."

"Not when the treats are this small and she gets proper walks where she can run around and work off that energy she has in spades." She waved at Giselle. "Your turn."

"What? No. I'd rather just watch. This time." Giselle felt clumsy and awkward, certain her dog wouldn't obey her. Charley took Giselle's commands as pure recommendations that she could choose to follow—or not.

"Aw, come on. This is your dog. You're the one she should want to please more than anyone else. Here, take a few treats, and make sure she knows you have them, but don't offer any unless she does something you want. Like, if she comes up to you and sits down without bouncing around you like a crazy dog, she can have a treat and praise."

Cornered, Giselle pressed her lips together and approached Tierney and Charley. The latter stomped a little, but she was still sitting down. Had Tierney glued the foolish dog to the ground? Giselle accepted a few of the fragrant treats and merely looked dumbfounded at her dog. As if on cue, Charley stood and walked over to Giselle, stopped in front of her, and sat down. She waved her right paw in the air as if to say hi or do a high-five. She looked so adorable, Giselle had to give a faint smile and praise her. She offered her a miniscule treat, which made Charley give her a pleading look.

"Tell her to do something. You know. Any basic command." Tierney had taken a seat on one of the stone benches along the flagstone path.

Giselle's mind went blank for a moment, but then she said, "Come here." She hoped she sounded as assertive as Tierney, or Charley would ignore her. She couldn't even begin to count the times she'd chased the dog across the lawn, having to use a broom handle to herd the stubborn animal into the house in the late afternoon. Now, Charley cocked her head as if to judge Giselle's sincerity. She stood and sniffed the air for a few moments, but then she rounded Giselle and sat down on her left side. When Giselle didn't move for a few flabbergasted seconds, Charley gave a soft "moff" and looked pointedly at Giselle's right hand.

"Good girl," Giselle said, having to clear her throat while she gave Charley two treats at the same time. This offering went down very well, and Charley licked her lips and then did what Giselle referred to as her retriever smile.

"Why don't you go to the end of the path, and we'll try this again? Making her come to you on cue is *the* most important command. Sure, it's fun to teach them to play dead, roll over, balance something on their noses. And there is a reason all that's good for dogs. But this, coming to you on cue—priceless."

"Why are such circus tricks good for dogs?" Giselle thought they sounded like a frivolous waste of time.

"Dogs need to work out problems to stimulate their brain. You know, the same reason we do Sudoku and crossword puzzles. Need to use the old gray matter." Tierney came closer and scratched the back of Charley's head in passing. "What do you do to keep your mind agile and in shape?" She gazed at Giselle in an interested way.

"I write music." She had no time for anything else, but of course, this young woman wouldn't know what it took to give so much of yourself to your work.

"That's your job, though. How do you recharge your batteries?" Sitting down next to Charley, her arm around the panting dog, Tierney looked genuinely interested.

Giselle wasn't sure why she didn't find the question as intrusive as she would have expected. Perhaps it was the clear, guileless look in Tierney's eyes or the complete trust her dog showed the virtual stranger.

"Hmm. Actually, I go for a drive." Giselle's cheeks warmed, but she had no idea why. "Alone," she added quickly. "In the Jeep to my favorite spots in the countryside."

"Sounds like an enjoyable way to get a change of scenery. So, no walks?"

"No. At least not outside my property." Wanting to take the words back, Giselle closed her hands into tight fists. "And you?" She wanted to shift the attention from herself back to Tierney.

"I like to write. Poetry. Lyrics. And I enjoy singing."

"Really?" A suspicious thought seeped into Giselle's mind. "Anything you'd like to share with me?" she asked, setting the trap she was certain Tierney would fall right into. "I mean, you've already made friends with Vivian and Mike today."

It was Tierney's turn to blush. "You're kidding, right? Nobody would want to hear something so amateurish. I do dream of becoming good at one point, but right now? I think not." Laughing self-deprecatingly, Tierney ruffled Charley's ears and stood. "I'm not here to score, Giselle," she said seriously. "I'm here to help you in whatever capacity you need me. If you let me stay on a little longer than two days, I can train Charley to be much more useful to you than a snuggle bunny. She has the potential to become a great service dog."

Clearly Tierney saw right through her. She knew, or guessed, that Giselle had implied Tierney was out to exploit her presence among famous musicians. Giselle still wasn't sure, but something about Tierney's demeanor and voice spoke of her being truthful.

"Fine," Giselle heard herself say. "You can stay two weeks. By then I'll know more about when Frances intends to return." *If ever.*

"Really? Great!" Tierney appeared on the brink of embracing Giselle, which would have been catastrophic. Nobody had hugged her in a very long time. Two outcomes could have resulted. Giselle groaned inwardly. Either she would have passed out or clung to Tierney in desperation, yearning for some human touch.

"Two weeks. I won't promise anything beyond that."

"That's still awesome." Tierney beamed. "I'll work with Charley every day between chores. She'll do great. Perhaps even Mister will pick up a few tricks."

"Dream on," Giselle muttered, but she had to force herself not to reciprocate Tierney's warm smile. She had to keep her distance, even if this young woman's charisma was chipping away at her armor. That couldn't happen, as it would only lead to heartache. Giselle's solitude was her safety. Without it, if she let people in and allowed them to see her vulnerability, she would eventually have to accept their inevitable departure after witnessing constant anxiety attacks that always made her think she would actually die this time. What would she do then? She knew exactly what would happen. She would lock herself into her bedroom and curl up on the bed in the dark. That had happened after her parents died. And even if she had prevented such an attack from occurring for quite a while now, she could envision what it would be like if she lost someone she'd dared invite into her life. "Why don't you get cleaned up and check out the freezer? I'll...I'll go back to work."

Tierney studied her for a few moments but broke eye contact before Giselle began to feel cornered. "Sure thing, Boss." Tierney turned and walked toward the guesthouse.

Looking down at Charley, Giselle expected the dog to trot after her new trainer, but instead the retriever cocked her head and seemed to study her with a glance that eerily resembled Tierney's.

Muttering under her breath, Giselle returned to the house and locked herself into her music room. She stared at the music sheet, using the fingers of her right hand to pinch the skin between her thumb and index finger on her left. This was one of the tricks she used to snap out of unfavorable moods. It succeeded, as always, but when she started to play what she had written down earlier, the image of Tierney's unwavering gaze returned. Frustrated, Giselle yanked her hands from the keys. She had to start working on another song, something with a less sultry melody. It was that or fear she might be losing her mind.

CHAPTER FIVE

Tierney wiped off the kitchen counter and then turned to her audience. Mister and Charley regarded her intently, the latter switching her gaze to the large sack of dog food visible through the open door leading to the mudroom.

"Pretty obvious, aren't you, girl?" Tierney said and walked over to read the sack. Following the chart on the back, she estimated Charley's weight and measured the dry food into a pink bowl with the dog's name on it. She repeated the process with the cat food and made sure they had plenty of clean water.

Dinner had been a tense experience between the two humans in the house. Giselle hadn't said more than ten words before returning to the music room, and Tierney had felt a strange variety of being tongue-tied. She didn't want to tick Giselle off. Her position as assistant was precarious as it was. Poking the Moroccan-chicken dish with her fork, Tierney had tried to create some appetite, but the more she chewed each mouthful, the more it seemed to grow.

When she was done, Giselle sat very still, gazing out the window for several moments. She looked forlorn and distant, which made Tierney suspect that composing hadn't gone very smoothly.

"Thank you," Giselle said, startling Tierney before she stood and took her plate to the dishwasher. "It was very tasty. You're a good cook."

"You're welcome," Tierney said quietly. "Will you need me for anything else after I feed the menagerie and take care of the kitchen?"

Giselle grew visibly tenser, if that was even possible. "No. You can do what you want. The guesthouse should have everything you need, including Wi-Fi and cable television."

"Sounds great." Tierney stood, but remained at the table since Giselle looked like she might run away if she came to close. "Breakfast at…?"

"Eight's fine. I normally have oatmeal or cereal. And coffee."

"Got it."

They stood looking at each other, the air around them electrified, which was mindboggling. Tierney had known this woman for about ten hours, and still she was dying to learn everything about her. How on earth had Giselle, so remote in her ways and clearly struggling with some sort of phobia or something, gotten under her skin so quickly and thoroughly? Tierney took pride in not letting anyone close, unless it was for happy-go-lucky purposes, such as going clubbing or hiking through nature. When things got serious, or when someone tried to use her as a crutch, it was time to move on. Why didn't Giselle, who truly needed assistance, repel her like other people had over time?

When Giselle nodded curtly and left, Tierney finished the rest of her chores, walked Charley for fifteen minutes, and then headed for the guesthouse. Giselle had showed her how to set the alarm before leaving the main residence. The guesthouse had a similar setup, but oddly enough it made Tierney feel trapped rather than safe.

The cabin really was too cute for words. Something told her Giselle had hired someone to decorate it, as she didn't seem like the type that went for cute. Unless you counted Charley and Mister. They were cute enough.

She turned on the TV and zapped through the channels available. It took a while since there seemed to be hundreds. After clicking through ten different infomercial channels in a row, Tierney sighed, pulled out her laptop, and hooked it up to the internet. She thought about googling Giselle but refrained from it as it felt like prying. Instead she logged into a closed forum on Facebook called Surviving the System USA.

Tierney read through some messages and commented on a few. A woman, Suki, was going through a tough time, having flashbacks from her teenage years.

I saw this guy at the supermarket today, and he looked just like the husband in the last foster home I was in. He was either totally uninterested in me and the younger boy they were fostering, or he was way too attentive. He ignored the boy, but he would come into my room claiming he needed to check for drugs or make sure I was studying and didn't have any boys hiding in there. He would grab me, insist he needed to check for needle marks. He would stroke up and down my arms—and I felt so cornered, so humiliated. I have never tried drugs. And I was sixteen. It was obvious he was feeling me up. It never went any further than that, but it still made me feel so unsure, you know. Unsafe.

Tierney grew angry, and she began to type.

Suki, you're not alone. I had similar things happen to me in a group home. I was sent there because I smacked the shit out of the husband in my previous foster home after he tried that crap with a girl younger than me. I think she was twelve. He reported me for being violent, and they sent me a group home. If I hadn't met my counselor at that point, who knows what route I would've gone down. I'm sure she would still be disappointed in me for being a vagabond of sorts, but she saved my ass back then. So, no wonder we have flashbacks, Suki. We had to fight to stay sane so many times.

Tierney read on, kept commenting briefly, but her mind had become stuck in the memory of the man who was supposed to be the father figure for the four foster children in his and his wife's care. The wife had been okay, if a bit too uncoordinated and not very organized. She often forgot their lunches or to make sure the smaller kids brushed their teeth, but Tierney took up the slack. That's just what you did as the oldest foster kid in your current home.

Her cellphone rang, startling her. She glanced at the display, and a trembling smile formed on her lips when she saw the photo indicating the caller. Swiping her finger toward the thumbnail of a green receiver, Tierney grinned as she answered.

"Hi, Dina. Long time, no see."

"And whose fault is that? I called the last three times. I was starting to think you'd keeled over or something." Medina Pachis, Dina to her friends, huffed. "That aside, I had a sudden urge to keep tabs on you. Must be my clairvoyant streak." Dina had stayed at the same group home in Chicago as Tierney when they were sixteen and seventeen. It wasn't one of the better homes, and both of them had suffered at the hands of a very strict and religious management.

"That, or you broke up with your latest hunk and needed to tell me all the sudden details." Tierney curled up in the corner of the couch, making herself comfortable. No doubt the story would be entertaining. Dina's life was colorful in a way Tierney's had never been—and never would be. She was far too jaded and careful to take the risks Dina constantly did.

"How did you know? Actually, it's a double whammy. I think I've gone through two lovers since we talked last. One guy and one girl."

Tierney groaned. "Whoa. You're terrible. Honestly, Dina. You're burning your candle at both ends. I'm the one who needs to worry."

"Nah. It wasn't that bad really. The guy sort of was a weekend fling, but the girl…" Dina cleared her throat. "Being bi is sometimes rather confusing. The guy was lovely, very sweet, but I knew going in that he'd just be like a carnival attraction. Susannah though…it was different. *She* was different."

Frowning, Tierney gripped the phone harder. "You sound heartbroken, Dina." She spoke lightly, but she meant it.

"Can't hide anything from you, can I?" Dina gave something that sounded like a mix of a sob and a laugh. "Susannah is great. Perfect— or as close to perfect as a person can get without being Mother Theresa, I suppose."

Tierney ached for her friend. Dina wasn't about one-night stands. For Dina, it was about potential love with each of the people she hooked up with, and each breakup, whether after a week, a month, or a year, ate away at her heart a little more. The analogy ran even more true than usual as Dina sounded hollow. "So, this Susannah is the one, you think?"

"God, I hope not. If she is, I'm screwed." Dina laughed unhappily. "If I meet any more girls like her, and it ends the same way, I'll be in real trouble." She cleared her throat. "Enough about my life. Where are you keeping yourself these days?"

"I'm in East Quay," Tierney said lightly.

"East Quay? That's Rhode Island, isn't it?"

"Yes. An hour or so east of Providence. I'm working as a temp assistant to a composer. You might have heard of her since you're such a music buff. Giselle Bonnaire." Tierney felt safe sharing this information with Dina, as her friend was extremely loyal.

"Giselle Bonnaire? The mysterious woman behind so many hit songs? I've only seen a few photos of her. And I think they were taken at least ten years ago. She was gorgeous back then. Please tell me she still is." Her tone brighter now, Dina chuckled.

"She is. I mean, she's not a classic beauty, but she has this special, well, I don't know, charisma doesn't cover it. It's more than that." Relieved she could talk to Dina about her confusion, Tierney curled up further against the pillows. "It's like she's frail and strong at the same time. She's a bit of a hermit, I think. She lives in the countryside with her pets, and apart from the people she works with, she doesn't seem to socialize much."

"So, lonely, huh?" Dina sounded apprehensive. "I know you have a knack for helping others, but you're not trying to save Giselle Bonnaire, are you?"

"Not sure what you're talking about, but no. I'm not. I'm here for two weeks, at best, and then I'll be on my merry way toward new adventures." *And be utterly alone again.* That normally didn't bother Tierney, since she was used to it, but now it did. She wanted to take the thought back and not acknowledge the way hitting the road yet again made her feel.

"You've been there for, what is it, a day or so? And yet you're head over heels, if not in love, so totally interested and mesmerized. And before you object to my estimate, then realize how long I've known you. If anyone can see a pattern form when it comes to you, it's me."

"I hate to admit it, but you're right. She has a way of pulling me in. Perhaps she does that to everyone—apart from some witches in town— what do I know?"

"True. It might be a gift, or something she does, being fully aware how it affects people. I can't say either way, of course."

Tierney doubted Giselle was manipulative. Nothing about her seemed false in that way. Instead, she seemed too reserved to be inclined to take part in power games like that. "She's not the calculating type.

I don't know her at all, but I have a pretty sizable radar when it comes to bullshit. I can tell you the bullshit meter went all the way to the bell when I ran into two women in the center of East Quay. They were quick to try to make me what I interpreted as their mole in Giselle's home."

"What? Really? But why?" Dina sounded shocked.

Tierney rose and went into the kitchenette. She opened the cabinet doors one after another, searching for tea or coffee, and found both. Pouring water into an electric kettle, she squeezed her cellphone between her shoulder and jaw. "I got the impression that they'd, or some friend of theirs, tried to stick their noses into Giselle's business, with a less than amicable response from her. They seemed really overbearing, but I'll make some extra cash walking their dogs and perhaps even babysitting, once they check my potential rap sheet."

"Oh, God. Tell me it's still sealed. I mean, that old stuff?" Dina squeaked. "All that happened when we were like fifteen."

"Sure it is. That won't surface." Tierney put some instant coffee into a mug, hoping she was right. Someone with connections could always circumvent the rules. "I'll be trotting along with kids and dogs before you know it. Right now, I'm in this super-cute cottage on Giselle's property, but I'll have to go back to camping when I don't have anything but the dog-walking money. Also, what I earn here, I can set aside. Meals are included."

"She sounds generous, your Giselle," Dina said softly.

"She is. But she's not my anything." The mere idea was preposterous. A vagabond chick and a well-spoken, famous composer. Tierney made a face at her reflection in the kitchenette window. After returning to the living-room area, she placed the mug on the small coffee table. "I'm going to make use of what happened to me today and write some lyrics," she said and pulled her laptop onto her thighs. "Whenever I have days like these, out of the ordinary, my muse starts dancing a goddamn jig on my shoulder."

"Ah, that muse of yours. You need to show your texts to Giselle. Perhaps she'll be inspired and write some beautiful music for you to sing. That could even be your demo."

Dina's idea made a cold knot twist her bowels together. "Don't even say that. I can't think of anything triter and more clichéd than that."

"Perhaps it's trite and a cliché because it actually happens sometimes."

"In Hollywood, maybe. In real life? Not so much." Tierney knew she sounded testy, but the mere idea of making a fool of herself like that nauseated her.

"Hey. Don't bite my head off, T." Dina had clearly retreated. "I was only kidding."

"Sorry!" Wanting to stomp on her own foot, Tierney made sure her voice mellowed. "I'm still a bit nervous about this job, even if it's only for a couple of weeks. I guess I really want to be useful. You know, train her dog and make sure those women don't poke their heads inside her property or start some odd rumors."

"Oh, God," Dina said again. "You've got it bad, sweetie. You're hooked. I haven't heard you talk about anybody else that way...well, except me, back in the day. And this after only knowing this woman for a few hours, really."

"You're reading too much into it." Tierney tried to weasel her way out of the entire topic. "She's my employer, whom I happen to admire. I'd just hate for her to be the topic of town gossip."

"Just saying." Dina made a kissing sound. "You know you can call me anytime you need to. Even if it's in the middle of the night."

Appalled at how tears welled up in her eyes, Tierney murmured, "You too. Any time. And don't give up on this Susannah you're so gone on. She may just realize what a catch you are."

"Same for your Giselle."

"Please." Tierney groaned. "I swear I'll—"

"All right, all right. I'll behave." Dina giggled.

They spoke about less turbulent topics for a few more minutes and then hung up after agreeing to catch up the upcoming weekend, which was in three days.

Tierney turned on Word and her favorite sites for rhymes and thesauruses. She stared at the blank page for a moment, and then her hands took on a life of their own, something they did when she just *had* to write down a song lyric. Only when she reached the chorus did she realize how this song could be interpreted, at least by someone reasonably aware of her current circumstances.

Chorus:
She looks at me
And I wish I could undo
How she seems to be
Lost in every shade of blue
If she dared trust in me
I would make the magic flow
Fireflies among the trees
As we sit and watch them glow

Tierney hid her face in her hands, but the image persisted of Giselle when she stood next to her dog in the garden, looking amazed at Charley wagging her tail as if saying, "See, Mom. See what I can do?" Tierney couldn't fathom how such a simple thing could tug at her heart strings enough to wind them up so taut it hurt.

Maybe Dina was right.

CHAPTER SIX

Two days later, on that Saturday, Giselle watched Tierney leave through the gate with Charley. It was time for her dog's long walk, and Charley was bouncing at the end of the leash. Tierney let her work off some of her exuberance and then reeled her in. Charley looked adoringly at the young woman and seemed to be eager to please her trainer.

Giselle confessed to herself that she would have given anything to join them. Why was it so difficult, so downright impossible to go outside her gate? A couple of years ago, she'd enjoyed walking in the woods and along the deserted gravel roads around the neighborhood. Now, she felt only reasonably safe from having one of her panic attacks when she stayed at the house or in her garden. It was ridiculous, and since Tierney had begun training Charley, she felt cheated. Three nights had passed since Tierney had talked her way into working for her. Each day that passed made her question how the hell she'd make her days work after Tierney left. The last two days had gone very smoothly, making Giselle wonder if either she was transparent or if Tierney was clairvoyant, since the other woman often picked up on what Giselle wanted before she'd said a word.

Giselle stood by the window, holding her cooling cup of tea. Tierney and Charley were out of sight, but she couldn't tear herself away from the view of the flowerbed that Tierney had begun weeding. Frances was still the one Giselle would rely on, no questions asked, but the woman was in her late sixties, and her back often acted up. Gardening was getting too hard on her—and who knew when she'd return home to the US. Giselle had received a short email from her in which she wrote that her sister would need around-the-clock care for the foreseeable future. The mere fact that Frances hadn't asked if Giselle had found a replacement spoke of Frances's concern for her sister. Normally, she was extremely protective of Giselle and thoroughly dedicated to her work as assistant and housekeeper. Giselle wrote an equally brief note back, stating she understood that Frances needed—and should—prioritize her family members and that she had employed someone else. She didn't see any need to mention that Tierney would be staying with her for only two weeks. Giselle knew Tierney would stay longer if she asked, but for some unfathomable reason, that seemed ill-advised.

Her cellphone rang, and she glanced at the screen. Vivian. Straightening her back as if the world-renowned mezzo-soprano could see her, Giselle answered.

"Dearest!" Vivian sounded like she was in the same room with Giselle. "I'm just calling to confirm our meeting tomorrow."

"We're on, Vivian. How are you?" Giselle walked to the music room, still speaking. "And Mike?"

"We're both splendid. I saw my eye doctor last week, and he thinks the progression of the disease has stopped, at least for now. That means I can identify shadows and brightness and that I'll keep that ability for an extended period. I was really dreading complete blackness."

Giselle closed her eyes hard, as if trying to experience being visually challenged. She saw a bright pattern on the inside of her eyelids from squeezing her eyelids too tight. "I'm glad you have some good news, medically speaking, Vivian."

"And you, dearest? Anything looking up for you when it comes to your diagnosis?" Vivian spoke matter-of-factly, clearly not considering her question intrusive. Perhaps it was because Vivian, and the rest of Chicory Ariose, didn't regard mental-health issues as any type of a stigma.

"I haven't seen a doctor or a therapist in more than a year. The last one suggested hypno-therapy, but the mere idea gave me such anxiety, I…I just couldn't." Giselle sat down on the piano stool. "I have found a routine that works. I can still write music, and with Tierney here—"

"Ah, that sweet girl! She showed up in the nick of time, I understand. Poor Frances has her hands full in the UK, I imagine."

"Tierney is very conscientious and a nice young woman." Trying to speak without inflection in her voice, Giselle played with the edge of her mug.

"Very nice," Vivian said. "And, according to Mike, very striking."

Images of Tierney's long, dark-auburn hair and light-gray eyes, the slightly upturned nose, which boasted a band of pink freckles against her pale complexion, appeared. The way she moved with such ease and confidence, like she was a woman of the world and knew exactly what to do, or not, at any given time, made Giselle want to ask Tierney about her past. The story she had given Giselle about looking at colleges didn't ring true, but as far as she knew that was the only thing Tierney had deliberately lied about.

"She's very beautiful. Outdoorsy." Giselle could hear the awe in her own voice. She had to stop talking about Tierney altogether. "Please tell me you and Mike are staying for dinner. We have plenty since Tierney stocked up the pantry and the freezer as if food is going out of style."

"We'd love to. Should we shoot for two p.m.?" Vivian's voice gave her smile away.

"Sounds good. Just come directly to the music room if I'm working. I have some new pieces and need your feedback."

"Exciting. See you tomorrow then, dearest." True to her nature, Vivian blew her a kiss over the phone and disconnected the call.

Turning toward the grand piano, Giselle began playing the soft, slow piece she'd been working on the last few days. Every time she thought she was onto something, it sounded too sweet, too romantic. She saw nothing wrong with music being romantic, but this melody needed a chorus that was gentle yet not ingratiating. Words for a potential lyric were floating in her mind, but nothing had manifested itself as solid. After all, she wasn't a lyricist. Chicory Ariose would have to decide whom they wanted to write the lyrics for Giselle's songs. Perhaps Eryn, their electric guitarist, who also was a journalist, had the required skills?

The verse flowed so well when she played it, but when she attempted to let her fingers run over the keys and flow into the chorus, she came to a stop.

"So beautiful," Tierney said from the doorway, and only now did Giselle realize she'd forgotten to lock the door.

"Thank you. It's not ready yet. Not by far." She couldn't fault Tierney for poking her head in when the door was open. To date, she'd never disturbed Giselle when it was closed.

"I could tell you're struggling with the chorus. May I hear the verses again? And perhaps the bridge, if that's ready?" Tierney smiled encouragingly.

About to refuse and break off the writing session, Giselle couldn't make herself extinguish the light in Tierney's eyes. "Sure. Take a seat here." She pulled a round stool close and patted it. "You're a music lover. Tell me what you think." She played the intro and moved on to the verse. Then she went on to play the bridge, a melody that would challenge the singer, in this case Vivian. After she finished, she lowered her hands onto her lap and turned to Tierney. "Yes?"

"Stunning verse and bridge. I'm sure nobody but Vivian could ever manage that last note." Tierney hummed the melody of the bridge, and even if her voice was quiet, it was pitch-perfect.

Giselle stared at Tierney. "You can sing?"

"I can carry a tune." Tierney tucked her hands under her thighs, as if to keep from nervously fiddling with them.

"Can you just hum along as I play, you think?" She was all professional now and only regarding Tierney as an unexpected tool in the process.

"Um. Sure. Why not?" Tierney colored faintly.

Giselle played the intro again, and when she came to the verse, Tierney began to sing rather than hum, a wordless sound of different vowels, following the melody. When they reached the chorus, Giselle managed to keep at it for a few moments, creating a melody that didn't seem too saccharine.

"Better," Giselle muttered and wrote down several rows of music on her sheet. "Besides, you seemed to hit that note just fine, even using your chest voice."

"Yeah?" Tierney seemed to relax. "I really love the melody, and you played more of the chorus this time."

"That's why I had to write it down instantly. When I'm at this stage, experimenting with the music so much for hours, I need to make sure I know which version I saw some potential in." Enthusiastic now, Giselle immersed herself in the melody and chorus of one of the other songs, for which she had a decent first draft ready. "This one then? Keep in mind it's a rough draft."

"Wow." Tierney looked dazed. "A rough draft? It's…I hate to keep repeating myself, but it's beautiful." Blinking, Tierney shook her head slightly. "If I wasn't a down-to-earth person, I'd say ghosts or other spiritual critters are at work."

"What do you mean?" Giselle's lips parted. "Ghosts?"

Tierney lowered her gaze, and Giselle could feel her withdraw. What was wrong now?

❖

Why couldn't she simply think before she spoke? Tierney pinched her thigh to punish herself. What would she say now that sounded at all plausible? Giselle was still studying her closely, and even if Tierney would have given a lot to have such attention directed at her from the exciting mystery of a woman that was her employer, this wasn't what she had in mind.

"I only meant—"

"You've heard this melody before?" Clearly stricken at the thought of her song not being original enough, Giselle laced her hands together. She looked like she couldn't bear to play her instrument right now, not even touch it. This reaction in turn shocked Tierney into action. No way could she let Giselle think that.

"Never in my life have I heard anything like that." Tierney didn't think but reached out and placed her hand on Giselle's right arm. "That wasn't what I meant. Please don't take this the wrong way, but something I wrote my first night in the guesthouse has pretty much the same cadence as your melody. I mean, my stuff is amateurish and not anything special unless you—well, unless you're me, or know me really well."

"You wrote something? A text? Lyrics? And they fit this piece?" Giselle now placed her hand over Tierney's. "Do you know it by heart well enough to sing it with my composition? It doesn't matter if it is nonsense or less than perfect, but it would really help for me to hear lyrics, *any* lyrics, with this melody."

Tierney sighed. Oh, she was in so much trouble. The text was about her, how she felt, and a portrait at this point in her life. Sighing inaudibly, Tierney nodded. "Just take it a little slower and let me find where I need to start. The verse and the chorus are dead-on, but I haven't written any words to fit the bridge."

"All right. No pressure, Tierney. Just hum if you don't remember or have any words."

Tierney rubbed her now-sweaty palms on her thighs. This was crazy, but she wanted to help Giselle, and if she had to expose herself to do it, it couldn't be helped.

Giselle began playing, and Tierney listened intently to the melody. Joining in with the lyric to the first verse, she hoped nothing would make this moment any more awkward or, worse, get her prematurely fired.

The sunlight bathed her
Drowned her with its gold
Proved it had the power
To keep her from the cold

Still she played it safe
Tried staying in the shade
Wary of the sunshine
Mindful of the shame

Giselle stopped playing. Her slender hands with their long fingers lay like slain birds on the keys of the piano. She slowly turned her head toward Tierney. "What…" She cleared her throat and drew a deep breath. "What, or who, is that song about, Tierney?" Before Tierney had a chance to answer, Giselle snapped her eyes wide open and captured her. "And be honest."

Tierney blinked and dug her blunt nails into her palms. With more confidence than she felt, she jutted her chin out and answered truthfully. "You."

Chapter Seven

Giselle wasn't sure she'd heard Tierney right. Had she really said "you"? Trying to collect her whirling thoughts, she asked, "About me? Guess it is a recent piece then?" Cringing, Giselle dragged her fingers through her hair and dislodged her headband, causing it to land on the hardwood floor with a resounding clatter. Giselle did her best to control her breathing before it escalated until she couldn't stave off a panic attack. Usually she scoffed at her former therapist's use of mantras, but now she let the word *andante* resound in the back of her mind.

Tierney bent and picked up the headband, handing it back to Giselle. "Yes. Very recent. I'm sorry. I shouldn't have been so forward. I never meant for you to know about my writing or my singing." She pushed her hands flat under her thighs again, something Giselle had noticed Tierney often did when she seemed awkward or nervous.

"If you think about it, I asked you to listen in and have an opinion." Giselle smiled politely, her lips tense enough to make her feel they would crack. *Andante, andante.*

"Guess you got more than you asked for." Tierney shifted on top of her hands. "Thanks for not assuming the worst though."

"What 'worst' are we talking about here?" Her stomach ached as Giselle forced her breathing to remain even, calm. Her fingertips tingled, and she didn't dare analyze Tierney's lyrics. Blinking slowly, another method to calm her mind, she regarded Tierney closely.

"It wouldn't be a far stretch to assume that I was trying to take advantage of the fact that you have connections in the music industry.

All I can say is that it's not the case." Pulling her hands free, Tierney rubbed her palms on her jeans. "Not at all."

"Can you try to sing the text to the melody again?" Giselle heard herself say. "If you want to? *Calando.*"

Tierney gaped. "For real?"

"Again. I asked, didn't I?"

"Um. Yeah. You did." Blinking fast a few times, Tierney squared her shoulders. "All right. From the top?"

Giselle nodded and played the rudimentary intro. It needed more work, but right now she was only interested in determining if Tierney's lyrics really had anything to do with her. If they did, she wasn't sure how she would deal with that situation. Explore what this young woman's motives were? Why she would write something deeply personal about a woman she'd known for a few days? Returning to the part where she felt safe and in control, Giselle kept mentally murmuring *andante* over and over, while she let her fingers play along the keys, coaxing out the music, listening with both anticipation and dread—at least with more passion than she could ever remember feeling.

Tierney cleared her throat softly and sang the same lyrics as before. When Giselle moved on to the chorus, Tierney followed, stumbling on a few words when the syllables didn't quite fit. This didn't matter, as the song came alive right before Giselle. As they reached the crescendo, Tierney had closed her eyes and swayed to the dramatic melody.

> *Her dreams rarely come true*
> *And still I try to give her everything*
> *She carries that old stake in her heart*
> *It tears me to shreds when she screams*
>
> *When nightmares steal her soul*
> *And she won't let me in*
> *All I can do is sit outside her door*
> *And pray she'll hear me sing*

Slowly, Giselle pulled her hands from the keyboard, suddenly spent and completely exhausted. "And how can that be about me?" she asked quietly.

"I don't know," Tierney said, her hands back under her thighs. "Not literally, of course."

"I daresay not." Giselle stood so quickly, the piano stool crashed back against the wall behind her. "I'm…I'm going to work out. You can take the rest of the day off once you're back from grocery shopping."

"What?" Tierney looked alarmed as she stood also. "What about dinner?"

"I'm not entirely helpless in the kitchen. I'll make myself something from the freezer. You have a decent selection to choose from at the guesthouse." Feeling her heart pick up speed with each passing moment, Giselle knew she had to get into the room behind the garage and throw herself into a massive workout session. Sometimes that warded off a panic attack and kept her from having to take the medication she had if everything else failed. She realized today was a "just grab the damn pill" day.

"All right." Tierney looked concerned as she took a hesitant step toward the door. "If you're sure."

"Of course, I'm sure." Giselle spat the words and just wanted Tierney to get away from the door, so she could pass her at a safe distance. If someone touched her at this point, it would hurt physically. Wound up enough for her teeth to clatter, she clenched her jaws and darted past Tierney. She hurried toward the garage, where she had everything she needed, casting a quick glance behind her.

Tierney had followed her to the door leading into the gym and stood there with the softest expression in her eyes. Giselle saw no pity, or signs of anything but concern, which made her draw several deep breaths as she headed to the changing area of her gym. Tearing her clothes off and pulling on her gym outfit, Giselle stepped onto the treadmill and started at the highest setting she could safely maneuver. She ran as if the devil were coming up behind her, the lyrics Tierney had sung with that sultry, slightly husky voice marching through her mind. Especially the part that said, "*She carries that old stake in her heart,/It tears me apart when she screams,/When nightmares steal her soul.*"

The gym door opened, startling Giselle. Tierney came in and strode over to the cross-trainer. She mounted it, created new settings, and began her workout, not even glancing at Giselle. This woman was infuriating but somehow had to care, or she wouldn't have given Giselle so much thought that she could write that song. Or disregard her orders to make sure she was all right. Tears rose in Giselle's eyes, and she let go with one hand to wipe at her wet eyelashes. She had to get a grip on herself. If Tierney could get to her like this, in her home where her privacy was paramount, she could very likely fall apart at any given time.

Eventually, she'd run so far, she'd set a record on her treadmill. Stepping off, she grimaced at the pain and stiffness in her legs, remembering belatedly that she hadn't warmed up. She hadn't had time. Ignoring the agony building in her system, Giselle moved to the side of the gym that held her weights. She strapped some around her wrists and carried out the exercises a personal trainer had showed her, exercises meant to keep her from injuring her hands and arms. She depended on them for her career and livelihood, after all.

Out of the corners of her eyes, she saw Tierney leave the gym without a word, and twenty minutes later a familiar noise indicated that Tierney had taken the Jeep out of the garage. Soon the house would be empty, and Giselle could shower and then retire to her bedroom. There she would use her Roland electric piano and work on some of the other music she had written for Chicory Ariose. Just not *that* song. With sorrow flooding her chest, Giselle wondered if she would ever be able to play that song again—let alone hear Tierney's haunting voice sing it—without ending up in the gym like now.

Tierney was relieved Giselle hadn't chewed her out for not following orders. No way could she drive away to the damn grocery store unless she made sure Giselle was doing okay. Stopping to cuddle Charley and scratch Mister's ears, she let her mind replay what had taken place in the music room. Yes, she hadn't been smart when it came to her audacity to sing her original lyrics to one of Giselle's compositions. When she thought about it, she realized that must have been downright insulting. Talk about stomping on an established artist's work and with a deeply personal text about the composer herself. Groaning, she stood and grabbed the car keys and Giselle's debit card, which she still couldn't fathom Giselle letting her use. She'd probably set a limit on how much could be spent at a time. That would make sense.

As she drove down the gravel road and then turned out onto the main road leading to East Quay, her mind teemed with images of today and fear of what might happen tomorrow. Thinking about Vivian and Mike coming for dinner made her nervous. Tierney was a decent cook, but what if she made a mess of the meal? That would surely be the last straw that would lead to her being fired immediately. And she hardly dared picture what the guests would think of the stunt she'd pulled today, no matter that it hadn't been a calculated move—not at all. No matter why Giselle had fled from the music room earlier, it hadn't seemed to be because of Tierney's text. At least not only because of that. Giselle had asked her to sing—and liked her voice.

Rubbing the back of her neck, she maneuvered the Jeep along the curvy road. Why had she sung such a personal lyric? A new one, with elements of Giselle in it! "Fuck." Tierney sighed. "She probably thinks I have no sense of propriety. Just a lot of pretentiousness." Mulling her dark thoughts over, Tierney was aware of how she skidded around the fear lurking in the depths of her mind. She truly didn't want to leave Giselle and her work as her assistant and dog trainer. Tierney had such plans for turning Charley into the perfect dog for Giselle. She'd spent a very happy hour before she fell asleep last night, imagining how amazed and thrilled Giselle would become when she saw what Charley was capable of, so excited that Giselle would let her stay on. It was quite ironic. Here she'd plotted to find diverse ways to make herself indispensable and walked right into the trap of doing the exact opposite.

Gripping the wheel, Tierney pressed the accelerator harder and headed for the health-food supermarket in East Quay. She would simply do her shopping, put the groceries away when she got home, and then go to bed, no matter how early it was when she finished.

Only when she grabbed a shopping cart at the store did she realize she'd referred to Giselle's house as "home."

CHAPTER EIGHT

Tierney confessed to herself that she was hiding. Standing by the kitchen counter, she was preparing some of the ingredients for the dinner Giselle was hosting for Vivian and Mike. They hadn't spoken more than ten words to each other, if that, since Tierney had come over to the main house this morning to make breakfast. Giselle had been pale and only answered Tierney's questions with one-syllable words. Not that Tierney wanted to have a long heart-to-heart, but this was torture. She'd tried to figure out how to remedy the situation, which was foggy at best, and so had suffered from insomnia all night. She had battled this condition for as long as she could remember. Whenever something was unresolved, or she was worried about something, sleep eluded her. She'd ended up writing three more lyrics, despite whatever damage the first one had caused yesterday.

Checking the clock and realizing it was lunchtime, Tierney arranged a plate containing some light salad with croutons and dressing on the side on a tray for Giselle. She poured mineral water into a tall glass, hesitated, but then added two slices of lemon on a small plate beside it. After grabbing the tray, she forced herself to walk with determined steps to the music room. She could hear faint music and stopped, not ashamed to eavesdrop. It turned out not to be one of Giselle's compositions, but one of Chopin's etudes. Tierney wasn't such a complete classical-music aficionado that she could pinpoint the exact one, but she could tell it was played with passion—perhaps even fury? It could well be that Giselle would be pissed off for being disturbed, but so be it. The woman had to eat. She knocked hard on the door to try to drown out the piano.

The music stopped so fast, Tierney snapped her head up in alarm. Great. Now she'd gone and done it. She didn't hear the steps due to the insulation and jumped when Giselle yanked the door open. Good thing it went inward, or the tray's contents would have spilled all over the place. Giselle stared darkly at Tierney with her head tossed back slightly, as in a challenge, but stayed silent. Her chest heaved in quick breaths, and Tierney realized she must have put all her soul into the Chopin piece.

"Your lunch," Tierney said, indicating the tray with her chin. "Want it over on the table?"

Blinking, Giselle took a step back. "Yes." She was quiet for a moment and then added, "Thank you."

"I'm going to take Charley for a walk after I eat." Tierney didn't detect Giselle warming up but pushed forward. If she was going to be fired soon, she might as well try to make her mark as fully as possible. "I was thinking, since you'll be indoors most of today, you might want to come along?" Tierney regarded Giselle cautiously, waiting for an eruption or icy, dead quiet.

"No." Giselle sat down by the table and unfolded the linen napkin. "But you go ahead."

"The sooner you interject yourself into Charley's training, the easier you'll find it to continue after I'm gone."

Giselle dropped her fork onto the plate, wincing at the clattering noise. "Gone? Have you decided to leave earlier than agreed?" She didn't turn to meet Tierney's gaze but picked up her fork and stabbed an innocent piece of the salad and placed it in her mouth. Chewing with much more elegance than should have been possible for anyone to pull off, she placed the two lemon slices in the water.

"No. No. Not at all. I'll stay as long as you need me," Tierney said quickly. It would be disastrous if Giselle made her mind up that Tierney was leaving long before it was time. She groaned inwardly at how good she often was at digging herself into a hole and then pulling the dirt in over herself.

"Even if it's longer than the agreed-upon two weeks?" Giselle still kept her eyes on the salad.

"Sure. I'm, um, you know, flexible." Wanting to hide her face in her palms, Tierney remained standing there, back straight and trying to look like she wasn't embarrassed.

"All right." Putting down her fork, with obvious care this time, Giselle finally turned her head toward Tierney. "How far?"

"Excuse me?" Frowning now as she'd lost track of what Giselle could mean, Tierney stepped closer.

"Your walk. How far?"

"Depends," Tierney said with new enthusiasm as the coldness had disappeared from Giselle's demeanor, leaving only slight apprehension. "If you want to come with us, we can walk up and down your gravel road a few times. That way, we don't risk anyone stumbling upon us and confusing Charley."

Giselle's expression softened. "Well. Yes. We wouldn't want the dog to become confused."

"We sure wouldn't." Tierney smiled broadly. "In half an hour then? I mean, that gives us time before Vivian and Mike arrive."

"Sounds good." Looking a bit ill at ease, Giselle returned to her plate. "See you out front."

Perhaps she was starting to have second thoughts, but Tierney refused to give her time to back out. Pivoting on her heels, she closed the door behind her and returned to the kitchen. As she sat at the table eating her own salad, it dawned on Tierney what Giselle had implied. Perhaps she wouldn't expect Tierney to leave after two weeks after all. It was a strange sensation to feel relieved about something like that, but Tierney did. Given she lived such a nomadic life by choice, it was even more unexpected.

CHAPTER NINE

G iselle had tried to think up anything that wouldn't sound totally manufactured and cowardly, so as not to have to go on the damn walk. Had it been inside her fence, she could have done it easily enough, but moving about in open terrain—not so much. In the end, she realized that Tierney's happy expression tipped the scale in favor of a walk. Her assistant had looked so excited to involve her in Charley's training, which reminded Giselle of Tierney's offhand comment about her leaving. Why this had brought everything inside Giselle's mind to a complete stop, she couldn't figure out, only that it didn't sit well with her. Tierney had worked for her only five days, but it seemed much longer.

She pulled on her hiking boots, which felt like overkill for a walk back and forth on her gravel road, but knowing Charley's antics, she'd need something with a good grip. The weather looked nice, and Giselle opted for a light windbreaker. When she walked out the door, she found Tierney and Charley waiting for her. Charley was sitting by Tierney's left side but looked like she might shiver out of her skin from sheer happiness. When she saw Giselle, she made a half a move, as if she was about to jump up on her, something Giselle had found it impossible to teach her not to do.

"Ah-ah, Charley," Tierney said, her voice low and firm. "Stay."

To Giselle's amazement, Charley remained sitting, even if her tail did its usual frenetic wagging.

"Why don't we walk up to the meadow and let her run off-leash a little?" Tierney smiled. "If she burns off some steam, she'll listen more carefully to us later."

"To you, no doubt. To me? We'll see." Giselle walked to Tierney's right, not at all comfortable as they approached the gate. Normally, she ventured outside her property only in her car, which she could reach indoors by way of the garage door that led to the mudroom.

"Oh, you'll be surprised. Just use the same tone you use when I annoy you." Grinning, Tierney winked at Giselle, who wondered if she was imagining the tiny hurt tone in Tierney's voice.

Tierney smiled warmly and the moment passed. "Charley needs a firm hand but also a very loving one. You can easily break a retriever's spirit if you're too angry, but you can also be too lenient with them as well, since they're such goofballs."

"And here I thought it was just my dog." Giselle spoke tongue-in-cheek, but her remark had some truth to it. Whenever she would see well-behaved dogs with good manners, she wondered what she was doing wrong with Charley. Had she given up when nothing seemed to go right? Yes. She had. She'd settled for Charley running wild on the property. Frances had taken her for walks, and it had stung that Charley usually minded her better. "I think it has more to do with me than her."

Tierney snorted irreverently. "Perhaps to a degree, but retrievers usually mature later in life. They're cheeky brats for the first three years, I'd say."

"How do you know so much about dogs?" Giselle asked.

"One of the places where I stayed had a kennel. It was the one place I really liked. I lived there only six months, but I soaked up everything they taught me about dogs, training them, and different breeds. I practically camped out at the libraries of the towns where I stayed, reading all kinds of books about dogs. Occasionally I read about other pets, but dogs are my favorites." Tierney shrugged. "Guess I can be educated, right?"

Giselle tried to wrap her brain around what Tierney had just said. "You said 'one of the places you stayed.' What do you mean?"

"I…oh, damn. You know I was in the system for most of my childhood and adolescence. In fact, I stayed in several different foster homes. Much like being an army brat, you know. A lot of moving."

Tierney sounded like she'd repeated this information a million times. Dispassionately, she talked about what had to have been a hard childhood and adolescence as if it meant nothing. But this was clearly not the case. Aware that she didn't know Tierney deep down, Giselle still could tell with reasonable accuracy that Tierney had to hide strong emotions to keep them from taking over. She recognized that particular trait, as she was the same way.

"Guess it can be hard to feel at home at any given place after such a start in life." Giselle kept close to the tree line of the woods to their left as she spoke. The stunning vision of the open fields to the right elevated her pulse.

"Sure can." Tierney eyed her carefully. "How long have you had problems with being outside?"

Guess that was only fair. Giselle rarely talked about her phobia with anyone, since the people around her already knew. "Always. It's grown worse over time. Crowded places and stress make it even worse."

"Do you feel safe only at the house?"

"My property, the car, and once I was on a secluded island when I wrote music for a movie." The tropical island had been remote and heavily guarded, but very few people could live like that. "Like this, surrounded by woods, is all right. Open areas…are difficult for me."

"What do you miss the most?" Tierney bent down and unhooked the leash from Charley's collar.

"I didn't know this walk would turn into a therapy session." Tensing, Giselle shoved her hands into her pockets. Was this when she asked Tierney why the hell she'd written that song about her? She hedged. Did she really want to know? Could she handle that?

"Oh, God. It's not that. We're just talking about our illustrious pasts." Tierney laughed, and again it dawned on Giselle how irreverent she sounded—but not callous. Perhaps that bubbling laughter was a coping mechanism. And who was playing psychologist now? Giselle sighed and was about to keep walking when she realized the tree line had ended and they stood several yards into the open field that was now twice the size of the former one.

"No." Taking two steps back, she bumped into Tierney. "No."

Tierney placed a gentle hand at the small of her back, not to stop her, Giselle realized, but to keep her from falling on the uneven ground. "Easy there." Her voice wasn't cheery now, but instead calm and with a tinge of alto. Much like her singing voice sounded. "It's just us here. And Charley. Look at her. That proves my point." She pointed at the racing dog that every now and then came to a dead stop, listened, sniffed, performed a ninja roll, and went on running again. "Goofball."

Giselle remained where she was. Tierney's hand against her back grounded her somehow, and she could breathe without wheezing. "She has so much energy."

"Dogs are nuts that way. They can go at it until they're totally bushed, and then they rest for twenty minutes, only to be ready for round two. I think they invented the term power nap."

"I think you're right." Giselle glanced at Tierney, who stood so close, her presence should have crowded all her senses. Instead it felt reassuring and not invasive in any way. That was so strange. "I don't think I want to go farther out into the field."

"Then Charley better come on cue, because I'm not leaving you alone here." Tierney stuck two fingers of her free hand into her mouth and gave a piercing whistle. "Charley. Come!"

Charley stopped so fast, she nearly fell. Looking over at them, she seemed to ponder if she could get away with tearing around the field one more time. If it was the fact that they gave her time to figure it out, Giselle had no way of knowing, but Charley gave a muted "woof" and came running.

"Here. Give her these and praise her to bits." Tierney handed Giselle five treats.

Charley came to a sudden halt, nearly slamming into Giselle's legs, and then sat down, her tongue lolling as she panted happily.

"Clever dog. Good girl." Giselle gave Charley the treats and was rewarded with an affectionate lick along the back of her hand. "You're such a clever dog. "

Charley clearly took that as an invitation and threw herself in her favorite position, on her back with her legs waving madly. Unable to resist, Giselle chuckled and crouched next to her crazy dog and rubbed her belly. "Such a lovebug, aren't you?"

"Moff," Charley replied.

Standing up, Giselle smiled at Tierney. "This is new. I mean, she's always been cuddly, but this, coming to me, especially when you're right next to me, is very special."

Tierney blinked and looked bewildered. Clasping her hands behind her back, she opened her mouth twice to speak before she said,

"She wants to please you, but she needs to learn what you want from her. Once dogs, especially retrievers, learn what you expect and that they have no other option than to obey, they love working. And if Charley spends more time with you, working together, her training will go exponentially faster."

"I believe you. You've done more with her than I've managed to accomplish in two years." Still mystified at why Tierney seemed to feel awkward and now also appeared flustered, Giselle spoke quickly before she lost her nerve. "I realize this takes longer than we first agreed on. I mean, training both me and Charley."

"I'm game if you are," Tierney said lightly, shaking her arms loose.

"I am. If you can imagine remaining in East Quay for a little while longer, I'd be very grateful."

Tierney now beamed, her open smile making her eyes sparkle. "I'll stay as long as you need me, okay?"

Taken aback, Giselle could barely breathe. "How can…you can't just say that." Nobody could promise such a thing, give a carte blanche of promised time. "What if something happens to your family or friends?"

"I don't have any family, remember? And as for my friends, I mostly see them online. I'm in contact with a few of my former foster-siblings and others with the same past."

"But still—"

"I'm a nomad. I confess. But as out of character as it is for you to let me, a stranger, into your home, it's just as strange for me to really want to stay and be of help to you."

So. There it was. Giselle needed an assistant to help with her dog, take care of the house, and run errands. Tierney saw herself as the one for the job. Still, it was more than that. "You realize you sell yourself short, don't you?" Giselle narrowed her eyes, rather pleased at the effect her expression had on Tierney. Back went her hands behind her again.

"What do you mean?"

"You offer to be my assistant and help train my dog. That's great, but I need you in another capacity. It would be a crime to overlook that skill. Vivian and Mike arrive in an hour. I want you to bring more of whatever lyrics you have, and we can try to fit them to my melodies."

"And the lyrics from earlier?" Tierney asked carefully.

Giselle wanted to say no, which would have been her usual method of operation. She always protected herself at all costs to keep from having that final panic attack that would defy what all her doctors or therapists claimed wasn't possible—and kill her. And now, here she stood, next to a young woman who wasn't free of scars. Tierney possessed the heart of a warrior. Giselle could feel it. She seemed to lead a nomadic life, so perhaps she was running from something, or someone. Still, she dared to write such revealing lyrics that they might well have caused her to be fired, but instead she had, in a moment of wanting to help Giselle, bared them, and herself.

This woman was vibrant and ready for whatever she could do to help, and then some. The lyrics scared Giselle, but she had to put them together with her melody, regardless of her own fears. Her heart landed with a sickening sound in the center of her abdomen. "Even those."

Chapter Ten

The doorbell rang, and Tierney quickly dried her hands on the tea towel she'd tucked into the waistband of her jeans. Nervously, she cleared her throat as she walked to the front door and opened it. Outside, Mike and Vivian stood, hand in hand, while Charley bounced around them.

"Charley, down." Gratefully slipping into her dog-trainer role, Tierney looked sternly at the exuberant retriever. "No jumping."

"Wow," Mike said. "That's the first time I've seen her actually obey without trying to get away with another jump. You're clearly onto this little sweetheart."

"Sweet and sweet. Let's not exaggerate," Giselle said from behind. "Welcome, both of you." She waved them in.

"Here. Let me take your jackets." Tierney hung the garments on wooden hangers in the closet next to the front door. "May I get you something to drink? It's actually quite hot today."

"Why, thank you, Tierney," Vivian said. "I'd love some iced tea if you have any."

"Me too," Mike said and put an arm around Vivian's shoulder. "Music room?"

"Yes. I thought we'd get some work done before we have dinner. It'll be early, around four, if that's all right?" Giselle moved toward the music room. "Iced tea for me as well. Unsweetened. And make some for yourself."

"Sounds perfect." Vivian followed alongside Mike, and if Tierney hadn't known the woman was legally blind, she wouldn't have noticed the subtle hints Mike gave her partner as they maneuvered among the furniture.

Back in the kitchen, Tierney placed a pitcher of unsweetened iced tea on a tray and added some sugar and sweeteners beside four glasses, in case someone changed her mind. Taking a breath, and then a second one, she carried the tray to the music room. For once the door was wide open, and Giselle sat at the piano, smiling warmly at her friends.

"Ah, that looks great," Mike said and helped Tierney place the glasses on coasters within reach of everybody. "And there's extra sugar here as well. Very thoughtful, Tierney."

Not knowing where to sit, or if she should remain standing in case Giselle needed her to fetch something, Tierney sipped her iced tea, desperate to moisten her throat.

"Come sit with me, Tierney," Giselle said, sounding as if that was a frequent practice between them. "I want you to sing something you know that I can play. I want Mike and Vivian to hear you sing."

"Now?" Already? Tierney's cheeks warmed. She'd thought she might be some oddity Giselle would display at the end of their working session, but Giselle evidently wanted her to jump in with both feet. "I'm rather embarrassed since I'm in the presence of professional musicians and am just a happy-go-lucky amateur." She put her glass down on the tray. "I'm sure you have more urgent business to—"

"Come now, Tierney," Giselle said, her voice softer. "You have a good voice. I just want you to warm up before we get to the original pieces. All right?"

"Okay." Tierney looked apologetically at Vivian and Mike. "Do remember that I mainly sing in the shower." This wasn't entirely true. She'd sung at train stations, malls, squares, farmers' markets, and even on open-mic nights.

"Do you know 'Summertime,' from *Porgy and Bess*?" Giselle asked. "Or you pick something."

"'Summertime.' Sure." Cringing at the idea that Vivian might well have sung that song at one point in her career, Tierney sat down next to Giselle on the piano stool. It was barely large enough for them both, and their legs pressed against each other.

"A-minor." Giselle played the easily recognizable intro, and Tierney tried to get into the zone. Her voice wobbled some during the first few words, but then she found her equilibrium and tried to sing the song as the lullaby it was. She closed her eyes briefly and relaxed the muscles around her throat, letting her voice track the resonance cavities within her. Giselle's music wrapped around her, and the soft touch with which she accompanied Tierney made her lean in a little, as if to maintain the connection.

When the last tone rang out, Tierney blinked, feeling slightly disoriented. She looked at Giselle, who had her hands folded on her lap. "Was it okay?" Tierney whispered.

"You're kidding, right?" Mike had pulled her feet up under her where she sat on the love seat with Vivian. "Those are some pipes you have, Tierney. I still have goose bumps." She held up her arm to prove it.

"Vivian?" Giselle tilted her head.

"Tierney, as Mike said, you have a stunning voice. I hear soul, pop, some folk-music tones, and then there's that something that's uniquely you. You don't mimic any of the popular singers, which is a very good thing. However, you should focus on a genre other than musical theater. You have to find a genre that speaks to you."

"And Tierney's already done that. Why don't I play one of the songs I've composed with Chicory Ariose in mind, and then Tierney can join in with lyrics she wrote."

Still taken aback, no, shocked, by the accolades from Vivian and Mike, Tierney barely registered Giselle's words. Then her anger rose. Had she really agreed to this? She was supposed to sing the song that was so deeply personal to her, and such a testament to how she saw Giselle, in front of these women, though nice as they were, she didn't really know? She had begun shaking her head at Giselle when she saw a range of emotions in those blue eyes. For whatever reason, Giselle was challenging both of them. Tierney had no idea why. Or perhaps she could guess. The lyrics had hit home. Maybe Giselle was going to stand her ground this time. If that was it, Tierney had to help. She couldn't refuse to be there for her. She swallowed so hard it hurt. "Sure."

Looking pleased, Giselle began to play the bittersweet melody that had almost caused them to part ways. Tierney could tell Giselle had changed some of it, and only when Giselle played the chorus a second time did she realize it was to accommodate Tierney's words.

Had Giselle memorized the lyrics Tierney had sung for her so well she knew where to change the melody? That accomplishment really demonstrated Giselle's genius.

Giselle let the melody fade out and turned to Vivian and Mike. "First, do you like the instrumental version?" She looked relaxed, but Tierney felt fine tremors against her left thigh.

"You never disappoint," Vivian said and wiped at her eyelashes. "And you say Tierney wrote some lyrics for this song?" She raised her eyebrows.

"No, well, yes, in a way. She already had lyrics, since writing is her favorite pastime, or so I understand." Giselle looked at Tierney with a smile. "Am I right?"

"Yes." Tierney pressed her hands under her thighs, which she belatedly realized meant she touched Giselle's right thigh as well.

"All right," Giselle said huskily, but didn't move away from Tierney's hand. "Two verses, one chorus, one more verse, the bridge, and last chorus. Is that okay?"

Tierney now wondered, and quite seriously, if Giselle could read minds. "I did write a suggestion for the bridge earlier," she said quietly.

"You did? When? You've been preparing food and setting the table since we got back from walking Charley." Giselle frowned.

"I wrote it in my head, while doing all that. I mean, cooking and setting the table are hardly rocket science." Tierney crinkled her nose.

"Of course, you did." Giselle began the intro again, nodding at Tierney to begin.

Tierney sang the beautiful song, so eager to make it her own, but mostly to do the song justice. When she neared the bridge, her nerves acted up, but she kept swaying to the rhythm while she continued to sing.

I never thought
I'd find the way
That she'd ever let me in
I hope she knows
I'm here to stay
I'm ready to begin

To love again

Tierney thought she could hear a soft gasp from the love seat but remained set on finishing the song. Once Giselle had played the chorus one more time, Tierney pulled her hands free and got ready to stand. A gentle hand on her arm stopped her, and she looked helplessly into Giselle's darkening eyes.

"Thank you," Giselle said. "I think we need to talk later. Don't you?"

Trembling now, with so many emotions fluttering through her system, Tierney nodded wordlessly. She wanted to sound cool and casual, but her old façade simply didn't work. "All right," she replied, relieved to get some coherent words out.

"I realize this must be your first draft, and it can use some polishing, Tierney, but it fits the song perfectly," Mike said and joined them at the piano with Vivian. "Do you have them written down, Tierney? Or recorded, which would be even better."

Glad now that they all liked her lyrics, Tierney pulled out her smartphone. "If we play it one more time, we can record it on my phone, and I can send it to you guys via my cloud."

Vivian looked confused. "Cloud?"

"This stunning lady of mine doesn't appreciate computers as much as I do," Mike said and snickered. "It means it's safe for us to listen to, but only us, since Tierney will send us a link to where she'll store the text online."

"I'm sure that's fantastically practical," Vivian said regally, but then laughed. What a fantastically melodious sound. "I heard a beautiful potential for harmonies in that song, Giselle. If you'll sing it again, Tierney, I'll try to add a lower harmony."

Singing harmonies with *the* Vivian Harding. Tierney could only smile and shook her head when a chuckle erupted from within her. She giggled, and Mike joined in.

"Not sure what's so funny," Mike said, wiping under her eyes with tapered fingertips, "but your laughter can set off a mega giggle-party."

"Goodness." Giselle clearly attempted to sound stern and get them back on track, but a broad smile stretched her pink lips.

Eventually, Tierney controlled herself and set her phone to record. As she sang the now-so-familiar song, Vivian let wordless tones simmer just below Tierney's vocals. When they finished, Vivian nodded, looking pleased. "I thought as much."

Tierney wanted to ask what Vivian thought but merely sat there, waiting for the pros to figure things out. She'd done her part for now.

"Play the first verse of the song back on the phone, please," Vivian said. "I want to hear if it sounded as good as it felt singing it."

Tierney placed the phone on top of the grand piano and then felt Giselle's hand pull her down next to her again. "Just in case we need to redo or alter anything."

Vivian and Mike ended up insisting on hearing the song sung in harmony twice before they were pleased. "We need to include Eryn and Manon," Vivian said brightly. "Mike and I can't speak for them regarding something so…so amazing. They need to hear it, and then all four of us can decide. We're a team and always decide together."

"Terrific," Giselle said. Checking her watch, she turned to Tierney. "Why don't you do what needs to be done to the food, and I'll play the rest of the songs after dinner. We can all benefit from stretching our legs."

"Absolutely." Tierney stood. "I'll be in the kitchen if you need something."

"Thank you." Giselle spoke matter-of-factly, but the expression on her face and the way her blue eyes sparkled reminded Tierney about the talk Giselle wanted to have. Would there be more interrogating regarding the fact Tierney had started out by writing the text about her impression of Giselle—or would they have an actual conversation without tons of preconceived ideas?

As she walked out of the room and headed to the kitchen, Vivian stood as well. "Tierney, I promise not to help you in any way, as my aim when I chop carrots is less than accurate, but may I still join you in the kitchen?"

"Of course." Looking at Mike, Tierney gently placed her hand around Vivian's elbow. "Like this?"

"Perfect. The others can play with that menace of a dog while the two of us chat."

Oh, no. Another deep conversation where someone wanted to know where she came from, how she could sing and write lyrics, and what made her tick. Could she perhaps take her words back and insist that she needed to focus on cooking? But that was a downright lie, as she had most of the food already prepared.

Tierney walked with Vivian to the kitchen. Why was she suddenly the center of attention? This was so not her style. She preferred to slip through cracks, skim along the surface of her life. No deep forays into her past, which would only lead to pity or dismay. And certainly, no confessions on her part about her true feelings about...anything or anyone.

Absolutely none.

CHAPTER ELEVEN

Giselle stood next to Mike as Charley gallivanted among the trees toward the back of the property. She could sense her friend was curious, but true to Mike's nature, she waited patiently.

"Yes, my dear?" Giselle asked teasingly. "Something on your mind?"

"You know what I'm wondering." Mike chuckled. "Those lyrics, and from such an unassuming woman like Tierney. Pretty daring. Bold."

"Mike…" Now Giselle made sure she interjected a warning into her voice.

"No need to be offended. You must realize that both Vivian and I care deeply for you. And when such a perfect individual shows up just when you need assistance the most and she turns out to be so talented… add to that how the words she wrote fit you. Not to mention the current between the two of you. Every time you accidentally touched, both of you literally jumped." Mike gently placed a hand on Giselle's shoulder. "And don't tell me I'm imagining things."

"Are you going to interrogate me all through dinner, too?" Giselle wasn't sure what she felt about Mike asking her questions, only that she'd rather pull out a tooth than answer.

"Interro—no! It's not like that at all. It's just that I see such a difference in you since the last time we met, and the only thing that has changed, as far as I know, is that Frances had to leave, and you have Tierney here."

That was some accurate pinpointing. Giselle did feel different. She was completely at a loss as to what way she'd changed, but she had. Tierney had a lot to do with it, but something unfathomable was happening regardless. "You're asking the wrong person, Mike. Tierney *is* a bit of fresh air around here. Frances and I have trotted along the same paths for years. I've felt safe that way. Now that she's in the UK—and I finally heard from her, by the way, a text message—she plans to stay with her sister and her sister's family for quite a while."

"Don't change the subject," Mike said and moved to let Charley pass, holding a long branch in her mouth. "God, is Tierney training her to fight with weapons?"

"No. That's an old skill. Be grateful she wasn't carrying it far out on the end. She could have sent you sprawling." Giselle watched her dog run like lightning across the lawn.

"So, back to the topic of changes and how Tierney factors in." Mike motioned toward a wooden bench, and they sat down. Immediately, Charley returned and laid her stick in front of them, sinking down with a silly grin.

"*You* are like a dog with a bone," Giselle said to Mike and made a face. "The most astonishing thing that happened was when she talked me into walking up to the fields with Charley earlier today. I was so sure it would end in disaster, and it nearly did, but I managed to stave off the panic attack...and not by running back to the house, but standing right there, several steps out in the field."

"That's a huge deal." Mike squeezed Giselle's hand lightly. "Was it the combo of her and the dog, you think?"

"Could be." Giselle lowered her gaze, not wanting to meet Mike's glance.

"Ah. So, something else as well."

"God." Giselle ran her hand under her hair, which she kept in a low bun. "She placed her hand on my back." Why was she being this upfront with Mike? Yes, they were friends and had collaborated several times and known each other since Chicory Ariose was formed, but still. She never talked about personal things with anyone. Was that yet another change that had come about since her everyday life was altered? All she knew was how good it felt to have this conversation with Mike.

"Where? Bra-level, waistline, or near your ass?" Mike asked seriously, but her eyes sparkled.

"Mike!" Flustered now, Giselle realized Mike was being facetious, but her own response to Tierney's touch had been so unexpected. Giselle could feel the impact of it even now. "If you must know, the small of my back." And it had felt so good, so reassuring. Tierney's touch had centered Giselle enough for her to simmer down and just stand there. Her presence had wrapped around Giselle, and the scent of her mixed with the fresh one from the woods and the field had made her dizzy in a much more enticing way.

"Ah. Very gentlewomanish." Mike gave Giselle's hand a quick squeeze. "And I'm teasing you. You realize that, don't you? I'm just so glad to see you so…well, so alive. Normally I glimpse that vitality in you only when you're at the piano."

Giselle hadn't known that. Of course, she had lived her life the same way for years and convinced herself this was what she had to settle for. Tierney's influence was altering her situation, day by day. Now, though, she'd had enough of them digging through her emotional state. "She has some voice, doesn't she?"

Mike brightened. "Oh, does she ever. It's very unusual, as it goes back and forth between being raw and unkempt to smooth and almost sounding like she had classical training."

"I can promise you that she's entirely a natural." Not wanting to break any of the confidences Tierney had shared, Giselle didn't mention the young woman's rough start in life. "Not only does she sing well, but she can emote, and I suspect she has perfect pitch. She heard me play that song once, recognized that her lyrics could fit, and sang it back to me as if she'd practiced for a week. I'm not sure she realizes she has that ability, but I'm willing to bet money on it."

"Coming from you, that's not a moneymaking bet, so I'll take your word for it." Mike nodded emphatically. "I could tell Vivian was taken with her voice. Since Vivi lost more of her vision, she's become even more auditorily sensitive. She can determine now whether it's Perry or Mason barking. I think they sound entirely the same, but she's always right, so what do I know?" Mike bent and scratched Charley's head. "Our boys are getting old. They're already on borrowed time. Great Danes don't live very long compared to some other dogs. They're quite rambunctious though, and our vet says that for the most part they're doing well."

"You must bring them next time. We can keep Charley from chasing them if they think she's too much."

"Sounds like a great idea. Vivian would like that." Mike looked up at the house. "I wonder if she's giving poor Tierney the third degree."

"Like you did with me?" Giselle said, raising her eyebrows deliberately.

"Ha. Well, yeah, kind of." Mike began to laugh. "Busted, huh?"

"I'll say." Giselle nudged Mike in a friendly way. "Should we go rescue Tierney before she decides her job doesn't have enough perks?"

"Not a chance. Tierney won't quit that easily. Even Vivian could 'see' the main reason for that." Mike winked at her and laughed.

Giselle covered her eyes with her hand. "A mad dog, a high-maintenance cat, and crazy friends. Must be bad karma reasserting itself."

Mike only kept laughing as they walked to rejoin the other two women.

Tierney put the salmon on the griddle, checked on the potato salad, and then fetched the pitchers of iced tea and lemon water from the fridge. Perhaps if she stayed busy enough, she could dodge the third degree. Sure, Vivian was lovely, but she was also curious. Curious, and protective of Giselle, no doubt. Tierney was certain that she would be out, headfirst, if Vivian thought she was taking advantage of her friend.

"Did Giselle corner you in there, my dear? I hope you had agreed to sing beforehand?" Vivian sat at the small breakfast-nook table, her head accurately following Tierney as she readied their dinner.

"Sure. Of course. I didn't mind." Tierney wasn't entirely certain how she felt about singing in front of professional performers. And not just your average local talent, but *the* Vivian Harding. "I just hope you weren't taken aback. I mean, it's not easy to have to find something nice to say, just to avoid hurting someone's feelings."

"Excuse me?" Vivian blinked. "Are you saying you think Mike and I praised you so you, or Giselle, wouldn't feel bad? When it comes to our career, we don't risk it by being afraid of rubbing someone the wrong way. Granted, I believe in letting people down gently if they're not good enough, for whatever reason. No need to hit them over the head." Vivian smiled wryly. "A tactic I wish some of my former voice coaches and directors had adopted. You, my dear, have a remarkable voice and the incredible gift of writing lyrics that fit the melody. Clearly you haven't yet been given the chance to break into the industry—if that's what you want."

Tierney knew she was standing there openmouthed. And she wasn't sure what she wanted, not really. "For now, I want to help Giselle," she said quietly. "No matter what, she needs me until this Frances comes back—if she does."

"As far as I understand, if she comes back, it won't happen very soon. But," Vivian said thoughtfully, "are you saying you're not aiming for a career in the music industry?"

Sitting down on the chair opposite Vivian, merely because her knees were growing increasingly weaker, Tierney gripped the top with cold hands. "Until now, I always assumed I'd need connections to have even a remote chance. I write lyrics and poetry because it keeps me sane. Well, more or less." Snorting, Tierney clasped her hands. "I'm really as far down the social ladder as anyone can be. Who would listen to my words?"

Vivian nodded slowly. "I understand what you're saying, but clearly Giselle listened and found you worth paying attention to. Worthy enough for her to coax you into singing for us."

"So, not a commonplace occurrence?" Tierney briefly stopped breathing.

"Not all. Unprecedented, in fact. I've never heard her sound this enthralled with anyone outside her small circle of friends and colleagues."

Her cheeks warming now, Tierney rose to turn over the pieces of salmon. "Really?"

"Really."

Pivoting, Tierney scrutinized Vivian, seeing nothing but complete straightforwardness. She had to change the subject before she self-combusted, so she tossed out the first question that came to mind. "How did you and Mike meet?"

Vivian chuckled. "Had enough, dear?" Then her expression changed into something soft and warm. "Mike is my knight in shining armor," she said, her voice low and intense. "I walked into her coffeehouse on the marina one day, shortly after finding out I was going blind. She was there, behind the counter, looking young, strong, and with a kind of sorrow about her that echoed my own. I quickly found out she had a strong protective side, and soon she kept showing up when I needed her the most. Fortunately, she seemed to want and need me just as much."

"She seems to have the protective side figured out." Tierney tried to find the words for what she meant to ask. "I mean, she helps you, but she seems to do it in a way that doesn't turn her into a caregiver. I'm not sure I'm making sense."

"But you are." A gentle smiled passed over Vivian's elegant features. She wore bright-red lipstick and her blond hair in a rolled-up braid. "Mike is my equal in every sense of the word, but it took me a while to make her see that. And to be totally honest, she had to persuade me about the age difference." Tilting her head, Vivian pursed her lips. "Are you asking me this as Giselle's assistant or as…well, from another perspective?"

Tierney grew cold. How could she be so careless? Vivian's kindness had lulled her into feeling safe about sharing almost anything, but she had to remember that this woman was Giselle's friend. Not hers. "Her assistant. Naturally. I'm not sure what other capacity I could possibly have here."

"Of course." Vivian reached out to Tierney. "Now I'm the one putting you on the spot. I'm sorry. I didn't mean for it to come across like that—all busybody."

Unable to resist the sincerity and, yes, honest charm Vivian exuded, Tierney took the proffered hand. "No need to apologize. I've often been told I'm overly sensitive." Mostly by foster parents who seemed amazed their foster child didn't take being locked in the basement as punishment very well.

"No such thing. Either a person is sensitive, or they aren't. In my opinion, we fluctuate depending on our situation in life. I get the feeling your childhood wasn't all that easy." Vivian squeezed Tierney's hand lightly.

"No. It wasn't. But I was often my own worst enemy, and I paid the price for it a few times."

"I would like to hear about that one day, if you feel like sharing. You interest me, and I know Mike feels the same way. She says you feel like a kindred spirit, and since her childhood was no picnic either... perhaps she's right." Pulling her hand back, Vivian changed the subject. "Food smells divine. Salmon?"

"Shi—shoot." Tierney flew off the chair and headed over to the stove. She pulled off the griddle pan and placed the salmon on warmed plates. "I think we need to get the others and—"

"No need. We're here," Mike said from the doorway to the foyer. "The great smell made it easy to find you. Where are we eating? I can help you, Tierney."

"Thanks. We've set the table in the conservatory." Tierney handed Mike the two tall pitchers. "They're heavy."

"Hey! What do I look like? Boiled pasta?" Mike grinned. "You okay, Vivi?"

"I can find my way unless Giselle suddenly rearranged her furniture." Vivian stood. "I won't offer to carry anything though." Vivian laughed.

They moved into the white and blue conservatory. Surrounded by glass on three sides, it was like sitting outdoors, but in more comfort. Tierney had picked a few wildflowers and placed them in a small vase as a humble centerpiece.

"So pretty," Mike said and then described the table to Vivian.

"It's Tierney's doing, mostly." Giselle turned toward the table but then stopped and scanned it. "Wait. We're missing one plate."

"Yes, we are." Mike looked over Vivian's head at Tierney.

"Tierney?" Giselle said, frowning."

"I set the table for you and your guests, Giselle. That makes three." Not sure what she'd done wrong, Tierney returned Mike's glance.

"Go get a plate for yourself. Of course you're eating with us." Scowling, Giselle motioned for Tierney to hurry.

When Tierney returned holding a plate, a glass, and utensils, Giselle pointed to the chair next to her. "Please have a seat."

Tierney watched Vivian and Mike sitting together and moaned inwardly. It was one thing to sit across from someone at a breakfast table, but this...Tierney yanked out the chair and sat down. She accidentally kicked the table leg, making the plates jump. "Oh, God. Sorry. I have big feet." Tierney felt her cheeks color.

"No, you don't." Mike winked.

Giselle reached for her napkin and draped it over her lap. "This looks wonderful. Thank you for cooking, Tierney. That saved me a lot of time. And I rather dislike having to resort to caterers."

"Unless it's something you order off the menu from the Sea Stone Café," Mike said. "And have it delivered by yours truly."

"Of course." Giselle looked like she was relaxing more and more.

"You're still actively managing your coffeehouse?" Tierney asked, curious.

"Only when we're in town. I have a great manager who takes care of things when we're in the studio or on tour." Mike arranged the food on Vivian's plate and murmured something in her ear. Vivian nodded and began eating as if nothing was wrong with her eyes at all.

"Speaking of that. Do you have a date for when you go in to the studio next time? I know you said something about this fall." Giselle cut through the salmon, and to Tierney's relief, the inside boasted the perfect, slightly pink color.

"Actually, we'll start in two weeks," Mike said. "We have four tracks ready to be cut. You don't have to stress yourself out, though. We're taking a long-overdue vacation, Vivian and I, after that. When we get back, in late September, we'll start recording your songs."

"I'll send them to you one by one so you can have your lyricist—"

"That's just it," Mike said. She made an apologetic gesture for interrupting. "I want to take Tierney's lyrics to Manon and Eryn and have them listen. If they like them as much as Vivi and I do, perhaps we'll commission more." She looked over at Tierney. "What do you think? Interested?"

Tierney felt trapped by her rampaging emotions. To have established artists interested in her texts was amazing, but what if accepting such a chance pulled her away from Giselle, who needed her? "I, uh…It's flattering, but—"

"Don't turn them down," Giselle said. She gave Tierney a pointed look. "If the rest of your lyrics are good enough, this could become your stepping stone to a better future. After all, your employment here is temporary."

The thud in the pit of her stomach had to be her heart breaking from its moorings. Rapidly, her untethered heart fluttered like a fish pulled up on the dock. "But…"

"Tierney." Giselle's voice held some caution but mainly sounded kind.

Slowly slumping against the backrest of the wicker chair, Tierney held on so hard to her utensils, her knuckles whitened. "So, late September. Sounds fantastic. Count me in." This would give her about eight weeks with Giselle.

Trying not to devour Giselle with her eyes, Tierney assumed her trademark broad, sparkling smile even as a tiny, unwelcome voice inside her head kept repeating, "Eight weeks to last you a lifetime."

Chapter Twelve

Exhausted after a day of music mixed with too much introspection, Giselle stretched her arms toward the ceiling. Her muscles ached, especially after playing one of the more passionate and up-tempo pieces. A hot shower had helped some, but sitting at her vanity, treating her face and décolleté with her Exquisite moisturizer, Giselle examined her face closely. What did Tierney see when she looked at her? Granted, the light makeup she wore every day out of habit helped her look more awake. Younger, in a sense. Not that it mattered. It never had. Perhaps she should be grateful she had been involved with a few people before the agoraphobia and anxiety disorder had placed her in a lifelong harness that pulled her away from…from civilization, to be blunt.

She wasn't being overly dramatic, even if a few people had suggested that. They weren't in her life anymore, as their negativity and general shaming weren't doing her any good. Instead, looking back at the girls she'd flirted with and come close to having a physical relationship with, Giselle found it bittersweet as well as fortunate to have lived through that period of her life at all, while she still had the chance.

Now, at thirty-eight, some days she felt much older. Compared to Tierney, who was, what—in her mid or late twenties—she felt ancient. As exuberant as Tierney was on the surface, she had an old-soul darkness sometimes. She wanted to ask Tierney what her past had been like. It surprised Giselle how much she wanted to know every little detail about Tierney. What had happened to her when she was very young to have her end up in the system? No matter what it was, it hadn't seemed to snuff out her spark. Not the spark that looked fake and too glittery, but that fire in Tierney that allowed her to train Charley—and yes, reach Giselle when anyone else would've been hard-pressed to do so. It was as mindboggling as it was puzzling.

Giselle wasn't so naive that she thought another person could ever cure her of her deep-rooted anxiety, but she had to concede that Tierney got under her skin like nobody else had ever done. Yes, her friends, whom she mostly knew through her line of work, had proved to be very understanding and accommodating. Tierney, though, had a way of gently coaxing her, and God knew this woman was persuasive.

Pulling off her robe, Giselle reached for a new nightgown, a cobalt-blue satin slip that reached her mid-thigh. After brushing her hair, she rubbed lotion on her hands, extending the fingers and balling them into fists repeatedly. Her first piano teacher had instilled this habit in her from an early age. Always tend to your hands, as they are your prize possession. It was true, but at age six, she'd found the advice hilarious.

She was about to slip into bed when she stopped, trying to remember if she'd made sure Tierney set the alarm before she returned to the guesthouse. Padding out into the hallway on bare feet, Giselle read the setting on the console next to the front door. Locked and alarm set. Of course. Tierney was conscientious and careful.

A knock on the door made her jump. She pressed a button on the alarm console, and a video feed of the person outside her door came into view on the small screen. Tierney. Giselle opened the door, glaring at her late visitor.

"What on earth are you doing here at this hour?" She put her left hand on her hip.

"I'm so sorry for disturbing you, but it's an emergency. I need to borrow your phone charger. Mine just won't work. It must be broken. I was in the middle of a call and—"

"And this call can't wait until tomorrow?" Giselle asked, knowing full well she sounded disdainful.

"No. No, it can't. If it could, I would never disturb you at this hour. Please, Giselle. I think I saw you have an iPhone. My other cord doesn't fit." Looking panicky now, Tierney shifted her weight from one foot to the other.

"All right." Giselle motioned for Tierney to step inside. Like herself, Tierney was dressed in sleepwear, in Tierney's case a tank top and boxers. Tierney stared at Giselle as if she'd turned blue all over—wait, blue. Realizing she was wearing only her satin nightgown, Giselle hurried to the bathroom and grabbed her robe, pulling it on. Grabbing her phone charger, she went back to Tierney and handed her the cord, which attached to a plug. "Here you go. You can give it back to me in the morning."

"There isn't time." Tierney sobbed and pushed the cord into the bottom of her phone and the plug into the closest socket. She sank down, her back against the wall. "Please, hurry." She closed her eyes, her face pale and her lips tense.

Uncertain what to do, let alone say, Giselle followed her intuition and sat down in one of the small armchairs next to Tierney. Tierney flinched and punched in a number with trembling fingers. "Pick up, kiddo. Please."

Kiddo? Giselle wanted to know whom Tierney was calling so frenziedly. Feeling she wasn't meant to overhear any of what was going on, Giselle rose from her chair.

"No. Please. Stay here?" Tierney looked up, panic still in her eyes.

Giselle wanted to ask why, but instead she made a detour to her bedroom and put on her slippers. Her feet were already ice-cold, and she could only imagine how Tierney had to be freezing sitting on the floor in barely more than underwear. Tugging her dusty-pink throw with her, she reentered the foyer. She walked over to Tierney and wrapped the blanket around her narrow shoulders.

"Thank you," Tierney whispered.

Giselle retook her seat in the chair and watched Tierney rap her fingertips against the floor. The signals she was sending the person at the other end went unanswered for a while, but Tierney kept dialing. Eventually, someone answered, and Tierney nearly toppled over. She ended up with her head against Giselle's thigh, her free hand grasping for the bottom hem of the robe.

"Hey, Stephanie. It's me again. My phone lost power. I had to ask my…my friend for a charger."

Giselle heard a mumbling sound when this Stephanie answered.

"No, you can't. I know it's bad, but doing something like that is worse. Listen. I can come get you. If that's what it takes, I'll come, and tomorrow we'll call your social worker and tell him what's been going on."

A new murmur. This time more intense.

"Stephanie, please." Tears ran down Tierney's cheeks. "Please listen to me. If you stand up for yourself and tell them what he's done, then they'll move you. I'll testify, if need be. Remember, I stayed in that home when I was your age. Clearly nothing has changed." Wiping at her cheeks, Tierney pressed her face against Giselle. "He was younger then, but still a creep. I suppose they stopped adopting kids about then."

The woman, or girl, wailed now, loudly enough for Giselle to hear. Tierney trembled and pushed closer to Giselle, who, not knowing she intended to, ran her fingers through Tierney's hair. Over and over, she combed through the silky tresses.

"Wait a second, Stephanie. Stay on the line." Glancing up, Tierney pressed the mute symbol on her phone and looked pleadingly at Giselle. "Please. May I borrow the Jeep and go get Stephanie? It's not far from here. Two hours at the most, one way. She can't stay in that house with that man after her. She doesn't have anywhere else to go."

"How do you know this Stephanie?" Giselle asked, not knowing what to think. "And why does she need rescuing this late in the evening?"

"She's fourteen and at a place where I stayed when I was her age. The foster parents had seven other foster kids when I was there, and they ended up adopting three of them. One of the kids acted strange already then, but now, he's a grown man...he still lives there and has set his sights on Stephanie. I've never met her." Wiping at her eyes again, Tierney pleaded her case. "We connected through the Facebook page for foster kids we both belong to. When I understood where she was living, I reached out to her."

"And you want to bring this child here?" Giselle wanted to pull back, but the tears streaming down Tierney's pale cheeks made it impossible.

"Yes. It's late. I can bring her here to the guesthouse and then call her social worker tomorrow morning and drive her back. You can take the money for the gas out of my salary."

Giselle thought fast. The idea of Tierney going straight into a potentially volatile situation and assuming responsibility for a child didn't sit well with her. It was dark outside, and Giselle normally did better outside then. Not being able to see the vastness around her wrapped her in a protective cocoon.

"One condition," Giselle said slowly. "We'll both go. I'm not letting you put yourself in danger, and I think Stephanie would be the first to think so too—if she truly is your friend."

"She is, and I can take care of myself, of both of us." Tierney stopped talking, tipping her head back to study Giselle. "So, you're prepared to face your demons for a perfect stranger?"

"Yes. And you've never been a stranger to me." She had probably gone too far with that last statement, but she needed to make Tierney see how dangerous it was to go out alone.

"All right. I'll drive. We need blankets and water. She's been hiding underneath the back porch for hours. Her phone is about to die as well." Placing her phone to her ear again, Tierney unmuted it. "Sweetie. Listen to me. I'm coming to get you. A friend of mine will be with me. She's really great, and she wants to help as well."

A slightly modified truth. Giselle walked back to her bedroom and dressed in jeans and a plain white shirt. Pulling on a windbreaker, as the nights were sometimes chilly, she walked back to the foyer where Tierney stood, still in her nightwear, looking indecisive.

"You need to put on some clothes. We should get going. The girl can't stay under the porch indefinitely." And to be selfish, she couldn't risk being outside with Tierney and a stranger after it was light. The mere idea of facing rush-hour traffic in the morning, no matter how safe she felt in the car, was enough to make her question her decision.

"Two minutes." It was as if Tierney had awoken from some sort of sedation. She rushed out the door and ran toward the guesthouse.

Giselle fetched the car keys, closed the front door, and set the alarm. While walking out into the garage, she decided to drive the Jeep out to the driveway. As she sat waiting for Tierney, she wondered where her determination came from. Why would she risk a severe anxiety attack to go pick up a total stranger?

The answer presented itself as she moved to the passenger seat. Tierney came running down the path toward her, flinging herself in behind the wheel. It wasn't for a stranger, no matter how heart-wrenching the girl's situation was. She was doing this for Tierney.

CHAPTER THIRTEEN

The road was deserted as Tierney drove through the countryside. She checked the time. They'd been on the move for almost an hour, and Giselle had perhaps spoken ten words to her. Quickly glancing to her right, she saw Giselle firmly holding on to the sides of her seat. This wouldn't do.

"Want to listen to some music?" Tierney motioned to the radio on the dashboard.

"Sure."

Well, that was eloquent. "Any particular genre?"

"No. You choose."

"Are musical-theater songs—"

"I. Said. You. Choose." Giselle squeezed the seat hard enough for the leather to squeak.

Wanting to smack herself over the head, Tierney realized that Giselle was struggling to remain calm. How could she have forgotten how hard this was for her? The fact that the woman was ready to go with her to a strange house proved how courageous she could be on occasion.

"Okay." With her eyes on the road, Tierney felt among the buttons and dials, and after a quick glance, she found the right channel. Soon the music from *Les Misérables* echoed through the car. Tierney loved the sad, heartfelt songs, but what if the emotional charge of the songs made this trip harder for Giselle?

They rode in silence for a while, and then Giselle gently cleared her throat. "Is this music meant to cheer me up?"

Cringing, Tierney sent her a quick glance. "Er...I know it's kind of sad, but—"

"I'm trying to lighten the mood, since your choice of music is a little gloomy." Though her tone was solemn, it charmed Tierney to see a faint smile on Giselle's lips.

"I had no idea they'd play half the songs. I hoped they'd intersperse them with something cheery." Tierney took one hand off the wheel and rubbed her neck. Giselle's obvious discomfort had begun to stress her out.

"Like *Sweeney Todd*? Now there's something upbeat for you." Giselle placed her hand over her mouth, and for a moment Tierney didn't get it, fearing Giselle was about to get car sick or something.

"No. For heaven's sake..." Then she snorted. "You're really having me on, aren't you?"

"And it's so easy." Giselle chuckled. "If you could have seen your face when they started singing "Bring Him Home"."

"Oh, God." Was she that transparent? "I really am trying to distract you."

"I'd say you do that better than any music." Now folding her hands loosely in her lap, Giselle kept her gaze steadily forward.

"I—what? I do?" That didn't make sense. Unless she was so exasperating that Giselle couldn't keep focusing on being afraid.

"Sure. So, what song's up after this one, do you think? Should we make a bet? My guess is one from *Miss Saigon*."

That did it. Tierney started laughing, unable to restrain herself. Holding on to the wheel and trying to keep the Jeep on the empty road, she shook her head and giggled until her sides ached and tears streamed down her face.

"That's not a commonplace reaction when listening to that particular musical." Giselle snickered.

"I would think not."

The radio began playing "For Good" from *Wicked*. The beautiful declaration of friendship, love, and forgiveness had always been one of Tierney's favorites. Without really being conscious of it, she began singing along, assuming Glinda's role in the duet. When she reached the part where Elphaba, the wicked witch of the west, took over, Giselle started singing her part.

Like a punch in her solar plexus, Tierney listened to the surprisingly rich alto voice emanating from Giselle. Why hadn't she told Tierney she could sing? She listened so intently, she nearly missed her turn to take the lead. Drumming the slow rhythm against the wheel, Tierney grew wrapped up in the beautiful song and even more so in Giselle's performance. When it was over, another, lesser-known musical number began.

"You have a great voice," Tierney said breathlessly. "I had no idea."

"I used to sing a lot…before. Nowadays I stick to my profession and write songs. Play the piano." Giselle sounded casual and matter-of-fact. "I'm not a performer. Obviously."

"I didn't mean you had to be, just that I truly enjoyed how you sound. And singing together. I rarely have someone to sing with." Or ever. Regretting her words, as she feared they might sound like she was having a pity party, Tierney glanced at the GPS above the radio on the dashboard. According to it they had about forty-five minutes left to go. "When did you sing?"

"I belonged to a choir when I attended Juilliard." At first it didn't seem as if Giselle would volunteer any more information, but then she continued. "It was a singing group, really. Eight girls and two boys. We used to sing à capella at different venues. Weddings, churches, that sort of thing."

"And after Juilliard?"

Giselle sighed. "As I said, I haven't sung in a long time. Whenever one of my compositions has ready-made lyrics, I will demonstrate it for the client to make it clearer what the final product might sound like."

"I see." That was incredibly sad. If someone liked to sing, it was awful to refrain from it, no matter the reason. "Unless you think me too forward, perhaps we can sing my lyrics if the other women in Chicory Ariose like my stuff."

"Really?" Giselle turned toward Tierney. "You know your own texts so well, how they're meant to be performed. I'm not sure I'd be able to add anything."

Tierney reached out and patted Giselle's knee, only to yank her hand back when she realized her mistake. "Ahem. You're wrong." Perhaps that wasn't a clever way to start persuading Giselle, but Tierney pushed on. "I mean, the songs are meant to be performed by Vivian and a few, also with Noelle Laurent, right? If we show them what they sound like when sung in harmony, it will make it easier, right?"

Giselle didn't speak for the next few hundred yards. Tierney was beginning to think she'd gone too far.

"You may just have a point. I'm going to play two melodies for them when they all return, Noelle included, and if we can harmonize, it may crystalize which one is the best choice. Or if neither of them fits the album."

"No negative thinking. They wouldn't ask you to compose their music if they weren't sure your style is for them."

"That's just it," Giselle said slowly. "Those two melodies aren't what you would call my trademark brand of music. They just may hate them."

"Any lyrics for them yet?" Tierney asked. "I'm not fishing for anything, honestly, but the right lyricist could help the group understand them."

"Great lyricists are hard to come by. Lesser ones can destroy a song. You may get the job, whether you meant to bring it up or not." Giselle didn't sound unkind, but the guarded tone in her voice was back. "We might just need one chorus and one verse to convey what the final product could sound like."

"If I can help, I will."

"Thank you." Her voice tense, Giselle rolled her shoulder. But her hands still lay relaxed in her lap, which was a good sign.

"Half an hour until we're there," Tierney said. Her phone pinged. "Can you check that message?" She gave Giselle her pin code.

"One new one. It says, 'Some other people are at the house. Please hurry.'" Giselle sounded clearly alarmed.

"Fuck. Does she know them?"

"I'll ask." Giselle tapped in the short question while Tierney pushed harder on the accelerator.

"She's such a cool kid. It's not her fault she was born into a meth factory. It was a good thing she was at school when the damn place exploded, but her parents were, along with a bunch of other people, bagging the crystal meth. She was ten at the time."

"Ten. Oh, my God." Pressing her hand against her chest, Giselle groaned. "That's crazy."

"Sure is. And she doesn't go down without a fight, which tells me she's really freaked out right now. The guy who's been harassing her is an adult now and only stays in the foster home because he can't hold down a job—and the foster parents like him for some unfathomable reason."

"And they still place young kids with them?" Pulling her upper lip back, Giselle snarled.

"They do. In their defense, foster-home slots aren't easy to come by. Especially for teens. Foster parents are wary of accepting teenagers. I don't know. It's like everybody thinks someone else is taking care of these children. In this case, this family is trying to care for a young man who's been with them since he was eight. His name is Dylan, and he's my age, perhaps one or two years younger." She clenched her jaw at the memory of how Dylan had tormented her, and how, being shrewd rather than intelligent, he'd often made it look like she started the fights. Eventually, Tierney had stopped hoping anyone would see what was going on. "I don't know what they were thinking, placing a young girl like Steph there."

"We'll be there soon. And, I know you said you want to take her back with us, but I'm sure you realize that could result in kidnapping charges." Giselle's voice was soft but also firm.

"I know. I know. But I just can't let them keep her there." Slamming her left palm against the wheel, she grunted at the stinging sensation. "She knows she's in trouble with this guy, and I know how it feels to be at the mercy of someone else."

"In a way, so do I." Giselle placed her hand on Tierney's knee. "The GPS says we'll be there in two minutes."

"Yeah. I recognize the neighborhood. It's been a while since I was here, but it hasn't changed all that much." She turned left at the next intersection, and her heart seemed to drop into the depths of her stomach. Two police cars and one ambulance were lined up next to Stephanie's foster home, the blue lights swirling, lighting up the entire street. They had clearly woken up a lot of the neighbors, who were gathering at a distance, some remaining on their doorsteps.

"What's happened?" Giselle covered her mouth. "She never responded to our question as to who the people arriving were. Did she mean the emergency responders?"

"I have no idea, but I'm going to find out." Tierney parked behind the nearest police car. Turning to Giselle, she spoke fast. "You stay here in the car. I have my cell in my pocket. If I call and ask you to take the wheel, can you do that?"

"Of course, but what—"

"It might not come to that. Perhaps she's fine and we can figure things out right here. Will you be okay?"

Giselle nodded, though her hands trembled visibly. "Yes. Go find her."

Tierney nodded briskly in return. "I will." She closed the door behind her and started running toward the house where she'd gone through hell.

CHAPTER FOURTEEN

L oud voices drowned out every other sound as a female police officer tried to talk to the woman on the garden path. Tierney recognized Barbie Brody, even if the years hadn't been kind to her. Behind her, doing his best to talk louder than his wife, stood her husband Victor. He was waving his arms, and Tierney realized he was one step away from being hauled into the backseat of a police car.

"Sir. Ma'am. Calm down. We're going to get to the bottom of this, but we need to find out what the problem is."

"I can tell you," Tierney said and stepped closer.

The Brodys stared at her, clearly not recognizing her, but that might well be because they were simply not expecting her to be there. And why would they? When she left their so so-called care for a group home, she had sworn to never return.

"And you are, Miss…?" The female police officer, whose nametag said Connor, turned to face her.

"My name is Tierney Edwards. I used to live here as a foster kid. I'm good friends with Stephanie Wilson, who is currently in the Brodys' care. She called me earlier this evening in a panic—"

"This young woman has nothing to do with our children." Barbie pointed a trembling finger at Tierney. "She hasn't set foot in our house in fifteen years, and she has no idea what we're dealing with here. Go back to where you came from." She glared at Tierney.

"A neighbor called 911 because of loud screams coming from your property, Mrs. Brody," Sergeant Connor said. "Where is your foster child now?"

"Oh, she's hopeless," Barbie groused. "If you had any idea of what we've gone through with that girl—"

"Her whereabouts, Mrs. Brody? Mr. Brody?" Sergeant Connor's voice grew sharper.

"I wouldn't be surprised if she's out with that little tramp Gloria." Barbie folded her arms across her chest.

"Last I heard from Stephanie, she was hiding under the back porch," Tierney said. Raising her chin, she returned Barbie's furious gaze. "As her curfew is seven p.m., she's not out partying."

"Hiding?" Sergeant Connor now turned completely toward Tierney. "Why?" She waved over two colleagues.

"She's afraid of the Brodys' adopted son, Dylan, who's a grown man. He harasses her, just like he did me, when we were both foster kids here."

"Davies, Crowe, go check under the back porch." Connor tilted her head. "Since this girl knows you, you can go with them." She turned back to the Brodys. "And I want to hear more about Dylan."

"He's a gentle giant," Barbie wailed. "He wouldn't hurt a fly. He's just misunderstood."

"And where is he?" Connor asked.

Tierney didn't hear Barbie's reply as she hurried after the two cops. Rounding the house, she saw the garden where Barbie had made her work hours on end, maintaining the perfection she demanded. The multitude of colorful birdhouses lit by little LED lights was new. The cop closest to her, Crowe, turned on his flashlight, but Tierney held up her hand toward him. "Don't use that.' If you shine that into her face, she'll freak out. Let me talk to her."

"All right." Crowe motioned for Tierney to go ahead. "We're right behind you."

"Thanks." Not even remotely concerned with going down on all fours in Barbie's perfect flowerbed, Tierney crawled toward the end of the porch, where there used to be a small hole. It had been her hideout when she just couldn't take anymore. She hoped this was where Steph had squeezed in under the wooden porch. It was eerily dark and cold under the house. Her knees and hands sank into the soggy ground, and Tierney remembered huddling in here, praying nobody found out where she was. She had to have been much smaller then. Even if she wasn't very tall now, it was still very cramped.

"Steph? Hey, kiddo? It's me, Tierney. Are you in here? You're safe now. My friend Giselle and I drove down to make sure everyone took this seriously."

"T-Tierney?" a faint, trembling voice said from far under the house. "Is that really you?"

"Sure is. Wait a sec." Tierney turned around and called out to Crowe. "May I borrow your flashlight, Officer?"

"Here you go, ma'am." The small Maglite entered through the hole.

Tierney switched it on and directed it to her face from a distance, so not to inadvertently do the scary mask by lighting it from below, like she'd done with her friends when telling ghost stories. "See. It's me."

"Tierney!" A shuffling noise came from Steph's direction.

After only a few moments, Tierney held a cold, shivering, teenaged girl in her arms under the porch. Stephanie sobbed, heartbreaking dry sobs, as if her tears had long given out. "Thank you. Oh, thank you for coming. Don't make me stay. Don't let *them* make me stay."

"We have a rather terrific cop out front who's questioning Barbie and Victor. Do you know where Dylan is?"

"N-no? He's been in the garden, calling my name, hissing at me. He may have started to suspect I was hiding underneath. Good thing he's so big he can't get under here. At least not fast enough to grab me."

"A really good thing. Now, why don't we crawl out of here and get you a blanket. Two cops are outside, Officers Crowe and Davies. They seem nice."

"Oh. Okay." Not sounding entirely convinced, Steph began to crawl along with Tierney. When they reached the opening, Tierney alerted Officer Crow. "Hey. We're on our way out. Can you step back just a little bit? I'm sure you're a great cop, but we foster kids aren't the most trusting people you'll ever meet."

"No problem, ma'am."

Ma'am? Tierney wasn't used to anyone calling her that. When she was on the road, the best she could hope for was "Hey, you." She opted to go through first so she could help Steph when she exited the cramped space. Having been in there for hours, the girl was bound to be stiff and cold.

It was a relief to stand up and stretch her legs. The damp dirt under the house had permeated her clothes. She hoped Giselle wouldn't mind if she messed up the seat in the car as she drove home. At least they were leather seats, and she would recondition the car until it looked brand-new as a thank you for helping her rescue Stephanie.

Stephanie poked her head out and took Tierney's hand. She rose on wobbly legs and wrapped her arms around Tierney's waist. Officer Davies, a tall African-American woman, unfolded a blanket and put it around them. As they made their way around the house to the front, the shrill voice originating from Barbie met them.

"There she is. Stephanie!" Barbie yelled and began walking toward them. "We've been so worried."

Stephanie pulled back, taking Tierney with her. "No!" Her voice was broken and terrified. "I can't. I can't."

"Step back, ma'am," Sergeant Connor said and took Barbie by the arm. "Give the girl some space. She seems to know and trust Ms. Edwards."

"They've never even met!" Victor decided to meddle. "This kid, she needs a firm hand, and she doesn't like Dylan because he's a godsend when it comes to helping us with the current foster kids."

"You have this man, who clearly scares the living daylights out of the girl here, helping you raise these children who have been placed in your care?" The low growl in Sergeant Connor's voice didn't escape Tierney.

"This man, as you put it, is our son!" Victor spat the words. "And what goes on in our house is no business of the police."

"That's where you're wrong again." Sergeant Connor shook her head. Turning to Davies, she spoke in a forced calm tone. "Get ahold of Child Protective Services. After what I've heard from these people, this girl isn't staying here."

Victor looked like he was about to object but instead turned to his wife. "I'm getting in touch with our lawyer. We're not letting them keep her."

"You're afraid of losing the only income you have, eh?" Tierney sneered as she kept her arm around Stephanie. "What about the other four kids in the house, Barbie?" She saw the surprise on Barbie's face. "Yes. I know everything about them. Two boys, eleven and eight, and two girls, twins, who are, ten, wasn't it, Steph?"

"Yeah," Stephanie whispered.

"You little rat." Barbie glowered at Stephanie. "That's how you show loyalty? Telling tales about our family?"

Stephanie was still shaking, but clearly Barbie's words ignited a fire in her. "This is not my family, not even *a* family. It's a business where you keep as many foster kids as CPS will place at your house, and you let the older kids take care of the younger ones. And do all the housework."

"Those are reasonable chores!" Victor was back and tucking a cellphone into his pants again.

"Reasonable? You went to Mexico with Barbie for a week and left us alone with that disgusting oaf you call a son." Suddenly looking unafraid, Stephanie broke free from Tierney's arms and stalked up to Victor. "You have no idea what I had to do to keep him away from the kids. We put mattresses on the floor in the twins' and my room and pushed the dresser across the doorway to make sure he didn't get in while we were sleeping."

Sergeant Connor gently pulled Stephanie back from Victor, and Tierney thought it was probably just in the nick of time. Steph looked like she was about to clock the man. Pulling her radio to her lips, Connor called for backup. "We need more case workers from the CPS," she said into the radio. "We have five underage children here that need to be examined at the hospital to make sure they're not undernourished or abused." She turned to Barbie and Victor. "Where's your son? Where's Dylan?"

"He's a grown man," Barbie said, averting her eyes. "He comes and goes as he pleases."

"No, he doesn't. He has a curfew," Stephanie said, her teeth beginning to clatter audibly again. "Dylan could be in the house. You need to go get the other kids."

"We're doing that." Connor pulled at the radio again but stopped in mid-motion when a loud growl echoed through the night. The closest neighbors took a step back toward their front door, and Tierney couldn't blame them. The horrible noise had emanated from the Brody house.

Staring in terror-filled fascination, Tierney saw a tall, burly man, whom she easily recognized as an aged version of Dylan, plow through the doorway, pushing the officers holding onto him away as if swatting at flies. Officer Davies was just returning from her patrol car and now pulled her Taser, aiming for the giant of a man. The wires shot through the air and hit Dylan on the side of his chest. At first the impact had hardly any effect, but then he went rigid and fell to the ground.

Tierney thought Stephanie had seen more than enough. "I'm taking Steph back to my car. Why don't you bring the other kids there while we wait for CPS?" She hoped Connor would see it her way. "The four younger ones probably rely on her, and I bet they'll be less traumatized in a civilian car than a black-and-white."

"Good point." Looking over to the Jeep, Connor asked, "Who's in the passenger seat?"

"That's Giselle, my friend. It's her car, actually." Tierney began to walk toward the Jeep, pulling Stephanie with her. "Hey, kiddo, they're going to bring the others to Giselle's car. She's really nice."

"Okay." Stephanie's voice was small again, and the fighting spirit she had demonstrated earlier was gone.

As they reached the vehicle, Tierney heard the click showing that Giselle had disengaged the central locking system. Opening the passenger door on the driver's side, Tierney motioned for Stephanie to get in. "Giselle, this is Stephanie. We're just waiting for the other four kids." She pleaded with her eyes for Giselle not to freak out.

"Hello, Stephanie. It's nice to meet you." Giselle extended her hand.

Stephanie shook it shyly. "Hi." She stared at Giselle, looking close to awestruck in the middle of all this drama.

"I see you have a blanket, and if you need more, you'll find three more in the back of the Jeep. If you lean over the backrest, you can reach them."

"Thanks." Stephanie pulled the blankets toward her and sat back down. Turning to Tierney, she whispered, "She's very beautiful."

Tierney glanced at Giselle and then returned her gaze to Stephanie. "That she is, kiddo."

It took about ten minutes, during which they sat in silence, before the officers and Sergeant Connor brought four wide-eyed children to the Jeep. Stephanie opened the door, climbed out, and motioned for the younger children to crawl inside. There she wrapped the blankets around them. Stephanie closed the door but kept the window rolled down so they could talk to Connor.

"Wow. It smells so good in here." One of the twins sniffed the air. "Like cookies."

Tierney chuckled. "I think it's Giselle's perfume."

Giselle looked like she wanted to swat Tierney over the head for that comment, but she merely smiled at the children. "You warm enough? Tell us if you're cold. We can start the car."

"I'm good with this fancy blanket," the oldest boy said. "My name's Lucas." He didn't extend his hand but merely wiggled his fingers just outside of the "fancy blanket."

"Lucas is eleven. This is Howie. He's eight. Lizzie and Meg are twins. They're ten." Stephanie sat with her arms around the two children closest to her. "We've been together at the Brodys' for almost one-and-a-half years."

"Are you okay, all of you?" Connor asked from outside the car. She had been talking into her radio on and off. "CPS is on its way. You won't go back to the Brodys tonight. My officers are in there, packing your things."

"Barbie won't let you take anything. She claims those clothes are really hers. She makes all the kids wear them, and then she keeps them when they leave." Lucas spoke matter-of-factly. "I had a really nice jacket before that my brother gave me when he grew out of it. When he turned eighteen, we couldn't be together anymore, but he's coming back for me once he has a good apartment." Jutting his chin out, Lucas defied anyone to contradict him. "The jacket is long gone. I think she sold it. It was made from real leather, and it smelled like him." He blinked several times.

"I could kill that woman," Tierney whispered to Giselle, mindful of the kids. "The one thing he had of his brother's."

"It is appalling." Giselle's eyes were darker than Tierney had ever seen them.

They chatted with the children, and soon the youngest boy, Howie, fell asleep. The older three were restless and kept turning their heads, as if looking for any of the Brodys.

"They can't get to you in here," Tierney said firmly. "Sergeant Connor is a good cop, and we're inside a locked car. You're safe."

"Unless the CPS has no open spots for us to go to, and they send us back. Dylan will be there." Lucas chewed on his bottom lip.

"I think they'll try very hard to help you guys now." Tierney wanted to promise him there would be foster homes, good ones, available to them, but it was impossible. The worst things for these children were broken promises.

Tierney heard voices outside the car. She could see Sergeant Connor talking to a middle-aged woman wearing a jacket over her pajamas and holding a tray in her hands. Connor tapped on the now-rolled-up window. Stephanie lowered it.

"This is Mrs. Lassiter. She has some cheese sandwiches and cartons of juice if anyone's hungry."

"Oh, I am!" Howie was apparently awake and now sat up straight, looking with huge eyes behind glasses at the tray. "May I have one, please?"

"Sure. Here, Stephanie. Take the tray. You'll find straws to go with the juice."

Connor pushed the tray through the window. "Thank you, Mrs. Lassiter."

"Claire, please. My husband is bringing another tray for the grownups."

For some reason, this kindness from a neighbor that Tierney didn't recognize from when she lived with the Brodys brought tears to her eyes. Clear drops hung from her eyelashes as she took a sandwich and handed one to Giselle. "Just when you think most people are scum, you run into someone like Claire Lassiter—or you." Tierney took Giselle's left hand in her free one.

"Or you," Giselle said, returning the compliment.

Another knock on the door indicated that CPS had arrived. A large van was parked behind the Jeep, and now two women and one man talked to Connor. It took them about ten minutes to discuss the situation at hand, and then Connor walked back to the Jeep, tapping on Tierney's window this time.

"For the most part, things are looking up," she said, rubbing the back of her neck.

"For the most part?" Tierney looked suspiciously at Connor.

"They have two different emergency foster homes that can take the four youngest. The girls in one, the boys in the other."

"And Stephanie?" Tierney gripped her sandwich harder, nearly poking her fingers straight through the slice of bread.

"They don't have a home for her yet. If nothing else comes up, we'll move her into a group home." Connor's expression showed she didn't like that solution one bit. "Who knows? A new placement can come available at any given time."

"Or not." Stephanie had scooted forward and regarded Connor with opaque eyes. "I'm not going back. Even a group home is a million times better." Her words were brave and she spoke with a firm tone, but a desolate expression ghosted over her face.

"Steph?" Howie said, clinging to her arm.

"Shh, cutie. It'll be all right." Stephanie squeezed his shoulder. "You're going to be fine, and me too."

"Yes, you are. Officer Connor, was it?" Giselle spoke, startling them all.

"Yes, ma'am." Connor nodded briskly.

"My name is Giselle Bonnaire. I live outside East Quay. Is there any chance Stephanie can come home with us?"

CHAPTER FIFTEEN

G iselle wasn't entirely sure where her words originating from. Considering she had tried her hardest to ward off Tierney less than a week ago, asking if Stephanie—a complete stranger, and a troubled teen at that—could come home with them was crazy. In fact, she'd rather not contemplate too closely the fact that she even thought of it as "coming home with *them*."

Sergeant Connor looked hesitant. "As heartwarming as that is, I'm not sure this will fly with the CPS. We have no idea who you really are."

"Yet CPS was willing to place five kids with family-of-the-year over there." Tierney motioned toward the Brodys, who stood together, still gesturing wildly in their direction.

"Hey, I hear you, but I don't call the shots when it comes to these matters."

Tierney sighed. "Giselle is a very famous composer and well known in the music industry, as well as in East Quay."

"Really?" Bending, Connor looked closely at Giselle, who wasn't sure she approved of Tierney's well-meant praise.

"Really," Giselle said. "If you, or the CPS, want references, you can call Manon Belmont, the president of the Belmont Foundation. I'm sure everyone in the state of Rhode Island has heard of her."

Connor nodded, looking impressed. "I sure have, ma'am. Let me check with CPS. They're looking exasperated over there. You may just stand a chance."

"Tierney?" Stephanie murmured from the backseat. "Are you sure? And, ma'am, please don't feel you have to do this. I'm just glad to get away from the Brodys. Especially Dylan." She shuddered.

"First of all, Stephanie, call me Giselle. All this ma'am business is getting on my nerves." Giselle smiled to show she was joking. Half-joking, at least. She had been teetering on the verge of a panic attack since the kids entered the car and the cops and CPS officials surrounded the vehicle. If she focused on Stephanie, perhaps she could disregard her anxiety. She thanked unnamed deities that it was still dark. She could pretend the darkness was a surrounding wall.

"Okay, Giselle. But still."

"Second," Giselle said, "I rarely do anything I don't want to. Not counting your friend Tierney here. She talked her way into her job as my assistant. Now, what I want you to understand, Stephanie, is that if they let you come with us, it is temporary. Tierney will eventually move on, and I'm pretty sure you won't want to stay after she's gone." Giselle's heart skipped several beats and then contracted painfully before it beat normally again.

"Yeah, I know." Stephanie let go of the now-sleeping girl and scooted forward. "It's really generous of you. I'd never dream of asking for something more permanent than that."

Giselle's heart did the stop-and-go trick again, making her fear she might go into a panic merely from sympathizing with Stephanie.

Sergeant Connor tapped on the window, and Tierney rolled it down. "Okay, folks. CPS can't get ahold of anyone at the Belmont Foundation, so I'm afraid Stephanie—"

"Oh, for heaven's sake." Pulling out her cellphone, Giselle found Manon's private number in her contacts. Though it was the middle of the night, she didn't hesitate to make the call. Four rings went through, and Giselle thought she would get Manon's voicemail, but then she heard a sleepy voice.

"Giselle?" Manon cleared her throat. "What's happened? Are you all right?"

"I'm sorry to call you like this, Manon. I'm all right, but I need your help." Giselle described the situation to the woman who was admired and respected throughout the state for her charity work and loved worldwide for being part of Chicory Ariose. "Can you talk to

Child Protective Services and let them know it's safe for them to let this girl come home with us?"

"Sure. Absolutely. Wait. Who is us? Your new assistant and you?" Manon sounded less sleepy now.

"Yes. Tierney and I." Giselle cringed but refused to let her reaction show.

"Okay. Put CPS on. I know most of those folks," Manon said.

Giselle handed the phone over to Connor, who took it to the group of social workers. It took less than a minute, and then Connor returned and gave the phone back. "That did it." She smiled. "You are free to drive home as soon as my officer has collected the girl's belongings."

Tierney wiped at her now-wet cheeks and then flung her arms around Giselle. "Oh, thank you! Thank you, thank you! You can't imagine how much this means. You're just so amazing and sweet that I'm at a loss for words."

Her cheeks warming, Giselle could hardly breathe as Tierney hugged her closer. The embrace was firm, but not hard, and Tierney smelled of soap and something resembling lilacs. Giselle trembled and couldn't stop no matter how she tried.

"You're welcome. And here comes an officer with a bag. That yours, Stephanie?" Giselle pointed when Tierney slowly let go of her. Oddly enough, this absence made Giselle shudder, mainly because she was cold and missed the warmth emanating from Tierney.

"Yes, it's mine." From the backseat, Stephanie sounded rather shell-shocked.

The CPS staff came to fetch the younger children, and Giselle's heart broke as she watched them cry and cling to Stephanie. The children relented only when Giselle raised her voice and firmly promised that they would get to see Stephanie again at some point.

"Don't make a promise you can't keep," Stephanie said after she pulled the door next to her closed. "We have trust issues as it is."

"I fully intend to take you to see the other children before they're permanently placed. I don't make promises I can't keep." She glanced back at the pale girl as Tierney started the car. "Why don't you try to get some sleep, Stephanie? The seat you're in folds back, and I believe you have enough pillows and blankets."

Stephanie studied Giselle in the faint light from the dashboard. Then she nodded firmly. "I believe you. Mostly because Tierney wouldn't have brought you unless she thought the world of you. I'll try to get some rest."

"Good." Giselle blinked at the young girl's words. So, Tierney thought the world of her? Perhaps her talent as a composer, but personally? How could that possibly be? Tierney didn't really know her.

Tierney drove back toward the main road and toward home. It was such a relief to think she'd be in her own house in mere hours. With a little luck, they'd be back in East Quay before the sun came up.

"I bet it weirds you out when I gush about stuff, but I'm so grateful that you stood up for Steph. It's odd, but it's as if someone had stood up for me when I was that age, like Steph's relief is rubbing off on me." Tierney shrugged. "I probably sound totally nuts."

"What you say is entirely plausible." Giselle tried to put her thoughts into words. "You were in the same situation at that age. Knowing exactly what Stephanie has been going through, not just tonight, but for years, you empathize—perhaps you even relive it some?"

"And then some."

"So, when I'm able to do something about it, with Manon's help, mind you, you're bound to feel some of the same relief. If we'd had to leave Stephanie behind to go to a group home, you would have felt that as well—only so much sadder." Letting herself act intuitively, she placed her hand on Tierney's knee. "Your heart is so big, it's as if you absorb the feelings from those around you. It goes beyond empathy. You wear their skin, and you respond like you've been there for their entire life. That's how I felt when you wrote those lyrics about me. It wasn't just a lucky guess on your part. You wrapped yourself in my persona and put it on paper. That's why I was so adamant that Vivian and Mike should hear it." Removing her hand, Giselle inhaled deeply and let the deep breath cleanse her.

They drove on in silence, but it wasn't uncomfortable. Instead it was calm and safe, a homey feeling that soothed Giselle's frayed nerves. Her inner panic-attack gauge lowered from red to green, which was such relief.

As they drove just outside East Quay, heading for Giselle's house, Tierney started to fidget. She let her fingers travel up and down the rim of the wheel, pulled at her sleeves, and pushed her hair from her face. Something was clearly wrong.

"Why don't you tell me what's bothering you? Preferably before we end up in a ditch." Giselle laced her fingers hard, bracing for impact.

"I—well, I mean—I…" Tierney rubbed her temple. "Okay. Listen. The cottage is amazing. But it'll be cramped with both Stephanie and me in there. She—can she stay in the main house?" Tierney glanced quickly at Giselle.

"You both should." Damn. She'd done it again. Giselle's words had come as if she was shooting from the hip, with little, if any, editing and certainly without consideration. "I have two spare rooms farther down the corridor from my bedroom. You will have to share a bath, but you'll still have your respective privacy." And she would have none whatsoever.

Giselle groaned inwardly. This would never have come to pass before Tierney showed up on her doorstep. Her safety, her hard-won control of her anxiety and panic attacks, had been at the forefront of her priorities. They came before even her music. She would never have been able to compose if she'd felt unsafe and about to spin out of control. And here she sat in her car, just before sunrise, with Tierney and a virtually unknown girl, offering them her guest rooms—*in her house.* And she couldn't take her words back. Human decency combined with determination kept her from changing her mind. And, yes, she would hate to read the disappointment on Tierney's face.

"You're sure? You're okay with that?" Slowing down, probably as not to have a last-minute accident, Tierney looked over at Giselle, her lips trembling. "I won't be offended if you decide to let just Steph stay in your house. Though, I can't lie, it'd be awesome if we could all be together." Tierney gripped the wheel harder. "Now, that sounded way too presumptuous. Sorry."

Tenderness erupted in Giselle, which took her by complete surprise, and she hid a smile at Tierney's obvious attempt to cover up her reaction to her own words. "It would be best for Stephanie."

"Yes. Of course." Tierney kept her eyes firmly on the road. "Perhaps we should wake the sleeping beauty in the back. We'll be at the house in less than five minutes."

Understanding that she was meant to perform the task, Giselle turned and gently nudged Stephanie. "Hey there. We're almost at the house. You all right?"

Slowly, Stephanie opened her dark-blue eyes. "I'm fine. Better than fine." She smiled faintly. "Exhausted though."

"I suppose we all are. We should get some sleep first thing." Giselle found it increasingly easier to communicate with the girl, perhaps because she could imagine a very young Tierney in Stephanie.

What that thought implied, she'd rather not dwell on in her fatigued state.

CHAPTER SIXTEEN

When Tierney came back from the guesthouse after fetching the bare necessities, she found Stephanie sitting on the floor in the foyer, her arms around one ecstatic Charley. The retriever wasn't just wagging her tail, but her entire backside, while trying to lick under Stephanie's chin. Stephanie giggled as Charley woofed softly in her ear and then plopped down on her back, hoping for a belly rub.

"I see Charley found you."

"I know you've mentioned your employer having a dog, but I had no idea it was so cool. I was just standing here, waiting for you, and—*bam*!—there she was, launching at me. At first, I was afraid she thought I was a burglar, but she just wanted me to cuddle her. She's awesome!"

"Don't let her fool you into giving her too many treats," Giselle said kindly as she returned from the corridor leading to her bedroom and the guest rooms. "She clearly likes you, Stephanie. Now, let me show you where you're staying." Giselle motioned for them both to follow her. "This way."

The guest rooms were large, almost the size of the guesthouse. Giselle assigned the farthest one to Stephanie. The color scheme ranged from soft, dusty pink to white and dark mauve. It could have been girly and too saccharine, but instead it was, like everything else about Giselle and her home, classy and sophisticated.

Stephanie took a deep breath but didn't move, and Tierney regarded her cautiously. "Steph?"

"I'm, eh, I'm okay. Really. Just a bit...you know..." Stephanie waved her hand in the air.

"Overwhelmed?" Carefully, Tierney put an arm around the girl. "I can imagine. Going from the Brodys' house to this in a few hours."

"Yeah. And escaping Dylan. And knowing the kids are out of there as well. It's been a lot lately, protecting them." Shuddering, Stephanie grabbed Tierney's hand that lay on her shoulder. "Thank you."

"No thanks needed, Steph. If you insist on thanking anyone, thank Giselle. It's her house. Her decision." Tierney's heart picked up speed when she thought about how Giselle had stepped in and taken command of the situation. This wasn't a side of Giselle Tierney had known about—not until now. When it came to so many other things, Giselle seemed frail and afraid. With an eerie feeling of having sold Giselle short, Tierney vowed to not make the same mistake again.

"Wow." Stephanie now said and stopped just inside the threshold. "This room really is amazing. And it's huge!"

"It's a decent size," Giselle said with a nod. "You'll share a bathroom with Tierney. It's located between your rooms."

"Sharing a bath with just one person is—I've never had that. At the Brodys' house, we were six people with one bathroom. Dylan had first dibs, always." She made a face but then scanned the room again, which made a new smile appear on her face. "I'll never forget that I got to stay in a room like this. Thank you."

Giselle blinked hard a few times but then motioned for Tierney to follow her. "This one's for you." Giselle opened the door to the second guest room, on the other side of the wall of Giselle's en suite bathroom. Here, the colors were off-white and forest green, with dark-maroon accents.

"This is just as beautiful. And I second Steph. It's an amazing room that I'll always remember staying in." Perhaps not so much for the room, but for the one offering it to her. Tierney closed her eyes for a moment. "And considering how many times I've had to share bathrooms, or even use the gymnasium showers to clean up in, this is a pretty cool deal." Placing her toiletries, sleepwear, and a change of clothes on the bed, she winked at Giselle, trying to lighten the mood.

"I'm glad you like it." Giselle stood there fidgeting for a moment but then turned around. "I'm going to set the alarm. Can you tell Stephanie how it works as soon as you can? I'd rather we didn't have a random visit from the security firm."

"No problem. I doubt she'll wake up before we do, so tomorrow should be fine. I'll just pop in and say good night—or good morning, as it were—before she goes to bed."

"All right." Giselle hesitated. "Do you think Charley will need to go out?"

"Yes, probably, or she may wake us up in an hour or two for her morning walk. Why don't I set the alarm after I walk her? That way you can just hit the sack."

Nodding, Giselle did look exhausted. It had been a long night and with enough emotional roller-coaster riding to last them a while.

"Thank you. See you when we wake up."

"No problem." Tierney half turned to get Charley but changed her mind. "Um, Giselle?"

"Yes?" Having also turned to enter her bedroom, Giselle stopped and placed a hand on the doorframe.

"I know I'm repeating myself, but thank you for doing this for Stephanie. I really care about this kid. She feels like a little sister, in a way, because of where she's had to stay." Walking up to Giselle, Tierney stopped just at the edge of her personal space. "I know it can't have been easy for you to not only accept a stranger into your house, but also to have us actually stay right next to you." Tierney motioned at the three rooms.

"I thought it'd be harder than it actually feels." Giselle had a wondrous expression on her face. "I think I dreaded the sunup more. Stephanie seems like a lovely girl. If I can help keep her away from people that might destroy that part of her..." Lowering her gaze for a moment, Giselle then raised it and locked her eyes on Tierney. "Also, I did it to keep you out of trouble. You would've moved heaven and earth to save that girl and the younger children. I'd rather you stay here with me than spend your life in prison for kidnapping and so on." Her voice was facetious, but her eyes were dark and serious.

Tierney's heart warmed, and the heat spread to her entire abdomen. "Glad you're keeping me from having to place my one phone call to try to find someone to bail me out."

"See. I did myself another favor too." Giselle smiled quickly and then walked into her bedroom, closing the door behind her.

Thankfully, Charley wasn't too eager to walk this early in the morning. She did her business and then trotted inside. Tierney hurried toward the bedrooms, but when she went to join her after setting the alarm—and placing a Post-it note on the front door telling Stephanie that the house had a security system—the dog was nowhere to be seen.

As Tierney saw that Stephanie's door was ajar halfway, she peered inside. Stephanie was already fast asleep on the bed, holding a pillow close. On the bed, by her feet, lay Charley, wagging her tail as she glanced over her shoulder at Tierney.

"You fell head over heels for Steph, didn't you, girl?" Tierney whispered. "Well, keep an eye on her for me, okay? She's precious."

After walking into her room, Tierney sat on the bed next to her things, closing her eyes. As tears, mainly of relief, began to stream down her face, she mimicked Stephanie and took a pillow in her arms. She didn't dare to hope this arrangement would last. That was asking for the impossible and would only lead to a world of pain. She had to settle for how Stephanie now stood a chance to go on to a new and better home. And until then, the young girl would get a chance to find her bearings.

Curling up on her side, still hugging the pillow, Tierney told herself she would only close her eyes for a few moments and then grab a quick shower. As it turned out, she was asleep before she'd finished the thought.

Giselle tossed and turned, twice getting up to straighten her bed, as she hated wrinkled bedsheets against her skin. She was exhausted but knew when she had exerted herself like this, being awake for an entire night, she went into mental overdrive. It could also trigger her anxiety, and knowing how important it was for her to get at least seven hours of sleep, that stressed her even more.

Sitting up in bed, she hugged her knees to her chest. The different faces she had seen during the drama playing out outside the Brodys' house flickered through her jumbled mind. First, Tierney's tense expression as she sped toward the town where Stephanie lived. Giselle had wanted to run her fingertips along Tierney's cheek, as if that would have smoothed out the small worry wrinkles at the outer corner of her eyes. Instead she had only dared to lay a careful hand on Tierney's knee, hoping to convey her sympathy. Tierney had done the same to her at one point, and only now did Giselle understand why she had literally yanked her hand away. The tingling sensation in her palm had turned to searing within a fraction of a second, which was not only unexpected, but also startling.

And how was it that Giselle had responded like that to Tierney? Was it just lust? Or pent-up desire since she hadn't allowed herself to let anyone close to her in ages? Giselle shuddered. Was she so starved for physical closeness that a mere pat on the knee, whether receiving or giving it, made her so hungry for more? Or was it because it was Tierney? Statistically, Tierney was probably straight and would be totally uncomfortable if she sensed Giselle's response. Thinking about it as she tugged at one of the large pillows, she realized that was perhaps not the whole truth. Several times since Tierney talked her way into her life, Giselle had found herself on the receiving end of one of Tierney's long gazes. She didn't stare, not at all, but she would look at Giselle, and her bright gray eyes would glitter like sun on the ocean.

Wrapping her arms around herself, Giselle pressed her forehead against her knees. Had she made a terrible mistake from day one with Tierney? Not to mention bringing her and Stephanie in under her roof? Now Giselle had two people, both virtual strangers, in her house, and she couldn't just throw them out. Stephanie was depending on them to keep her safe and cared for until she was offered a better place. And Tierney…Groaning, Giselle felt her nipples harden at the thought of Tierney sleeping on the other side of the wall. Her evil mind pictured the often-free-spirited Tierney sleeping in a severely messed-up bed, arms and legs flung in all directions, her hair fanned out over the pillows.

Giselle tried to take in long, even breaths, but her stomach clenched as the vision of Tierney moving restlessly while stuck in vivid dreams haunted her. Then the vision changed, and Giselle was there with her, her arms and legs wrapped around Tierney, reveling in the feel of her as she kept her from having nightmares. In her mind, Tierney turned toward her and reciprocated the embrace, Giselle free enough to accept the strong arms around her.

Whimpering, Giselle threw herself back against the pillows. This was insane. Crazy. She would drive herself nuts if she kept entertaining impossible scenarios that would end up breaking her heart.

Her treacherous body wouldn't slow down. Pushing her hands in between her thighs, Giselle tried to stave off the burning sensation permeating her lower stomach, radiating throughout her system. She didn't want to feel like this. It was such a solitary emotion, burning, pining for someone that would, or could, never be there with her. Yes, Tierney was in the next room, but she might as well have been in another star system. Ripping her hands away from her body, Giselle sobbed. Just once, but that was more than she had allowed herself to cry in years. Normally, she kept her equilibrium and remained cool and aloof. She would be damned if she was going to lie here, touching herself while aching for Tierney, only to end up even colder and lonelier than before.

Giselle shoved at her pillows, pushing them together. She pulled the covers up over her shoulders, which suddenly felt cold to the touch. She would go to sleep, forget about all this, and tomorrow focus on her music and on being a gracious hostess.

Eventually Tierney and Stephanie would move on, continue their lives elsewhere, and Giselle was fine with that. Burying her face into the soft pillow, she whimpered. She didn't have any alternative.

CHAPTER SEVENTEEN

Tierney entered the house after taking Charley on a quick walk before she started on, well, brunch, she supposed. It was after one p.m., and she had heard Giselle move about in her room when she woke up. After showering and making herself presentable, Tierney checked in on Stephanie, and that was where she'd found Charley, still curled up on Stephanie's bed.

Tierney set the breakfast-nook table, humming as she worked. The bright-yellow tablecloth made it look fresh and cozy.

She heard steps behind her and turned in time to see Giselle sweep into the kitchen and yank a plate from the table. Without saying anything, she passed Tierney, snagged some bacon and scrambled eggs, poured herself a glass of orange juice with her free hand, then left.

Standing there with her jaw sagging, Tierney heard the door to the music room close with a resounding bang. So, the composer wasn't in a good mood. Tierney would never pretend to know Giselle inside out, but Giselle's defense mechanism was obviously in action. If Tierney went after her and tried to ask her what was wrong, her attempt would only backfire.

Resetting the table for two, Tierney inwardly shook her head. It wasn't easy to understand Giselle, but this time, Tierney guessed that last night's ordeal, and her decision to bring Stephanie with them to stay at the main house, was at the core of Giselle's behavior. No doubt, Giselle was second-guessing herself, and perhaps she didn't want them to know, least of all Stephanie, most likely.

"Smells great," a quiet voice said from the doorway to the kitchen. "Bacon?"

"Good morning, Steph. And yes, bacon and eggs any way you want them. Scrambled?"

"Love scrambled eggs." Stephanie took a plate and added some bacon strips and eggs from the stove. "Giselle not up yet?" Stephanie looked refreshed, as if she hadn't gone through hell and back yesterday.

"Listen." Tierney held up a finger. When they were quiet, barely audible piano music filtered through the soundproofed room. Giselle was playing one of her more intense pieces.

"That's her playing?" Stephanie scooped some scrambled eggs into her mouth. Chewing, she blinked several times.

"Something wrong? Too much salt?" Tierney became concerned.

"Are these real eggs?" Eagerly, Stephanie took another mouthful.

"Sure." Not certain what Stephanie meant at first, Tierney then remembered. "Oh, please, don't tell me the Brodys still use powdered eggs?" Tierney remembered the bland, strange concoction that her former foster parents had claimed was scrambled eggs.

"They do. I got kind of used to them after a while. I don't think the little kids had ever tasted real eggs. Guess what you don't know, you don't miss." Shrugging, Stephanie took a bacon strip between her fingers and bit into it. "Oh, my God. Even this is the good kind. I had it a few times at a friend's house. When Barbie found out I'd gone to their house when school ended early because a teacher got sick, she grounded me for two weeks. Only time I could go out was when I ran errands for her. I wasn't even allowed to go to school during those weeks. I hated it."

"School?" Tierney poured coffee for herself. She raised the pot inquisitively toward Stephanie, who shook her head and poured herself some orange juice instead.

"No. I hated not being in school. School was sort of my safe place. I didn't have many friends, but I had a few, and they made life bearable. Together with the younger kids at the Brodys'."

"Those idiots...those..." Tierney didn't continue with the offensive word she meant to say about the Brodys, not wanting to set a bad example even if she knew Stephanie had heard worse than what Tierney could come up with, from Victor Brody.

"I know. Those." Stephanie looked pensively out through the window.

"As for what you asked earlier, yes, it's Giselle playing. She's composing for Chicory Ariose right now." Tierney was glad to change the subject.

Turning her head and looking much happier, Stephanie looked impressed. "That is beyond cool. Once they started to record a few songs with Noelle Laurent, a lot of the kids in my school started really getting into them. Some kids thought they were chill by saying they were too old, but even they had to surrender. I mean, they're from Rhode Island and everything. And Noelle is just the bomb."

"She sure is." Tierney wondered if the world-renowned soul-pop star would make an appearance at the house with Chicory Ariose. If she did, and if Stephanie was still here at that point, it would be an unforgettable experience for her young friend. Laughing inwardly at herself, Tierney confessed she wouldn't exactly say no to meeting Noelle in the flesh.

A strange, loud sound from the music room startled her. It sounded as if Giselle had slammed her fists into the piano keys and then slammed the lid. Hesitating, Tierney stood, not knowing what to do.

"Why don't you go see if she needs something?" Stephanie looked a little pale. "I can put the dishes away."

"You're not here to do chores," Tierney said absentmindedly. "That's my job."

"Yeah, that may be, but I'm a bit iffy about someone slamming doors and yelling. I don't know about you, but that may have been a musician's way of doing just that. Please, check on her?"

Tierney flinched and scanned Stephanie closely. Tension around the eyes and pale lips spoke of stress. "Okay. Thanks for dealing with the kitchen. Just put things wherever they fit in the dishwasher. I'll start it later if you can't figure it out." She patted Stephanie's shoulder in passing. Grabbing the coffee pot, to have a less-obvious reason to disturb Giselle, she walked quickly through the house toward the music room. After she knocked on the door, she opened it and peered inside. At first, she didn't spot Giselle, but then she saw her standing by the window, both palms against the glass.

"Giselle?" Tierney murmured, hoping she wouldn't frighten her.

Pivoting so quickly she had to grab the back of an armchair, Giselle glowered at her. "What do you want? I thought it would be obvious I don't want to be disturbed."

"Yeah, that. I just wanted to see if you needed a refill." Tierney wiggled the coffee pot for emphasis.

Giselle stared at it as if it was a completely alien object. "Coffee?"

"Yes." Walking closer, Tierney peered into the mug sitting on the small sideboard next to the grand piano. "This is empty."

"All right. If you insist. By all means, pour me some coffee." Flinging her hands into the air, Giselle turned back to the window.

"Please, Giselle. Tell me what's wrong. Maybe I can help?" Mentally ducking, waiting for Giselle's annoyance or anger, Tierney gripped the now-empty coffee pot harder.

"Either you are presumptuous or…I don't know, actually. What are you exactly, Tierney?" If Giselle's voice hadn't sounded so hollow, the scathing words would have been hurtful. Now, Tierney could look beyond what Giselle said and instead try to interpret what she meant.

"I'm not presumptuous. If anything, I feel I'm walking on thin ice." Tierney put the pot down and took a hesitant step toward Giselle. "We heard you all the way in the kitchen, despite the soundproofed walls. You startled Steph." It was a cheap trick, but Tierney was ready to say just about anything to get Giselle's attention.

"What?" Giselle turned much more slowly this time. "I didn't mean to. Please let Stephanie know that." Pressing her right hand to her midsection, she swallowed visibly.

"She knows. She's doing the dishes so I could go see you. I think you're upset because you have regrets. I'm not sure how I can make her understand that, but mainly you're just at a loss since you aren't used to this situation." Tierney stopped speaking, out of breath after rattling off the words.

"I don't regret anything, but my entire system is in uproar." Giselle made a face.

"And why the hammering on the poor piano?" Tierney asked lightly.

"It was there." Giselle growled. "I mean, I really disapprove of such displays, but it was as if I had ants crawling all over me. I couldn't think, and even worse, I couldn't hear the music. I hate that."

"I'm so sorry. I never meant for anything regarding my past or Steph's situation to affect you this way." Really upset now, Tierney wanted to snap her fingers and make herself go invisible, something she'd seen in a rerun of an old sitcom once. It had stuck in her mind, as she would have loved to be able to do that on more occasions than she could recall.

"Oh, for heaven's sake, it's not your fault. You're not responsible for my actions, or lack thereof." Annoyance barely hid the pain in Giselle's voice. She inhaled deeply and slammed her fist against the window. "Fuck."

Anger simmered beneath Tierney's skin now. "Am I supposed to apologize for apologizing now? I'm at a loss here, really." She was. How was this going to work when Giselle was in full panic mood?

Slowly turning back to face Tierney, Giselle was now clearly trembling, and her complexion had taken on a pale, grayish hue. "No. This…" She gestured at herself. "This is all on me." The desperation in her voice proved to Tierney that Giselle was fighting her demons right now.

Reacting purely on instinct, Tierney strode over to Giselle and wrapped her arms around her. Being the shorter of the two, she hugged the rigid woman tight around her waist. "Please. You're going to be fine. This is just the first day. Steph and I won't crowd you or demand stuff of you that you don't want to give, that you're not ready for." Hoping Giselle would take her suggestion the right way, she said, "If you want, I can ask Steph to walk Charley and play with her. That way, we could perhaps work more on the song combined with some lyrics. Perhaps the lyrics will suck, but that might just get you back on track. If not, yelling at me for being a musical moron could do the trick."

Giselle stood motionless for a few moments that seemed like minutes, but then relaxed some and lowered her head, pressing her forehead against Tierney's shoulder. "I hate myself when I get like this. I loathe not being in control. I apologize."

"All this apologizing is making me tired." Tierney had to joke, or the proximity to Giselle, standing in a full-frontal embrace, would make her knees give in.

"I agree." Lifting her head, Giselle looked wearily at Tierney. "Do you think Stephanie is all right and feeling secure enough to be on her own so soon?"

"I think so, but I'll ask. If she's uneasy about it, she can sit in the living room with my laptop and surf the net while we're in here with the door open. That sound okay?"

Giselle's expression softened, and color returned to her cheeks. "It does." She stepped back but slowly raised her hand and cupped Tierney's cheek. "You are something else."

Gasping, Tierney felt as if Giselle's touch ought to leave a permanent handprint on her cheek...or, rather, her heart. She slowly raised her own trembling hand and placed it on Giselle's, wanting to prolong the touch. "I'm not sure what you mean by that, exactly." Tierney smiled, or perhaps the attempt to do so was more like a wobbly stretching of the lips.

"You're not like anyone I've ever known." Giselle tilted her head, wearing a puzzled expression. "It's like as soon as I think I have you figured out, you surprise me by doing something completely unexpected." She removed her hand from Tierney's face, but turned it inside Tierney's hand and held it as she lowered it farther.

So, they were cupping cheeks and holding hands. "Talk about surprises. I didn't see this coming." Tierney swung their joined hands lightly. Her heart refused to be cautious as it sang in her chest.

Giselle blushed faintly but smiled. "Neither did I. And, somehow, you've helped pull me back—or reel me in, perhaps. I sometimes feel I'm this runaway freight train that barrels toward disaster and I can't stop it. Or myself. I'm not quite sure how it happens, even if I can recognize the triggers. And on occasion, I can't find any explanation for it. At all." Her smile turned wistful.

"I'm not sure what I did, but I bet you becoming annoyed at me, rather than panicked about something else, had something to do with it." Cautiously, Tierney peered at Giselle through her eyelashes.

"Probably." Now, Giselle chuckled, which warmed Tierney throughout. Why was it that whenever Giselle could freely smile or laugh, it meant more to Tierney than pretty much anything else in her life? It didn't happen often, but when it did, the moments were golden. Giselle squeezed Tierney's hand gently, then let go. "Why don't we try your suggestion? Go ask Steph if she wants to play with Charley or keep us company."

"All right." Missing Giselle's touch as if it was connected to the oxygen she required to breathe, Tierney returned to Stephanie in the kitchen. As it turned out, Stephanie wanted very much to play with Charley, but also asked if it was all right to tiptoe into the music room later. After reassurances from Tierney that she was welcome, Stephanie flung her arms around Tierney's neck and hugged her fiercely.

"Thank you so much. I know it's temporary, Tierney, I really do know that, but I'm so glad to be here right now. This is such a dreamy place, and if it takes me forever, this is how I want to live one day."

Trying to swallow the lump forming in her throat, Tierney hugged her young friend back, wishing she had a home of her own to offer Stephanie. Chiding herself, she knew that was only half the truth. She wished she belonged here and that she and Giselle could offer Stephanie *this* home. Stephanie was right. It was a dreamy place—and she couldn't indulge in dreams. She'd learned that hard fact as a child when the parents she'd hoped would find her irresistible and adopt her never came.

In a way, Tierney wished she would grow itchy feet again and want to move on to the next town soon. That was what she'd done since she was eighteen and out of the system. The nomadic life had suited her fine, but now she was straying far too long from the lessons she'd learned. Don't get attached, be friendly but don't make friends, and, most important of all, never let anyone see your heart bleed. Those were her mantras, and she feared they were starting to corrode. Tierney trembled as she thought of Stephanie's dreams. She was just a kid and still not jaded enough by her experiences. The Tierney pre-East Quay would have taken it upon herself to caution Stephanie against dreaming too big.

Now, she couldn't make herself do that. Stephanie had the right to dream, to plan, without someone shooting her down. Tierney rocked Stephanie gently. Stephanie had gone from a close online friend to an even closer friend, and a protégé of sorts, in the physical world.

Would these emotions be her downfall?

CHAPTER EIGHTEEN

Giselle had to fight not to stare at Tierney as she stood next to the piano, her eyes on the notebook she'd placed on the music stand in front of her. Focusing on playing the new chorus to one of the potential songs Chicory Ariose might choose, she was inspired to help Tierney find the passion the lyrics suggested by aiming for a heart-wrenching crescendo. The song was about profound longing, and Giselle wanted the listener to feel every single note and absorb every one of Tierney's words.

As they reached the end of the chorus, Tierney stopped singing and flipped her hair back over her shoulder, exasperation evident in the way she moved. "It needs more. Like a bridge with a whole different feeling, well, not feeling perhaps, but a change of pace."

Giselle kept her fingers moving on the keys as she thought about the suggestion. Tierney was right. They couldn't do one crescendo and go right into the last, even stronger one, without a break in between. They already had a bridge earlier in the song, though. Pondering their options, Giselle noticed the highlights glistening in Tierney's hair, small golden-auburn sparkles where the sun from the window found the shiny locks. The color of Tierney's eyebrows suggested the amazing mane was not dyed. Did Tierney realize, or even bother to notice, how beautiful she was? She had more than physical beauty; it was much deeper than that. The light emanating from her eyes, combined with the bright smile that could sweep someone off their feet when it was genuine, could drive a person crazy with need. Giselle found it easy to tell when Tierney used her broad grin deliberately. When it was real, it hit her eyes and made her cheeks flush a pretty pink.

"Yes," Tierney now called out, doing a twirl where she stood. "Just like that!"

"What?" Pulling out of her reverie, Giselle stopped, yanking her hands off the keys.

"Were you even listening to yourself?" Huffing, Tierney rounded the music stand and sat down next to Giselle on the piano stool. "Something like this. And don't have a cow now. Remember I really don't play the piano." Tierney slowly ran her fingers through a gentle string of notes, using just her right hand. She made a few mistakes the first time she tried. "Damn. Not like that. Wait." She tried again, and this time she got it right. The tones were ethereal in a way the other bridge, and the rest of the song, was not. Using her left hand, Tierney added a few simple chords. Her left arm kept touching Giselle's abdomen and even the side of her right breast as Tierney reached for the keys on the far left of the piano. "See what I mean? That okay?" Tierney turned to look at Giselle, who knew she was blushing.

"All right. Let me try." Still feeling like a fool for losing herself so much in thoughts of Tierney that she couldn't focus, Giselle played the melody. "Like this?"

"Yes!" Tierney began to get up, but Giselle tugged at her T-shirt.

"No. Grab your notebook and stay here." Giselle refused to examine why she thought having Tierney sit next to her would work better. Perhaps because she wouldn't be distracted by Tierney's face that way. Yes. That must be it.

"Want me to sing the words again?"

"Yes." Moving her fingers to loosen the joints, Giselle started from the beginning. When they reached the bridge Tierney had suggested, Giselle concentrated harder, at first only half listening to that part of the lyrics.

I hate that losing you makes me cry
Skinless, humiliated, afraid to try
Moving on alone
Dreading every storm
Scared to find out why

Giselle closed her eyes as she played, slowly letting the words permeate her. When had Tierney written this? Who had let her down so badly that these painful words paired with the music came off as pure torment?

When they ended the song, muted applause came at them from the settee by the window. Giselle blinked and looked at Stephanie, who sat there with Charley at her feet. Surprisingly, Mister was curled up on the top of the backrest, right beside Stephanie's neck.

"You like it?" Tierney leaned sideways, smiling at Stephanie.

"Are you kidding me? I felt you wrote this for me. And the music is…it's stunning. I've never felt so drawn in, I don't think. And you know I listen to a lot of music. All the time." She gazed down at her lap. "This ancient iPod is all I have, but as long as it's able to charge, I'll have my music with me."

"One of the few things they can't take from you." Tierney leaned back against Giselle's shoulder. "When you move from place to place, sometimes with your few belongings in a garbage bag, you get afraid of becoming attached to anything. I had a rabbit, a stuffed toy, that I'd had since I was three or four. When I was fourteen, the woman I was staying with gave it away to one of the younger kids, claiming I was way too old for stuffed toys. I was devastated, yet I couldn't take it back. The look in the little boy's eyes, the way he instantly loved my rabbit, made it impossible. So, when Steph talks about loving the music in her iPod, it's a big deal."

Giselle understood. "Then we shall make sure she has some new tunes on it." She stood. "Come with me, Stephanie." The girl followed her hesitantly. Charley and Mister trotted after them, and clearly Tierney was curious too as she rose from the piano stool as well.

"Here, Stephanie, is my collection of music. Some is digital, stored on that media machine over there. Some is on CD or vinyl. All I ask is that you be careful with everything and put it back in its place, but other than that, you can copy anything you want to your iPod. Do you have enough room on it?"

"What? I mean, really? I can…you're letting me use your music system?" Stephanie gaped. "Are you sure?"

"Of course. I think a true music lover should have a wide variety to choose from. I'm able to buy all the music I want, and I'm pretty picky. That's why my collection is so eclectic. I'm sure you'll find something you like though." Giselle hadn't been prepared for Stephanie's reaction to her offer. It dawned on her that this girl wasn't used to getting anything without a ton of strings attached to it. She turned to Tierney. "The same goes for you. Please use any of the music you might enjoy."

Tierney was focusing on Stephanie and her reaction, but now she blinked and looked almost as dazed as Stephanie. "You're more than generous, Giselle," she murmured.

"Nonsense. The least I can do is share something you can truly enjoy and is just sitting here." Smoothing down her light-yellow shirt, Giselle checked the time. "I have another two hours to go, but now that I'm over that hurdle, you're free to do what you want."

"Thanks. I'll inventory the fridge and the pantry. Maybe Steph and I can go grocery shopping later today, or tomorrow." Tierney nudged Stephanie's hand. "Up for it, kiddo?"

"Sure." Stephanie answered absentmindedly since she was already browsing the CDs. She had her head tilted sideways, skimming her right index finger along the backs of the plastic casings.

Right then, Tierney's cellphone rang, and everybody grew rigid. The reaction would have been funny if Tierney hadn't looked so startled, or if Giselle's heart hadn't jumped.

Answering, Tierney walked into the next room. She spoke quietly to the person on the other end, clearly asking some questions as well. When she returned, she gave a less-than-authentic smile. "That was one of the women I met in East Quay when I stepped off the bus. She needs me to walk Timo, her cocker spaniel. I'll be gone a couple of hours."

Stephanie sent Giselle a hesitant look. "That's okay," she said politely, but Giselle could see how out of sorts she suddenly was.

"We'll be fine. Stephanie can oversee Charley and Mister while I work. You can also take anything you want from the kitchen, Stephanie. You know where the entertainment room with the TV set is." She smiled reassuringly, and Stephanie looked marginally less stressed.

"If you'd rather I'd stay, Steph, I can call Leanne and cancel." Tierney placed a gentle hand on Stephanie's shoulder.

"Nah. I have your cellphone number, and so does Giselle, right?" Stephanie looked brave and stronger where she stood, squaring her shoulders. She pushed her hair back. "If you say no, she might not call you back. You'll lose a chance to make extra money."

"True." Tierney still didn't seem convinced. "I'd rather know you're all right than make a few extra bucks."

"I'm fine. I'm not a child anymore." Jutting her chin out, Stephanie looked every bit as stubborn as any other teenager Giselle had come across, not that there were a lot.

"Of course not. Well, I'm off then. We'll do the inventory of the groceries tomorrow, I think." Tierney began walking to her room. "Oh, by the way, I thought it would be good for little Timo if I could exercise him while riding a bike. I saw you have one in the garage. May I borrow it?"

"It's Frances's. Or, well, it's mine, but I bought it for Frances when she worked here." Giselle knew she sounded a bit unhinged. "You're welcome to use it. The key should be in the lock, as I keep it in the garage."

"Excellent. All right. Have fun, ladies." Tierney waved and walked to her room.

Nodding to Stephanie, Giselle headed for the kitchen. She fetched a small bottle of mineral water, stopped in mid-motion, and then pulled one out for Stephanie as well. Walking back to the music room, she gave the bottle to Stephanie without a word. Flanked by Charley and Mister, Stephanie was sitting on the floor, spreading CD covers and vinyl records over the coffee table. As Giselle turned to leave, Stephanie raised a hand.

"Thanks for the water. And just so you know, I've made a note on my phone where each of these goes so I can put them back when I'm done." She smiled carefully.

"Very clever idea. I'll remember that next time I want to listen to something." Giselle noticed the flickering in her eyes when she praised her. It warmed her, and for the first time she felt entirely comfortable around Stephanie. Tierney was right. Clever ideas aside, this girl was special. It dawned on Giselle that the longer this child stayed with them, with her, the harder it would be to have to let her move in with someone else. How would she know Stephanie didn't end up in a situation just as bad, or even worse than the one she'd lived through with the Brodys?

Mulling this unexpected sentiment over, Giselle walked over to the music room. She was just about to close the door merely from force of habit, when she realized that would shut Stephanie out. She left it open two inches and sat down on the piano stool, readying herself to put in a few more hours of work.

Tierney rode the fancy bike toward East Quay, glad a bicycle path ran the whole way since some cars appeared to be trying to set a speed record on the narrow country road. The sun was out, and she had to stop and remove her windbreaker. She tied the sleeves around her waist and made sure the old messenger bag she'd scored at a thrift store in Providence sat firmly slung across her chest and under the jacket.

Perhaps it was a good idea that Stephanie and Giselle had to communicate without her there to "translate," Tierney thought as she pedaled toward East Quay. She would have to cross the entire town to reach the posh area by the ocean, and that gave her plenty of time to consider what had occurred in the music room as well. Tierney had no idea where her strength had come from, going toe-to-toe with Giselle, especially since Giselle had been seconds from freaking out completely. Tierney never wanted to be the reason for Giselle to have a full-blown panic attack or something. That had to be a horrible feeling. She had read about it, and even if she couldn't picture it entirely, a lot of the people suffering from it claimed it felt as if they were about to die.

Then there was the physical thing. If it had been anyone else, Tierney's gaydar would have claimed Giselle was a lesbian, or at least bisexual. It was impossible to judge with someone as guarded as Giselle, and all she had to go on was the flustered look on Giselle's face and her clearly dilated pupils. Giselle responded to Tierney, of that she was certain, but it really didn't mean anything, as Giselle was entirely out of Tierney's league. And then there was the fact that Giselle was her employer and perhaps her ticket to the music industry. That alone made a potential attraction impossible. No way in hell she would have anyone think she'd slept her way to a job. And yet. Tierney pushed herself harder, pedaling up a hill, forcing her strong legs to propel the bicycle faster.

And yet, Tierney knew she was falling for Giselle, despite, or perhaps because of, her complex nature and vulnerability. Tierney was aware of her own strong protective side. When Giselle was struggling, whether it was with her music, walking out in an open field, or even going out in the car to rescue a young stranger, Tierney's gut reaction was to help her through it. Not necessarily make it easier for Giselle but to help empower her. It was perhaps arrogant to think she could dart into Giselle's life and be the catalyst to help improve it, but that wouldn't stop her from trying—if Giselle allowed it. Being a proud woman, Giselle wouldn't take kindly to any obvious attempts to "fix her," and it wasn't about that. Tierney was damaged enough and possessed enough self-awareness not to think she could "fix" anyone.

It was hard to explain, even to herself, but she truly felt she could make a difference when it came to Giselle—and Stephanie. Not only to train Charley as she had planned from day one, but also to show Giselle that it was okay to be different, that having a panic attack didn't have to mean the end of everything. Never had she felt so invested in helping someone. Thinking back, she realized it had probably started when she founded the Facebook group for young people in, or just out of, the system. That had been one of the first things she did after she saved up enough for a laptop with wireless internet.

Reaching an intersection, Tierney turned onto the road that led into the center of East Quay. That part of town was well maintained, with old houses in New England style. Clearly, the merchants had a hand in the upkeep, as this was a town that appreciated small, local stores, even if a shopping center sprawled near the outskirts. Mindful of the cars, Tierney pulled aside and double-checked the address on the map on her phone. It was reliable, and she could tell she had twenty minutes left before she reached Leanne's house.

Enjoying the exercise the bike ride gave her, Tierney smiled into the wind. She had never been this close to feeling content in her life.

CHAPTER NINETEEN

Tierney rang the doorbell and took a step back. A dog barked, and then Leanne opened the door, smiling brightly. "Welcome!" Timo the cocker spaniel came running and circled Tierney's feet, jumping up at her constantly. Only when he realized she wasn't impressed did he plop down on his butt and merely stare at her with his tongue lolling. Not unlike Charley, but smaller.

Leanne beamed. "This is great! I was actually pretty sure Ms. Bonnaire would have showed you the door that first day." She waved at Tierney to come inside. "I'll just get Timo's leash and collar." She opened the door to a narrow closet just inside the front door. "Tell me. Did the whole Frances-sent-me idea really work that well?" She strapped the collar around Timo's neck and handed the leash to Tierney, who hadn't found a large-enough pause in Leanne's word flow to answer her.

"I didn't lie to her," Tierney said, hoping Leanne wouldn't pry for information about Giselle or her.

"Just a white lie, if you ask me." Leanne winked, and her bright orange-red lips pulled into a wide smile. "All for a worthy cause."

"As I said, I didn't have to lie. Ms. Bonnaire hired me anyway. Full-time, really." Tierney motioned toward Timo, who was now tugging at the leash with his little white teeth. "I'll have him back in an hour."

"Oh. Okay. Sure. That'll be great." Leanne looked disappointed at Tierney's reluctance to gossip. "I'm working from home today. I'll be here."

"See you in an hour then." Nodding politely, Tierney gave a light tug at the leash and made a startling *ptcht* sound, which made Timo let go of the leash. "Now that's a good boy. Come on. Let's go for a walk." She strolled down the road leading to the marina and the beach beyond it. The parking lot was full of cars, which meant business was booming for Mike, as she owned the coffeehouse called the Sea Stone Café. Studying the many fancy yachts, sailboats, and motorboats along the docks for a moment, Tierney shook her head at how different her world must be from that of the people who owned them.

She followed the gravel path leading past the marina and headed toward the dunes that in turn would take her to the beach. She doubted dogs were allowed all the way down to the water at this time of year, but she hoped it would be possible farther north.

Timo seemed to be on his best behavior. Perhaps it was all the unfamiliar scents tempting his nose or the fact that Tierney spoke to him in a calm, friendly voice and wouldn't let him get away with pulling on the leash. He was no doubt used to his owner's chatty nature, even if she was more soft-spoken than the friend who had been with her that first day—Daphne, was it? Tierney couldn't remember.

As she walked up and down the dunes, which was great exercise for both of them, Tierney spotted a tall person walking two dogs. Huge dogs. It took Tierney only a second to realize it was Mike with hers and Vivian's dogs. Tierney waved, hoping to exchange a few words with the charismatic woman. If Tierney hadn't led such a nomadic life, Mike could have become a very good friend. She could feel it.

"Tierney!" Mike called out from a distance. "What a great surprise." She stopped a few yards from Tierney when she spotted Timo. "And who's that little fellow?"

Tierney introduced her new friend but refrained from telling Mike whose dog it was. Leanne might have other values in life when it came to matters of the truth, but she would still benefit from Tierney's rule of confidentiality.

"I recognize him, I think." Mike frowned. "Remember, I meet a lot of people when I'm at the café. I think that's the chief of police's cocker spaniel. He's met our boys before." Mike let the huge Great Danes closer. She had them on a joined leash, easily handling them. "Perry, Mason. Remember, he's little. Be gentle."

Perry and Mason resembled giraffes as they dipped their heads to sniff the now-dwarfed Timo. After yelping once at their towering over him, Timo seemed to recognize them and began to wag his tail.

"How about if we go farther up the dunes together? I know some great paths up there." Mike smiled. "I want to hear all about your progress with the music."

Tierney began walking next to Mike, glad she could combine work with some extra fun. "Actually, we made some headway today. It's quite the miracle, since we were driving all night."

Mike stopped so fast, Perry and Mason nearly made her topple over. "You were driving in the night with Giselle?" She gaped. "What the…I mean, why?"

Tierney saw no point in keeping Stephanie's presence a secret, since Vivian and Mike would meet her the next time they visited Giselle. Keeping most of the detail out of her recounting of last night's ordeal, she told Mike the gist of it all.

Mike began walking again but kept her eyes on Tierney. "Am I right to understand that you not only persuaded Giselle to keep you around, but you also talked her into making room for a kid in need of shelter—under her own roof?"

"That's about it, I suppose. You do make me out to be rather manipulative, you know." Only half joking, Tierney nudged Mike's arm with her shoulder.

"No, no. Not at all. In fact, I think it's great. If you only knew how many times Vivian and I, and the others in Chicory Ariose, have despaired at Giselle's solitude. Sometimes I've dreaded going to her house, as it pained me so bad that we had to leave her there alone when we went home to our respective happy relationships. She would stand in the window, holding Charley back so she wouldn't run out, jump the fence, and chase our cars. Don't get me wrong. Giselle is a formidable woman in her own right, but that doesn't make her less lonely. Your presence, and this kid, Stephanie, is just what she needs."

"From your mouth to…" She shrugged, afraid she might have let too much of her newfound, hopeless attraction—and affection—when it came to Giselle show. "It's temporary. All of it." Tierney's voice wobbled, and she coughed, embarrassed.

"Do you wish it would be more, well, permanent?" Mike asked gently.

"That'd be presumptuous, wouldn't it?" Tierney turned her head and focused on Timo, who was now busy digging a hole in the sand. One of the Great Danes looked longingly at him and then decided to stealthily assist Timo with one gentle paw.

"No. I don't think so. We feel what we feel. To hell with conventional ways to handle ourselves. I can tell you care for Giselle. At what level, and in what capacity, that's your business, and I won't pry."

It was as refreshing as it was intimidating to be with someone as straightforward as Mike. With her black hair and dark-blue eyes, she was such a stunning woman. She and Vivian had initially appeared mismatched, but one only had to be in their presence for ten minutes to feel the love between them. And if Tierney could sense that about them—after all, they were virtual strangers—perhaps it wasn't as unlikely that Mike could do the same when it came to Tierney's feelings for Giselle.

"Stephanie sounds like a terrific kid," Mike said, changing the subject. "I know quite a bit about growing up that way. I lived on the street for a while, before the Belmont Foundation gave me the chance of a lifetime. That's how I saw it. Thanks to them, I could buy the café, which was in poor condition, renovate it, and watch it grow into what it is today. That in turn sent Vivian my way, which later brought Manon and Erin. So, and I'm not trying to be a know-it-all here, please don't think that. Who knows what the future will bring for you, and for Stephanie?"

Tierney wanted to put on her usual armor and claim that no orphan, or kid in the system, would ever presume to dream that big—not if they knew what was good for them. Such high-flying dreams led to heartache and devastation. But this was Mike, someone with a similar background to her own, and that made it impossible to dismiss what she was saying.

Not wanting to comment on Mike's words, Tierney checked her phone. "Hey. It was nice to see you again, Mike. I better get Timo home. His owner is a bit…particular." She smiled, her less-than-authentic one that felt more like a grimace. "And I heard you," Tierney added, not wanting Mike to think otherwise. "Thanks."

Mike placed a hand on Tierney's shoulder. "Giselle has my number if you ever need to, you know, chat. About anything. And just so you know, I never gossip. Not even to the love of my life."

Thinking about the amazing, beautiful Vivian, who had captured the heart of the entire music world, Tierney could relax into a genuine smile. "Anything I share with you about myself, you can tell Vivian. She's cool."

Mike chuckled. "I'll tell her you said so. That'll make her day."

They parted after having to pull Timo away from his gigantic friends. As Tierney walked back toward his home, she pondered what Mike had said. She thought Tierney was good for Giselle. And coming from Mike, it hadn't sounded like she meant in more a professional capacity—more like personal. But how personal and in what way, exactly?

No matter what way, Tierney had risked her heart, whether Giselle was into women or not.

The walk back took only ten minutes, and Tierney found Leanne waiting for her on the sidewalk. She was frowning, and Tierney's heart sank. Now what?

"You're twelve minutes late. I was worried." Leanne bent and patted Timo. Being very excited to see her, he placed his paws on her thighs. "Timo! Where have you been? You're dirty!" Leanne didn't just frown anymore. She scowled at Tierney. "Where have you been walking him?"

"Among the dunes. And I know I said an hour, but he had so much fun with a couple of dogs we met and—"

"Dogs? You let him play with some strange dogs? Are you insane? They could have parasites, heartworm, or any other communicable disease. What were you thinking?"

Trembling now, from anger and from being upset, Tierney replied, "I never put him in danger. Mike said Timo knows Perry and Mason, and all they did was dig in the sand. See? It's falling right off when it dries." Tierney motioned toward Leanne's trousers.

Yanking the leash out of Tierney's hand, Leanne brushed her knees with her free hand. Then she stopped in mid-motion, her face mellowing. "Mike? As in Michaela Stone?"

"Yes."

"And you suddenly know her?" Leanne tapped her chin. "Ah, of course. She's been to Ms. Bonnaire's house. I've heard they sometimes collaborate. Well, then. That's all right then. Still, I loathe tardiness. Next time—"

"Excuse me." Furious still at the way Leanne had talked to her, Tierney held up a hand, palm forward. "I'm not so sure there'll be a next time. Timo is a great dog, and he listens very well once he understands that's what the person walking him wants. That said, I'm not going to subject myself to verbal abuse like this. You don't pay me well enough for that."

Leanne gaped. "Wait a minute. Who do you think you are? From where I'm standing, you're a stranger to our town, arriving here and looking for odd jobs. You claim you're touring colleges, but how do I know that's true. Maybe it's a good thing my husband insisted on running a nationwide search on you to make sure you wouldn't run off with Timo. He's our baby."

So cold now, Tierney pulled her hands into her sleeves. "Go right ahead. Do your searches. That won't change the fact that I did an excellent job walking your dog. Some sand between the toes never hurt anyone. Neither has going on an impromptu play date with a four-legged buddy. Just give me what we agreed on for today, and you won't have to deal with this insane, inept, and *tardy* person again."

"Hmm. I really should deduct for the time you made me wait, but nobody will ever say I'm not a woman of my word. Here." Holding out the money for Tierney, Leanne raised her chin in a clear challenge. "Don't get too comfortable at Ms. Bonnaire's. I'm sure she'll find it interesting to learn that you planned to trick your way into her house."

"I'm sure she will—oh, right—she already knows. I told her on the first day about the two helpful acquaintances of hers that I met in town, and how they encouraged me in a very special way to apply for the job as her assistant."

It would have been entertaining, if it hadn't been so appalling, to study Leanne's expression. She went from smirking superiority to furious apprehension in seconds.

After grabbing the bike she'd leaned against the fence, Tierney unlocked it and mounted it in one fluid movement. She didn't say good-bye—that would have been hypocritical—but she sped down the road where one posh, mansion-looking house after another seemed to lean toward her. She couldn't wait to get back to Giselle and Stephanie. Tierney groaned. Now she had a whole other problem to consider. Should she wait and see if Leanne's cop husband would find she had a sealed juvenile record or tell Giselle beforehand?

Turning the corner, Tierney was relieved that the return trip was downhill. She'd spent a lot of energy going off on the horrible dog-owner, and now she could just let the bicycle roll down the hill. The wind caressed her face, whipped her hair around her neck, and whistled where it found the maples and shrubbery.

As she reached the intersection at the bottom of the hill, she shifted her grip to squeeze the brakes on the handlebar. Nothing happened. Her heart thundering, Tierney tried again. And again. And again. Watching the traffic go by in the intersection, she put her feet down, trying to press her soles to the asphalt. She barely reached it with the tip of her toes. The cars and trucks seemed to approach sideways as they zoomed across the road she approached from.

"Ahh!" Judging that she had only one option to save herself from certain death, Tierney turned the handlebars a sharp right. The next thing she knew, everything blurred, a lot hurt, and then the blur turned black.

CHAPTER TWENTY

Giselle emerged from the music room, still humming the new bridge of the song she'd worked on with Tierney. Tierney was such a natural when it came to creating her lyrics, and she evoked a flood of emotions when she sang. Feeling excited, thrilled, and eager to hear more, Giselle smiled to herself as she walked toward the kitchen.

She saw no sign of Stephanie, but she could hear murmuring voices from the TV room. Walking over to it, Giselle peered around the doorframe. On the couch, with towels as protection, Charley and Mister flanked Stephanie, who was engrossed in something unfamiliar to Giselle. Perhaps a soap. She rarely watched TV, unless it was in the middle of the night and she couldn't sleep. Then, she would turn on the TV in her bedroom and indulge in popular science channels until fatigue claimed her. She rarely chose anything to do with music, as that was what her brain needed to rest from if she would have any chance of recharging her inner batteries.

"What are you watching?" Giselle asked and stepped into the room.

Stephanie flinched but then smiled shyly. "Just a rerun of a rerun, I think. I mean, I do love some of the soaps, but this, I think I've seen it more than four times. Wish they'd show something newer sometimes."

"I have tons of DVDs. You're welcome to pick out anything you want if nothing good's on." Feeling ridiculous as she tried to communicate with Stephanie, Giselle crossed the room and sat down in one of the massive armchairs.

"Oh, can I?" Bouncing up, Stephanie surprised Charley, who raised her left eyebrow. Mister stretched and moved to curl up on the backrest of the couch.

"Sure. They're in that cabinet over there. Double rows, so you'll have to rummage around. And like the CDs and vinyls, they're categorized and alphabetized."

"Makes it easier to find what you're looking for." Stephanie nodded approvingly. "I like when it's tidy. If you only knew how the Brodys lived. So much stuff everywhere. It was my job, and the younger kids', to clean up the mess, but it was hard. Every time we had it looking decent, Dylan, in particular, would throw things everywhere. Dirty clothes on the floor, pizza cartons everywhere, and tons of beer cans." Stephanie blinked. "Oh, man. I'm sorry. I didn't mean to shovel all that on you." She had been squatting on all fours by the film cabinet but now sat back on her heels, her shoulders slumping.

Giselle didn't want to see this defeated look in Stephanie's eyes. "Hey. I'm always interested in hearing what you've been through. Tierney told me a little bit—and she hasn't broken any confidences, just so you know—and I really want to know more if you feel like sharing." How odd that listening to Stephanie not only made her feel less selfish but also infinitely better. Her own demons pulled back some, like they weren't important when Stephanie described the conditions at the Brodys'. The thought that Tierney had gone through similar things while in the so-called care of those people pierced her heart.

"Thanks." Stephanie looked more at ease. "I'm relieved. I don't mean to generalize about foster homes. Thank God, I know a lot of kids from the Facebook group that lucked out and got to live with great people. Some were even adopted. That's the majority. Then there are those who've had it way worse than I did. Their stories are so heartbreaking, I can barely think about them without crying."

Giselle could understand that. She moved to the leather bench by the window, close to Stephanie. "I'm sure they're grateful for the group, for being able to share. What do the moderators do if they hear about unlawful treatment of these young people?"

"When I signed up for this group, one of the rules, stated very clearly, was that the moderators—Tierney is one, by the way—wouldn't hesitate to report such treatment to the authorities. I kind of hoped

Tierney would do that for me. I never could, as I've learned the hard way that the social workers and cops don't always take what a kid says at face value. If the foster parents are good at expressing themselves, they outmaneuver the kid and have the upper hand. They're all adults discussing things between themselves. It's hard to make yourself heard, and believed."

"Tierney was adamant to get to you. I—um—well, I have some phobias that I struggle with, but still I couldn't let Tierney drive alone in the middle of the night. I mean, I had no way of knowing where she'd end up and if she would have backup. I have some pull, in a way, in this state, as I'm pretty well connected. I hoped I wouldn't make things worse for her—or you—by having a panic attack. Luckily, I didn't." Giselle smiled gently.

"That has got to suck," Stephanie said and shifted to sit with her legs crossed. "I've never had a panic attack, but I've been panicky, which I assume is pretty close to it."

"I think so too." Folding her hands, Giselle wished she had the courage to hug Stephanie to show she cared. Still, this was a big step, moving within someone's personal space when she hardly knew them.

Her cellphone rang, making her jump. Fumbling, she dug it out of her cardigan pocket and checked the display. An unknown number. Most likely, it was someone trying to sell her something or ask her to donate money, but she still pressed the green receiver symbol on the screen. "Hello?"

"Is this Giselle?" an unknown woman asked. She didn't sound young.

"Yes. Who am I talking to?"

"Oh, dear. My name is Beatrice Nielsen. I'm afraid your friend, young Tierney here, has had a bit of an accident with her bicycle."

"What?" Giselle stood so fast, the room began to spin. "What happened? How is she?"

"She came down the hill like a bat out of you-know-where and slammed right into the side of our car. She flew across the hood. Fortunately, Mauritz, my husband, managed to slam on the brakes before he ran her over. She's sitting here on the curb now and looks a bit groggy. She refuses to let me call 911, though, but asked me to contact you."

"And why couldn't she phone me herself?" Giselle asked as her heart plummeted.

"She's got a cut right at her hairline, and some of the blood has gotten into her eyes. I still think she needs a doctor." Beatrice made a disapproving tsking sound with her tongue.

"Put her on, please, ma'am?" Gripping the cellphone harder, Giselle felt Stephanie at her side. Stephanie placed an arm around Giselle's waist while Giselle engaged the loudspeaker on the phone.

"Giselle?" It was Tierney, sounding pained but not slurred, thank God. "I'm a first-class idiot. I forgot the fucking helmet. The brakes failed somehow, and I hit a car. It wasn't their fault at all."

"Nor was it yours, dear," Beatrice said in the background. "It was an accident."

"You have to let them call 911, Tierney. Please." Giselle put her hand on Stephanie's where it rested at the side of her waist.

"Nah. I just need to go home and clean up. No hospital." Tierney spoke in a slow yet clipped way.

"But you may need an X-ray, and maybe stitches." Giselle was getting upset.

"No. No hospital." Tierney must've held the phone closer. "That's final."

Stephanie tugged at Giselle. "She can't afford it," she mouthed.

Annoyed at herself for not realizing such a basic fact, Giselle sighed. Of course. It was totally like her to not consider other people's economic situations. Another symptom of living a solitary life. "Tierney, listen to me. Stephanie and I will come and get you, and we'll drive down to the urgent-care clinic. If they say you can get away with stitches, we'll go home right away. And before you object again, this is on me. I'm your employer. What I say goes, right?" She waited until she heard Tierney draw a deep breath and most likely prepare to refuse again. Giselle drove her point home. "Tell me, Tierney, if I was sitting on a curb, wounded, bleeding, wouldn't you help me?"

A long silence made Giselle check her phone to make sure they were still connected.

"Yes," Tierney whispered. "I'd move heaven and earth."

Giselle nearly whimpered at the tenderness and something resembling awe in Tierney's voice. "Well then," she murmured after clearing her throat. "We're on our way. Give the phone back to Beatrice so she can let me know exactly where you are."

"Okay." A short scraping sound came over the loudspeaker and then Beatrice's throaty voice again. She gave them directions, and Stephanie impressed Giselle by taking notes and entering them into her own cellphone.

"Beatrice, are you staying with Tierney until we get there?" Giselle asked while she stood and walked out to the small cabinet in the kitchen that held all the keys.

"You couldn't drag us away. There's a bit of a crowd here, but Mauritz is keeping them from getting too close. It's mostly kids." Something in Beatrice's words gave Giselle the feeling that nobody messed with Mauritz, or Beatrice herself for that matter.

"Thanks. Call this cellphone again if something happens." *Please, God, don't let anything make her injuries get worse.* Hurrying into the garage, she jumped into the driver's seat and found Stephanie already on the passenger side. As Giselle turned the ignition key, she froze. She was about to press the button on the sunscreen to open the garage door, when it dawned on her. How could she have spoken without thinking? She couldn't possibly leave the house in daytime, let alone drive along the busy streets into East Quay.

"Giselle?" Stephanie asked, sounding confused. "What's wrong?"

"I can't. And you don't have a driver's license." Giselle could taste iron in her mouth when she clenched her teeth so hard she hurt herself. "We have to think of another way." But what way was there? Could she call Mike Stone? Or perhaps Manon? That would take too long.

"Why? Oh. One of your phobias?" Stephanie was pale in the fluorescent light in the garage. "But we have to get to her. Can't you just drive us there, and I'll go get her? Then you can take us to the doctor, and I'll go inside with her. Would that help?" Stephanie gripped Giselle's hand. "Please, Giselle?"

It wasn't hard to picture Tierney with blood pouring down her face. She might have a concussion or, worse, a serious head trauma. If there was a time to work past her agoraphobia, it was now. Still, it was one thing to rationalize like that and an entirely different matter to carry out her intention.

Giselle pressed the button on the garage opener. Slowly, she backed the Jeep out onto the driveway. After closing the garage, she looked around. The sun was low behind the forest across the gravel road. She spotted Mister, who had his own little door to go in and out as he pleased, sitting on the steps leading up to the front door. Everything looked peaceful. Perhaps she would be able to make it.

CHAPTER TWENTY-ONE

Feeling a bit nauseous, Tierney sat on the sidewalk. The lovely couple she'd hit full force had placed a fleece blanket with a pug motif around her shoulders. She really wasn't cold, but she couldn't stop shivering. Beatrice and Mauritz had taken her collision with them quite well, considering they had to be in their eighties. Beatrice looked very posh and well dressed, and Mauritz, with his plaid shirt and chinos, had that everybody-loves-granddad style.

"Here you go, ladies," an unfamiliar voice said. A man in his sixties came walking up with two camping chairs. Behind him, another man, this one slightly younger, carried a tray with what looked like iced tea.

Tierney stared. Was this how things were done in East Quay? Normally, a crowd of staring people would have formed, and people would film with their phone cameras, and at least someone would call 911 no matter what she said.

"I thought you might be thirsty," the younger man said, smiling reassuringly. "We live right up there and saw the whole thing from our deck. I'm glad you're sitting up." He directed the last part at Tierney.

"Paul? I remember you from school," Beatrice said and lit up somewhat as she accepted one of the chairs. Mauritz had fetched a second blanket for his wife, and now she pulled it closer.

"Yes, Mrs. Nielsen," the younger man, Paul, said. "I recognized you right away."

The older man unfolded the other chair next to Tierney. "What do you say I help haul you off that curb, miss?" he asked. "Oh, my. You sure did a number on your scalp."

"Yeah. Thanks." Tierney clung to his arm as he guided her into the chair. "And call me Tierney."

"I'm John." John smiled. He introduced himself to Beatrice and Mauritz, but Tierney only heard them talk very vaguely. It had dawned on her Giselle wouldn't possibly be able to drive in daylight, and in rush-hour traffic at that. It was that time of day. Perhaps she should call Giselle back. She looked around for her phone and spotted it in Beatrice's hand.

"I need to call Giselle back." Tierney reached for her phone.

"I'm sure she'll be here any minute." Beatrice calmly held on to the phone. "Just relax, girl. You'll be fine." She tilted her head. "Can you believe that young Paul there was my student in middle school? He was such a sweet boy. Very musical and very intelligent."

"Now you're making me blush, Mrs. Nielsen." Paul came up and crouched next to them. "You're a bit pale there, Tierney. You're not feeling faint, I hope."

"A bit nauseous," Tierney confessed. "And I need to call Giselle again. She's not, I mean, she shouldn't drive. Can I get a cab, do you think?" She wasn't sure she was making sense.

"Giselle? Giselle Bonnaire?" Paul looked astonished. "Talk about East Quay being smaller than you think at times. I know Giselle. We used to be neighbors. I'm older than she is, but we were both into music in a major way and found a certain kinship."

Since Giselle's property was isolated, that meant Giselle had to have lived somewhere else when she grew up. For some reason, Tierney had taken it for granted that Giselle had always lived in her remote house after she inherited it.

"I see. Well, perhaps you know why she can't drive here." Not wanting to betray Giselle's confidence, Tierney didn't elaborate.

"She was the nervous type even back when we were in our early teens. She was homeschooled for the most part, and her piano teacher came to her house to give her lessons. I think the only classes she attended away from home were our laboratory for chemistry and physics." Paul looked wistfully at Beatrice. "It would have been great for Giselle to have a teacher like Beatrice Nielsen. I saw her coax many students out of their shell. In fact, I was one of them."

Tierney leaned against the backrest. She was so tired, and the emotional outburst after the debacle with Leanne weighed on her. What if her police hubby found her sealed record? Yes, she'd been filled with bravado before the accident, but now she felt wary about the possibility. Cops here wouldn't be able to unseal her records, and it wasn't as if she'd committed a serious crime, yet the mere fact that she had such records could be used against her. Why had she been so scathing toward Leanne, a customer? Tierney needed the extra cash, and now she wouldn't have a chance to walk any other dogs. Leanne most likely had a long reach. One word from her and others were bound to listen.

A car pulled up outside the Nielsens' dented vehicle, and Tierney squinted at the agile figure jumping out from the passenger door. It was Steph. How was that even possible?

"Oh, Tierney." Steph knelt next to her. "You sure look a mess." She glanced around. "Thank you, everybody, for taking care of Tierney. I don't mean to be rude, but we need to take her to the doctor right away. We have your phone numbers, Mr. and Mrs. Nielsen. We'll be in touch, I promise."

"Here. Let me help you." Paul bent and lifted Tierney as if she weighed nothing. After carrying her to the Jeep, he waited until Stephanie had opened the door to the backseat. He helped Tierney inside and cast a glance at the driver. "Giselle. Nice to see you after all these years."

Tierney stared at her. Giselle appeared tense, and perspiration beaded on her forehead and upper lip. She looked like she was ready to faint. And her grip on the steering wheel was white-knuckled enough for Tierney to fear Giselle's pale skin might crack.

"Hey, you okay?" Paul asked, clearly having noticed the same.

"Nice to see you, Paul. I'm fine. We have to go." Maybe Giselle's grimace was meant to be a smile, but it looked more like a painful stretching of the lips.

"Why don't you jump back here with Tierney, and I'll drive you to the UCC?" Paul asked. "I think it'll go faster, and you can tend to your, um, friend."

Giselle glowered at him via the mirror. "Still playing big brother?" she murmured.

"You bet." Paul rounded the car, and Giselle climbed between the seats and sat down next to Tierney, who slumped sideways onto Giselle's shoulder. She didn't faint exactly; she could hear Giselle's worried voice, smell the fragrance of her perfume, and if she opened her eyes, she'd be able to see Giselle's beautiful face. But it was as if her resolve and strength had abandoned her now that Giselle was here. Giselle, who never in a million years would have ventured out, not to mention into the fray of things, at this hour.

"You're going to be fine," Giselle murmured. "They'll fix you up, and then we'll go home. All right?"

Stephanie had climbed into the backseat on the other side of Tierney, who was beginning to feel a bit ridiculous. Perhaps that was a sign that she really was all right? She smiled. Paul was already driving fast along a road lined with maples. The leaves were green now, Tierney thought, but they would be spectacularly on fire come fall. Rolling with the motions as Paul made several turns, she felt Giselle's arms come around her. It was strange, but the better Tierney began to feel, the more agitated Giselle seemed. Her chest was heaving, and her heartbeat, which Tierney heard loud and clear since her head had slid down to just above Giselle's breast, was rapid. Giselle was shivering, much like how Tierney had been only moments ago.

"Giselle?" Stephanie murmured. "You're doing fine. We came this far, and you can make it until we're home. Just breathe slower."

Paul turned in behind a hedge and stopped outside a low building. A sign showed this was the urgent-care clinic and they were outside the ambulance bay. Stephanie jumped out, and Paul poked his head in, looking worriedly at Tierney and Giselle. "Yikes. Which one of you needs the doctor most?"

"V-very funny, Paul. Move so I can help Tierney out."

Soon, they were in a corridor where two nurses met them with a gurney. They assisted Tierney as she climbed up and gratefully lay down. She did her best to keep her eyes locked on Giselle, who was now leaning against the wall. Her face was ashen, and Tierney was afraid she might faint or have a panic attack. She reached out for Giselle, who didn't seem to notice her hand at first but eventually took two steps toward her and gripped it. Her grasp bordered on painful, but Tierney figured that Giselle needed anchoring more than anything else. She squeezed the elegant, strong hand in hers and gazed up at her.

"Thank you," Tierney murmured. "You came. You didn't have to, but you did."

"Of course I had to. So did Stephanie." Giselle spoke through clenched teeth. Perhaps she feared they'd clatter if she relaxed her jaw. She walked next to the gurney when they wheeled Tierney into an exam room.

After the nurse cleaned the minor scrapes on Tierney's palms and knees, the doctor, a middle-aged brunette, who gave Tierney grief for not wearing a helmet, quickly stitched up the small gash at her hairline. The nurse bandaged it, and after making sure Tierney had never lost consciousness, something Stephanie verified by calling Beatrice and Mauritz, the doctor recommended Tylenol and some rest for the upcoming couple of days.

Paul was still there when they exited the exam room, and so was his partner, John. The kind interest was heartwarming, and Tierney could hardly believe her luck, in more ways than one. Luck that she had survived the collision and for literally running into such caring, nice people. "Thank you," she said, and hugged both men. "I'm so grateful for your help."

"How are you going to get home?" Paul asked, sending a hesitant look Giselle's way.

"I'll drive," Tierney said, but stopped talking when a firm hand gripped her elbow.

"No, you won't. If I've made it this far, I can drive home as well." Giselle spoke curtly, but Tierney knew she was trying to prevent the anxiety from gaining on her.

"You sure?" Paul asked. "I'd be happy to help."

"I'm sure. But thank you. I'm honestly glad to have met you again after all these years." Giselle extended her hand to Paul. "And, when Tierney's feeling herself again, you and—John, was it?—must come visit."

"We'd love to." Paul raised her hand to his lips. "Take care, and drive carefully."

Stephanie nodded. "I'll make sure she does."

Tierney snorted, not bothered by the mock glare Giselle gave her. Then she thought of something. "Hey, Paul? You can do me a huge favor, actually."

"Name it," Paul said.

"The bike. Can you take care of it? I think it's beyond repair, but I want to make sure. It's not even mine. It's Giselle's." She sighed and lowered her head. "You'll have to take that expense from my salary for the foreseeable future." Realizing what she'd just said, Tierney touched one of her own hot cheeks. Trust her to imply she'd be in Giselle's employ for months on end. Another part of her wondered how much such a bike went for. Probably more than five hundred dollars.

"I don't care about the bike. I'm just glad you're all right." Giselle put her arm around Tierney's shoulders.

"I'll take care of it and bring it out to you," Paul said reassuringly.

"Thank you, Paul," Giselle said and held Tierney closer. "Now, Tierney, let's go before you fall over. Again."

"Gee, thanks." Smiling wryly, Tierney was grateful that the car was still right outside. She sank into the passenger seat and buckled up. Stephanie did the same in the backseat, and Giselle started the Jeep. "I really do mean to pay for the bike, Giselle. It was my fault."

"I never ride it. Frances sometimes did, but who knows if she's ever coming back." Giselle shrugged as she turned the car out into the road. Rush hour was over, and Tierney thought she could see Giselle relax marginally.

"We'll examine it when Paul brings it over." Tierney knew it was sort of childish, but she wanted Giselle to know they hadn't closed the subject.

"How did it happen, Tierney?" Stephanie asked from the backseat. Her voice sounded close to shrill, and Tierney suspected the girl was tense about her and Giselle not agreeing regarding the bike.

"I was really upset after returning Timo to Leanne. I wanted out of there and forgot the helmet that I had strapped on the back of the bike." Tierney sighed. "I'm an idiot." She rubbed her temple, but that motion aggravated her sore forehead.

"Wait. Back up. What happened at Leanne Walters's?" Giselle gave Tierney a quick glance.

"I was twelve minutes late. Twelve. Leanne was throwing a fit right there on the sidewalk and made me feel like she thought I'd kidnapped her baby. I know I'd said an hour, but I ran into Mike, and we talked some while the dogs had fun. And yes, according to Leanne, I put her cocker spaniel in harm's way since the dogs in question could have had rabies and whatnot. She wouldn't listen to me. She said her husband the cop was going to run a search on me." Remembering her bravado when facing off with Leanne, Tierney now only felt her abdominal muscles tremble and her headache worsen. "Then the brakes didn't work, or maybe I maneuvered them wrong. I don't know. I saw the car and tried to turn, but I slammed into the driver's door. Oh, God." She covered her face with her hands. "I'm going to have to pay for the damages to the car, aren't I?" Where the hell would she get her hands on that kind of money? Perhaps she could sell her body to science?

"Stop." Giselle held up her hand. "I'm the first to recognize you're talking yourself into a panic attack. Everything will work out. I don't know them well, Beatrice and Mauritz, but I'm certain they're reasonable people. Don't worry about the money. Promise me that."

Tierney groaned. How was she supposed to promise such an impossible thing? "All right," she said anyway. "I'll try."

The drive home went well. Seeing the house in the distance made tears rise in Tierney's eyes. Never in her life had she felt as if she had a home like she did now. This was a recipe for disaster since she was very much a temporary guest in Giselle's house—and her life. That fact hurt, but she was still glad to be there. While walking from the garage toward her room, she glanced at the large clock in the hallway. Already nine p.m.? No wonder she was exhausted.

"I'm heading for bed," Tierney said, yawning.

"Wait. You shouldn't be alone. Why don't you change into your sleepwear and come to my bedroom," Giselle said, a faint blush coloring her cheekbones.

Tierney was sure she must have heard Giselle wrong. "What?"

"You need someone to check on you a few times during the night. The doctor asked me when you were busy suffering through the stitching up of your hairline. She wanted me to wake you at least once. If you sleep on the other side of my king-size bed, I can easily set the alarm and do so."

This was insane. Were all the deities in the universe out to torment her today? Tierney wanted to thud her head against the closest wall, but that would have ruptured her stitches, naturally. "Sure. Thank you," she heard herself say.

"Okay. I'll go feed the animals while you get ready. Stephanie? Can you take Charley out for her evening walk?"

"Sure thing." Stephanie winked at Tierney. "And if you'll show me how much food they get, I can do that from now on."

"That's sweet of you. Come on then." Giselle began walking toward the kitchen. Turning her head over her shoulder, she said, "Go get ready before we have to carry you. You're pale."

Tierney merely nodded and headed for the guest room she occupied. After she used the bathroom and brushed her teeth, she discarded her torn clothes and put on a tank top and sleep boxers. She was still shivering, so she wrapped a soft throw around her shoulders and tiptoed to Giselle's bedroom. She stopped at the threshold, as it felt wrong to enter before Giselle returned. Looking at the bed, she tried to picture herself sharing it with Giselle, but it was impossible. Only earlier that day she'd wondered about Giselle's sexual orientation and if she'd imagined the currents between them. Now she was here and—

"Get into bed. You're shivering." Giselle's voice behind her made her jump.

Giselle placed a hand at the small of Tierney's back and guided her to the right side of the bed. "I favor the left side, so I hope this is all right?"

"Sh-sure." Damn, her teeth were still clattering. After letting go of the bed throw, Tierney climbed into bed, sighing in bliss as Giselle covered her with the soft duvet. "Ahh. What a wonderful bed."

"I like it too." Giselle sat down on the side of the bed and placed a pitcher with a lid on it on the nightstand. A glass already sat there, upside down. Giselle turned it over and poured some water into it. After handing it to Tierney, she also produced two Tylenol Extra Strength caplets.

Sitting up so she wouldn't choke, Tierney washed down the pills with the water. "Thanks."

"Can I come in and say good night in case you turn in before I get back with Charley?" Stephanie asked from the doorway.

"Sure." Tierney held out her arms, and Stephanie crawled over to Giselle's side of the bed for a hug. "Sleep tight. You'll be sore tomorrow, but you know that, right?" She smiled sorrowfully.

"Yup. But I'll be fine in a day or two."

"I take that as a promise. 'Night."

"Good night."

Stephanie bounded out and called for Charley. Rapid claws on the tile floor proved that the retriever was excited about going for an evening walk with her.

"Wait a minute." Giselle rose and hurried out into the foyer. Tierney heard her call out. "Stephanie? Don't go so far you can't see the house, okay?"

"I won't, Giselle!" The door closed, and Giselle returned.

"Just had to make sure." Giselle shrugged. She sat down on the side of the bed again, taking Tierney's hand. "Are you truly all right? No nausea?"

"Not anymore. I was nauseous at first, but I feel better. I just need to shake the headache, and I think the Tylenol will do the trick. I'm not used to painkillers, so..." She managed to form another smile.

"All right." Giselle looked down at their joined hands. Her expression was pensive, and Tierney wasn't sure Giselle realized she was caressing the back of Tierney's hand with her thumb. "I was really afraid."

Blinking, Tierney mouth fell open. "I'm sorry?"

"No. Don't say you're sorry. What I mean is, I was more afraid than I would be if you were anyone else. I feared you were seriously injured or, worse, that you were in critical condition. All I could think of was how the hell I was going to find my way to you. Only when Stephanie questioned why I couldn't just drive did I figure that I might manage it. And when I started driving, I felt the panic come, but it had more to do with you than the fucking phobias."

Tierney couldn't remember Giselle ever swearing before. "I'm so impressed with how you handled that. I know some of what you deal with, as I've witnessed a fraction of it. For you to put me first and get there so fast—it means so much."

"That's why I'm begging you to forget about the damn bicycle. It doesn't mean a thing, all right? All I care about is that you're going to be okay. That's all that matters. For Stephanie as well." Giselle's head fell forward, and she was quiet for a long time. When she slowly raised her head again, her eyes had darkened. "I don't mean to make you uncomfortable."

"Never. You could never do that." Tierney curled up on her side, facing Giselle. "All I could think of when I sat on the curb surrounded by nice, helpful people was you. And Stephanie too, of course, but mainly you. I wanted to hear your voice and let you know I wasn't in any real danger."

"So, not just me, then." Giselle drew a tremulous breath.

"And not just me." Tierney was sinking farther into the pillows and the soft mattress. She pulled Giselle's hand in under the pillow. Closing her eyes, she murmured good night and allowed sleep to claim her, determined to not have any bad dreams.

CHAPTER TWENTY-TWO

Giselle crawled into bed after taking a long bath, something she confessed was in part to soothe her nerves, but it was also a way to procrastinate. She had sat on the side of the bed, her hand in Tierney's as the pale young woman had fallen asleep. The way Tierney had pushed both their hands in under her pillow and cradled them against her had stolen Giselle's breath. Only when her lower back began to ache from the uncomfortable position had she gently freed herself. After going out into the kitchen, she had spoken briefly to Stephanie, who was having some fruit and milk. She'd guessed right. Stephanie needed some reassurance.

"You sure she's okay?" Steph shoved her hands into her pockets after placing her empty glass into the dishwasher. "I mean, she looks awfully pale."

"She's been through quite the ordeal. So have we, you and I. For a moment I feared..." Angry at herself for not being able to stay calm, Giselle pressed her thumbnail against the nail bed of its counterpart. The sharp pain sometimes made her able to focus. "It's always worse when you don't know what's happened or the exact outcome. Now we've learned she's perhaps mildly concussed and has a few bumps and bruises. That's pretty lucky after the way she hit that car."

"Yeah." Stephanie lowered her eyes. "And then there was that bi—I mean woman, who treated her like shit." Stephanie raised her gaze, and her eyes blazed.

"That's a whole other matter. I know Leanne Walters is rude on any given day of the week, but this behavior is way over the top. Makes me wonder. Either way, Tierney shouldn't have to be the target of such vitriol. I plan to call Manon tomorrow and ask what she knows."

"Good that you have more connections around here than God." Stephanie smiled faintly. "I'm going to bed. For some reason, coming in from the cool air made me hungry and sleepy at the same time." She blushed. "Eh, you did say I could take anything I wanted from the kitchen, didn't you, and I didn't want to disturb you."

"It's fine." Giselle briefly squeezed Stephanie's shoulder. "I'm not hungry, despite the hour. I'll go to bed too."

"Take care of her. She's one of a kind, our Tierney." Stephanie gave a little wave. "Night."

"Good night. Sleep well."

One of a kind? That was an understatement.

Now she sat up in bed and set the alarm on her phone to one a.m. and five a.m. She would make sure Tierney wasn't disoriented or seemed worse off in any way. After lying down, she switched off the bedside lamp, leaving only the nightlight from near the door to the bathroom emanating a muted glow.

Rolling over onto her right side, she faced Tierney, who lay on her back now. The nightlight lit her profile, emphasizing her high forehead, slightly upturned nose, full lips, and softly rounded chin—all so familiar now. Tierney seemed mysterious and as if a painter had drawn her bathed in moonlight.

Giselle's breath hitched. She'd come so close to losing Tierney today. She'd been so worried. No. That didn't come close to describing it. She'd been so anguished and frightened that she'd pushed through the fear of a panic attack and driven into East Quay. To say it was a wake-up moment was an understatement. It was more like being part of the ice-bucket challenge. She'd pushed away the thought of Tierney moving on, told herself that would happen sooner or later, but probably far in the future, that she had time to perhaps convince Tierney to stay on. The phone call with the dire news had ripped at her heart so badly, she'd thought it might stop beating.

Shifting restlessly, Giselle inched closer to Tierney, who seemed to be deeply asleep. She placed a tentative hand on Tierney's upper arm, careful not to wake her. No doubt Tierney would be sore as hell tomorrow, but she was *alive* to be sore, so in that respect, it was a good thing.

Closing her eyes, Giselle thought back to the latter part of the day—how she'd come so close to a panic attack that she'd practically tasted the adrenaline that coursed through her system. By focusing on Tierney and letting Stephanie help her, she'd managed to keep it at bay, but she had been far too close to an attack to be a safe driver. Still, she couldn't very well let Tierney take the wheel in her condition, and of course, Stephanie was too young to have a license.

Giselle's mind stopped at the thought of the brave girl. Despite her rough life, she had something noble about her. Yes, she moved and spoke like a typical teenager for the most part, but her warm heart, dedication, and the way she'd comforted her foster siblings in the car— oh, my, was it only last night? It was as if they were stuck somewhere they could slow down time. Every hour meant something new, even revolutionary, for Giselle. Did the other two feel the same? Was their stay as life-altering as it was for her? Either way, Stephanie was a truly remarkable girl, and Giselle would love to follow her journey through life. She paused her train of thought. Of course, something of that nature would be impossible, other than from a distance.

With Manon's influence to help her, Stephanie would go to a good foster home. Giselle could only hope that Stephanie would like to keep in touch, perhaps by email, or, God forbid, Facebook. Why did this thought make yet another knot form in her stomach? Did she really think she could be enough for a teenage girl? She, who could barely walk all the way to the field with the dog or drive without hyperventilating? Weren't you supposed to drive kids all kinds of places? Sports activities, music lessons, and other extracurricular activities, those sorts of things?

Feeling utterly ridiculous for even allowing her fantasies to travel in this direction, Giselle closed her eyes and began her relaxation exercise. It normally put her to sleep, but she feared tonight it would take a while.

Something nudged Giselle, waking her up in a way she wasn't used to. As she sat up, she tried to fathom where she was and what, or who, was tugging at her. A husky voice murmured next to her, and a strong hand was tangled in the shoulder strap of her nightgown.

"Tierney, you're dreaming," Giselle said, keeping her voice low. "Wake up." She stroked the wild hair from Tierney's forehead. She could just make her out in the light of the nightlight, and she could feel a fine sheen of perspiration on Tierney's forehead.

"Have to find them," Tierney muttered. "Lost. All of them. Lost."

"You're okay. You're safe now. Wake up, Tierney."

Tierney stopped moving and seemed to hold her breath. "What?"

"You're here. With me. Look at me," Giselle said when Tierney's eyes darted from corner to corner in the dark bedroom. "Just look at me. See? It's me. Giselle."

"Giselle." Slow and slurred consonants proved Tierney wasn't entirely awake. That or she had taken a turn for the worse.

"That's right. You're in my bed, in my house, in East Quay. Stephanie is doing well and is sleeping in the guest room down the hall. Remember?"

"Yes. We have to get her away from Dylan. The Brodys. They're dangerous..." Tierney's head fell forward and landed on Giselle's shoulder.

Unable to resist, Giselle wrapped her arms around Tierney and held her close. The scent of shampoo and toothpaste mingled with Tierney's own scent, causing shivers along the inside of Giselle's legs. "Please, wake up. You must've had a nightmare." She pressed her lips to Tierney's temple, mindful of the bandage at her hairline. The last thing she wanted was to hurt Tierney.

"Uh-huh. Mm. Nightmare. I had to find the children. All gone. And it was dark." Tierney felt hot to the touch, yet her hands were so cold where they tugged at Giselle as if she couldn't get close enough.

"You did get all the kids away from the Brodys. They'll get new and better foster-care placements. You saw to that."

Tierney turned her head and pressed her face against Giselle's neck. "And you. You were amazing." She sounded awake now, but clearly not lucid enough to question why she was so close to Giselle—in bed.

"I just followed your lead."

"Nuh-uh. You brought up your connection with Manon Belmont. The cops were totally impressed. Especially that Connor woman. She gave you long, gooey looks." Tierney sounded slightly peeved.

"Long, gooey looks?" Giselle blinked. "You really must be concussed, Tierney. Nobody gave me any looks whatsoever."

"Blind. I mean, you. You're blind…and deaf." Tierney flung the hand not tangled in her spaghetti strap in the air.

"What makes you say that?" Giselle tried to follow Tierney's erratic thoughts.

"You can't even see how much I want you. I've been pouring my heart out in my lyrics, and you've got to be blind since I've been so damn obvious. About liking you."

Giselle could hardly breathe. "I see?" She really didn't.

"Case closed. Blind." Tierney sighed against Giselle's neck.

Small ripples of goose bumps traveled along Giselle's entire back and down the back of her legs. "You're saying you're attracted to me?" It was far too incredible to even attempt to imagine. Still, those long looks between them, which Giselle could perhaps count as "gooey" when she thought about it, had become more and more frequent.

"I am. And I don't even know if you're a lesbian, like me. I mean, you could of course be bi, or bi-curious. Or totally straight. Or—"

"Shh. I'm a very inexperienced lesbian. That ought to deter you." Giselle lowered her voice further.

"Really?" Tierney sounded more awake now. "You—really?"

"Yes. Really." Squirming, Giselle wanted to put some distance between them. She hoped Tierney wouldn't laugh at her. If she did, Giselle didn't think she would survive it. It was one thing to struggle with everything else in her life, but being mocked by the woman she'd come to…like…would be excruciating. Flashbacks to that horrible scene at the restaurant when she met Mary years ago flickered like a movie rolling on the inside of her eyelids.

"I'm so glad you told me. I've spent tons of time trying to figure out how to ask you, or if I should kiss you and try to draw conclusions from that. Then I thought, if you kissed me back, it could be for reasons that have nothing to do with your sexual orientation. And if you didn't want to kiss me, or didn't like it, it could have everything to do with me, and not with your preference." Drawing a deep breath after those declarations, Tierney carefully moved closer. "I'm fully awake now. Damn, it was hard to wake up from that nightmare."

"And what about your headache?" Giselle tried to focus on Tierney's condition instead of her own rampaging desires. "Anything new?"

"Better and no. Hardly any headache left. And nothing new as far as I can tell." Tierney tried to move closer but seemed to realize her left hand was caught in Giselle's shoulder strap. "What the…oh my God." Wiggling her fingers, Tierney freed herself. "Seems you caught me in your yarn, Giselle."

Gasping, Giselle held Tierney tight and kissed her temple again. "Seems like it." Warm waves rocked her, and all Giselle could think of was how Tierney felt against her. She tried to reel herself in since, though Tierney might feel better, she was still suffering the aftermath of the accident. "Just let me hold you, okay?"

The soft melody on the cellphone interrupted them. It was the time Giselle had set to check on Tierney. She muted the alarm and made sure the second one was still set.

"Okay," Tierney said and yawned. "I'll be good. For now. Now that I know you're a lesbian, I may just ask for a kiss sometime."

Whimpering, Giselle pulled the now-drowsy Tierney onto her shoulder. "Sure. I doubt I could resist you." Nor did she want to. That truth created a warmth in the center of her abdomen that fluttered in all directions, making her stomach clench and her legs feel restless. The heat grew inside her, and she began to tremble.

"Y'okay?" Tierney whispered.

"Yes. Go back to sleep." Giselle realized she sounded short, but the storm of emotions tearing through her wasn't what she'd expected. For years she'd surmised she wasn't very passionate, or even romantically inclined, unless it had to do with composing music. For her to lie here with Tierney and have images of ravaging her, despite the fact the poor woman was recuperating after an accident, blew her mind.

Tierney's right hand shifted, and her arm ended up around Giselle's waist. Giselle now knew Tierney would be the death of her. If she responded like this to a mere touch, what would happen if they kissed? What if that triggered a panic attack because of sensory overload? Giselle fought her abrupt desire to leave the bed. Part of her wanted to retreat to the music room and rid herself of these emotions by playing the piano until she was exhausted.

Huffing under her breath, she leveled with herself. Who was she kidding? She couldn't leave Tierney alone in here. Nothing could have persuaded her to move an inch away from the amazing creature that had tucked herself up along Giselle's body so sweetly. Giselle would just have to suffer through feeling the soft curves that caressed her when Tierney breathed and sometimes shifted a bit next to her.

"Sleep well, angel," Giselle mouthed inaudibly into the room. Closing her eyes, she hoped she'd be able to go back to sleep as well. She had a feeling she would need every bit of her strength tomorrow.

CHAPTER TWENTY-THREE

Tierney turned in bed, knowing even before she woke up that she was alone in the bedroom. She vaguely remembered Giselle waking her up in the early hours of the morning, asking her a few questions, and then letting her go back to sleep. Stretching, she felt sore, but her headache from yesterday and last night had almost disappeared. She carefully sat up and swung her legs over the edge of the bed.

A blue silk robe lay at the foot of her side of the bed. She guessed Giselle had put it there for her. Standing up, she put on the knee-length robe and tied the belt around her waist. After she padded over to the bathroom, she used the toilet and then turned to the sink to wash her hands. Glancing in the mirror, she stared at her bruised forehead. A small bandage covered the stitches at her hairline, but around it, her mottled skin was an ugly blue-green tint. Her left eye was swollen, and she'd scraped her cheekbone. After pulling up the sleeves of the robe, she saw more scrapes and a few bandages she couldn't remember anyone putting on her.

Groaning, she finished washing her hands and wiped them on a thick terry-cloth towel. Her stomach growled. Time to eat something. . On her way through the bedroom to the kitchen, she checked the alarm clock. Only eight thirty—hopefully not in the evening.

The kitchen was empty apart from Mister, who rushed in from the foyer, eagerly circling her feet when she opened the fridge. It was probably smart to start easy, so Tierney pulled out some strawberry yogurt and grabbed a spoon from the drawer. She sat down at the table in the breakfast nook, attempting to open the lid, but it was impossible, as her fingers were sore.

"Tierney?" Giselle's voice made Tierney lift her gaze, concerned. "What are you doing up?"

"I was hungry." Tierney watched Giselle hurry toward her.

"You should've called me. I was in the living room reading so I'd hear you." Giselle sat down beside her.

"But I'm okay. I mean, I'm not dizzy and my headache's pretty much gone. Sore everywhere else though." Tierney smiled encouragingly, as it didn't seem like Giselle quite believed her. "Could you open the yogurt for me?" She nudged it toward Giselle.

"Of course." Giselle pulled off the lid with ease. "Please tell me that's not all you're having."

"I'm starting with this, as I'm not sure how my stomach will react. I'm hungry, but it's not smart to overdo."

"You're not nauseous, are you?" New concern appeared on Giselle's face.

"No. Just kind of weak and trembly." Tierney shrugged and took a mouthful of yogurt. To her relief, it tasted great, and she quickly wolfed it down. "Ah. Nice."

"What else can I make you? Some eggs?" Giselle stood.

"No. Thank you. I would love some orange juice, though. And maybe a banana."

Giselle fetched everything for her and sat down again, peeling the banana. "I want you to take it really easy for a couple of days, all right? The nurse said we should change the bandage once a day but not disturb the stitches."

"I can manage that. And I'll probably bounce back sooner than you think. By the way, where's Steph?"

"She insists she's the new designated dog walker." Giselle smiled faintly. "As my dog and she are clearly joined at the hip, I knew better than to object."

"Yeah. Charley took to her immediately. And vice versa."

Something resembling remorse flicked across Giselle's face. She smoothed down her hair that she kept in a low ponytail. "Do you think Charley fulfills a need in Stephanie? I mean, on a very deep level?"

"I suppose, but why do you ask?" Tierney finished her banana.

"I don't want to cause her unnecessary pain when she has to move to her new foster home." Giselle rubbed her arms as if suddenly cold.

Tierney rested an elbow on the table and rested her chin in her palm. "Foster kids always live with that reality."

"That may be, but I don't want to cause her this pain. She's been through enough." Giselle's eyes flashed at Tierney.

"Well, unless you plan to send Charley with her when she leaves, it's unavoidable. You don't want to deprive her of the joy of bonding with a dog either, do you?" Tierney placed her free hand over Giselle's restless one.

"Of course not. Why does this have to be so damn complicated?"

Squeezing Tierney's hand too hard, probably out of frustration, Giselle sighed.

"Ouch."

She flinched. "Oh, God. Did I hurt you?" She cupped Tierney's hand in both of hers, examining it. "Damn. You must be sore. No wonder you couldn't open the yogurt on your own." She kissed the undamaged skin on the back of the hand.

Tierney stared at Giselle, and flashbacks from last night, the closeness, the embraces, the soft kisses on her skin, all flooded back. They'd talked about how they both were lesbians, about kissing and attraction—and, oh God—how Giselle had held Tierney as if she were irreplaceable...even precious. "Giselle?" she whispered now, her mouth dry.

"Yes?" Frowning, Giselle looked as if she regretted everything.

"You held me last night." Tierney tried to fathom how this could have happened but, more importantly, how she could have forgotten about it until now. Perhaps her concussion was more serious than she'd thought.

"I did. I had to."

"Had to?" What kind of word was that to use?

"I mean, I wanted to. For purely selfish reasons, I needed to feel that you were safe, breathing and, well, here." Small pink areas appeared on Giselle's cheekbones. "You did scare us."

"I know. We talked about that last night as well. You said you had a rather strong reaction to my being injured." Tierney couldn't stop asking for details. She needed to confirm what had taken place last night rather than what she'd dreamed.

"Yes." Giselle adjusted her shirt and again smoothed down her ponytail.

"And I said I might ask for a kiss?" Tierney phrased the words as a question since she thought they couldn't possibly be true. Where would she have gotten such a bout of courage?

"Yes." Not elaborating, Giselle looked down at their still-joined hands.

"You probably guessed that I really, really like you," Tierney whispered.

Giselle didn't answer, but her eyes darkened as she let go of Tierney's hand and gently placed her own on Tierney's undamaged cheek. Running her thumb along Tierney's lower lip, she leaned closer and gave her a chaste kiss on the lips. It lasted only a few seconds, but that was enough for Tierney to lose her breath. Sliding forward on the chair, she slipped a hand under Giselle's hair and cupped her neck. After she pulled her forward gently, she returned the kiss, only slightly less chaste and a few seconds longer.

A door opened and closed in the foyer. Dazed, Tierney pulled back, only to be attacked by a panting Charley, who seemed overjoyed to see her.

"Charley, down!" Giselle said firmly. The dog, normally so disobedient, sat down so fast she almost toppled over. "Good dog. Stay." Giselle put her hand on top of Charley's head. The dog wagged her tail frenetically as she looked back and forth between them.

"Hey, you're up!" Stephanie entered the kitchen, smiling broadly at Tierney. "You look better. All pink, like." She gazed back and forth between Tierney and Giselle, her grin growing even wider. "You too, Giselle. All pink. Imagine that."

"Brat." Tierney stuck her tongue out toward the now-giggling girl. "When did you get out of bed?"

"At seven. Charley woke me up by hogging the bed and making me too warm. I was reading a bit, and then I heard Giselle. We had breakfast, and then I walked Charley. She's so good at tracking. I was trying to hide in the woods, and she found me in five seconds."

Giselle looked tormented for a moment, obviously thinking of her statement earlier, about not wanting to hurt Stephanie. "She's practiced on the cat ever since she was a puppy. Mister would try to hide from her and her baby teeth, but she'd find him and chase him through the house."

"Oh, I would've liked to see that." Sitting down across the table, Stephanie sighed. "I bet she was a super-cute puppy."

"She was. Little did I know what was in store for me when she grew older." Giselle tried to scowl at her dog, but Tierney could tell she was hard-pressed not to smile. "I have to admit that the two of you are a good influence on her."

"Yeah?" Preening, Stephanie scratched behind Charley's ears. "She's a good girl. Aren't you, cutie?"

Charley looked like she agreed. Or, rather, like she thought it should be obvious. Walking over to her water bowl, she drank some and then flopped down on the floor with a thud.

Fatigue washed over Tierney. She'd been out of bed for less than an hour and was already exhausted. "I think I need to go back to bed, actually." Standing up, she found the floor tilting in a way it usually didn't. "Oy. A bit dizzy."

"Let me help you." Giselle stood and wrapped her arm around Tierney's waist. "Back to bed indeed." She turned to Stephanie. "Thanks for walking Charley. I'm going to help Tierney and then head to the music room for a few hours. Can you check on her in an hour?"

"Sure thing, Giselle." Making the thumbs-up sign, Stephanie stood. She took an apple from the fruit bowl on the counter, then tilted her head. "Okay if I watch a movie?"

"Absolutely. Don't let Charley onto the couch without putting one of the blankets on it first, though."

Nodding, Stephanie came over and kissed Tierney's cheek and then bounded off toward the living room, Charley right behind her.

"God, that energy," Tierney moaned. "Makes me feel old."

"And where does that leave me?" Giselle made a wry face. "Ancient."

"Hardly." Crinkling her nose, Tierney leaned on Giselle. "I mean, who's leaning on whom here?"

"For very different reasons." Giselle guided Tierney back to the bedroom.

"Eh. I'm doing much better, you know. No need for me to hog your bed."

Giselle stopped and looked down at her. "Would you rather be in the guest room?" Her expression didn't give anything away.

"That's a trick question, right?" What did Giselle want her to do? Stay in the main bedroom or, which was more reasonable, return to the guest room? She was still only an employee, wasn't she? Surely, they needed to set boundaries, or tear them down, before they took things further. If that was what they were doing?

Tierney shifted her feet restlessly. "I would never assume. I'm your assistant, after all. Or so far. You know?" She felt stupid now. If only a handy little sinkhole would swallow her.

"I didn't mean to make you feel uncomfortable." Giselle didn't let go of her but took half a step away, putting a distance between them. "Either way is fine with me." Her forlorn expression belied her words. She raised her chin in what could be taken for a clear challenge or a standoffish pose.

"Don't you know from the kiss in the kitchen how much I want to be close to you?" Tierney asked. Was she creating a terrible precedent by feeling she always had to take the first step and be the reassuring one? At least that was what it felt like.

"The kisses were sweet, but how do I know if you regret them now?" Rigid now, Giselle seemed to pull farther and farther away.

"I don't. Do you?" Making sure her voice was soft and non-challenging, Tierney tried to decipher why Giselle's eyes had suddenly grown flat and opaque and her body so braced for impact.

"I don't, no. So, which bedroom, Tierney?" Impatience seeped into Giselle's voice.

"I actually like both you and your bed," Tierney said, trying to lighten the mood.

Giselle didn't return the smile but stepped closer to Tierney again and helped her make it to the bed. She straightened the sheets, as the bed was still unmade, and pulled the covers up over Tierney when she lay down. "Rest for a few hours. Should I wake you up when it's time for lunch?"

"Yes, please. If you wake me up half an hour earlier, I can check the freezer—"

"Stephanie and I'll make lunch for the three of us. You're recuperating." Her eyes narrowing now, Giselle stood.

"All right, all right. Don't chew me out like that. Remember, I'm convalescing."

Giselle smiled faintly. "Glad you realize it. Yes, you're my assistant, but I hoped you'd realize you're much more than that by now." She kept her distance and held her hands loosely laced in front of her.

"How could I have realized anything of the sort?" Her lips trembling now, Tierney had no idea how everything could suddenly be her fault. "I'm not a mind reader."

Giselle looked like she was about to leave, but instead she bent and placed a gentle kiss on Tierney's temple. "Sleep well, angel." She straightened and walked rapidly out of the room.

Tierney raised her hand to her temple and placed two fingers where Giselle had kissed her. She tried to press the wonderful feeling the caress had left behind closer, to keep it with her forever. This woman was an enigma, so hard to read, and unpredictable in all sorts of ways.

Turning on her side, she grabbed one of Giselle's pillows and embraced it. The magical scent of citrus and flowers engulfed her, making her bury her face against the zillion-thread-count pillowcase. So exhausted that tears rose in her eyes, Tierney sobbed quietly into the pillow.

Then her mind pinged and something pierced her senses. *Angel*? Giselle had called her an angel. That had to mean something. She'd never called Tierney by any nickname, and why should she? Inhaling again, Tierney combined the memories of Giselle's voice and the touch of her lips with the scent of her on the pillow. Closing her eyes, she finally allowed herself to relax. It was extraordinarily easy to fall asleep in Giselle's bed. It wrapped around her aching body like a warm cloud of cotton, and the last image on her mind before sleep claimed her was how Giselle had looked when she kissed her in the kitchen.

CHAPTER TWENTY-FOUR

Four days after the horrible shock Giselle had lived through when Tierney had collided with a car, she strode toward the door after the gate bell rang. She opened it and saw two women and one man standing on the gravel road next to a Chevrolet SUV. Frowning, it took her a few moments to recognize the women. One was Daphne Croy, owner of one of the many gift shops in the artisan area of town. The other woman was Leanne Walters. The man was unfamiliar, but Giselle surmised it was Leanne's police husband.

Fighting a constricting sensation in her throat, Giselle felt her heart began to hammer. Why were they here? If what she'd heard about these women was true, they weren't here to apologize to Tierney. Groaning inwardly at having to deal with virtual strangers, Giselle told herself everything would be fine. It was broad daylight, and she was within her own fenced garden. Forcing herself to assume the role she'd had some success playing—that of a self-assured, worldly woman—she raised her chin and walked toward the three of them by the gate with long, certain steps.

"Hello," Giselle said calmly, proud her voice didn't wobble. "What can I do for you?"

"Ms. Bonnaire." The man extended his hand over the gate. Reluctantly, Giselle shook it. His grip was close to painful, and she nearly yanked her hand back. Instead she raised her right eyebrow at him until he let go. He obviously didn't care that she was a composer and her hands were her tools. "My name is Bob Walters. I'm the chief of police at the East Quay precinct."

"And you always take your wife and her friend with you on police business, Bob?" Giselle asked smoothly. Leanne pursed her lips, a reaction Giselle found quite satisfying.

"I'm not on duty today. Leanne wanted me to come along for two reasons. Could we perhaps go inside and discuss these matters?" He motioned toward the gate. "I see you have a good security system. Good thinking since you live alone out here."

Giselle wanted to smack the condescending little prick with the electric flyswatter Frances had bought her a year ago. "No. We can talk here." She wouldn't bother to be politer than that.

"Please, Giselle…may I call you Giselle?" Leanne smiled cordially.

"Ms. Bonnaire is fine since we're not actually acquainted." Returning the smile with her own, Giselle knew she gave a very aloof and close-to-rude impression.

"Very well." Leanne's bloodred lips became a narrow line. "We have reason for concern regarding the woman you have employed. It wouldn't be neighborly of us if we didn't inform you of what we've learned. As Bob said, after all, you live out here alone."

"And what, pray tell, have you discovered?" Giselle wasn't interested, but she wanted to know what gossip these three were spreading in town. She wasn't apprehensive regarding herself, but for Tierney, who did the shopping and drove into East Quay several times a week.

"Your employee, Tierney Edwards, has a record." Bob Walters frowned and clearly attempted to mimic a very worried "neighbor." "I did a background check on her, and at first I didn't find anything, but my wife had a hunch I should widen my search, which I did. When I tried Illinois, I found a sealed juvenile record. Of course, I can't access it without a court order, but it's enough to warrant alarm."

"I find all this concern and curiosity puzzling." Giselle forced herself to keep her hands loose at her side. If she impulsively folded them over her chest, she would only come across as defensive. "When you think about it, Mrs. Walters, you encouraged Tierney to apply for a job in my home. You suggested that she fake references from Frances, and by doing so you said it would be easier to gain my trust. But Tierney is far too honest and caring to do that."

"Honest and caring?" Leanne snorted derisively. "If you could have seen what she did to my dog five days ago, and heard what she said to me, you would think differently."

"The dog you hired her to take for a walk, which she let have some fun with dogs he had met before? That dog?" Giselle placed a hand on her hip. "Not to mention how rude and unappreciative you were when she returned."

"She was late!" Leanne's eyes glimmered. "For all I knew, she could have sold Timo for scientific experiments."

Leanne's husband shot his wife a surprised look. "That's taking it a bit too far, honey, but she should've been back on time. And being rude to strangers like that is a surefire sign she's not stable. Combine that with her juvie record, and we see a pattern."

"That's right," Leanne said and nodded.

"So you didn't tell her to lie to get a job here then?" Giselle tilted her head and let her gaze travel between Leanne and Daphne, her trusty sidekick.

"I—that's beside the point. I didn't know then what I know now." Leanne tugged at the zipper in her jacket.

"And what is that? Exactly." Giselle was getting entirely fed up with these three.

"She's unstable and has a record. What else do you need to know to take appropriate measures?" Leanne said, raising her voice. "I'd be very curious to see what's in her juvie records."

"Why don't you ask her yourself?" Giselle motioned farther down the gravel road. "She's right there with my dog Charley. Better keep your distance. Charley looks like she's been playing in the woods again. She's dirty."

"So was Timo. Full of sand. It took me forever to get all that dirt and knots out of his fur." Leanne took a step closer to her husband. "You talk to her, Bob. She hates me for no reason."

"Don't worry, honey," the burly man said and put his arm around her.

Tierney came closer, and to her credit she didn't slow down her stride for a moment. Instead she walked up to the trio and regarded them calmly. Her eyes, normally so sparkling, held a dark, stormy hue. "What's going on?" she asked.

"These concerned citizens of East Quay claim you're about to sell my dog to science and steal the silverware." Giselle spoke curtly.

"Not until I've burned down the house and let Charley destroy your roses." Tierney passed the visitors, who gave her a wide berth to enter the code and open the gate. "Come on, Charley." She walked up to Giselle. "You all right?" she murmured almost inaudibly.

"Yes."

"Okay." Tierney raised her voice. "Leanne, why did you come here? Is it to make matters worse than they are? You had your say five days ago. In my opinion, you showed your true colors, and I have no desire to have anything to do with you again."

"Now, wait a minute, little lady," Bob said, but his wife interrupted him.

"You're a criminal who has wormed your way into this poor woman's house and taken advantage of her disability. It's a horrible thing to do to someone fighting such weakness." Leanne huffed.

"Are we having guests? Should I start the coffeemaker?" Stephanie called from the front door.

"No, thank you, kiddo!" Tierney yelled back and then returned her focus to the trio. "I just assumed we'd skip the coffee today. We have other guests coming later and can't really afford to stand here and gossip."

"Who's that?" Daphne asked. "Good Lord, don't tell me this woman convinced you to take in another stray?" Gaping, she placed a hand on her forehead and clearly did her best to look aghast.

"Now wait a fucking minute," Tierney said with a growl. "Steph is not a stray. Nor am I. It's about time you learned how to treat people with respect." She scowled at the trio outside the gate. "Giselle may live in a beautiful house with all the privileges that come from being well off, yet that hasn't dented her humanity and her ability to care for those less fortunate. But when it comes to you, it's had the opposite effect. I doubt either of you has ever had to think about where to find your next meal—or when."

"You're shrewd. I'll give you that." Bob snickered. "You deflect and cast blame on your betters just so Ms. Bonnaire won't ask the tough questions. I know you have a juvie record, and even if I can't uncover any of the details just yet, I want you to know I'm watching you."

"In a perfect world, your presence ought to make me feel safer, but oddly enough it doesn't work. Oh, right. You're not here to protect me, but rather protect Giselle *from* me, and perhaps from Steph too. Do you need protection, Giselle?" Tierney looked at her, and despite her teasing tone, Tierney's eyes had dark shadows under them, as if she was exhausted.

"Not in the least. Come on. Let's go inside. We need to bathe Charley before the others arrive. They're bringing Helena and Noelle with them. And, God help me, Perry and Mason."

"Really?" Brightening, Tierney called Charley, and they began to walk up to the house.

"Hey. You can't just ignore our information," Leanne said loudly.

Giselle swiveled. "Oh, I heard you, Leanne. I plan to have my lawyer consider what the law says about defamation and the police conducting unwarranted computer searches. At the very least, we're filing a restraining order so you can't harass either of these young women. In the meantime, I suggest you leave my property. As it happens, the gravel road is my private property, in case you missed the sign by the main road."

Bob Walters grimaced as he turned to guide his wife and her friend back to the SUV. He shook his head and glared at Giselle. "This is how you repay people who care enough to get involved. Perhaps you deserve to have someone steal your property, or worse."

"And that sounded like a threat. Good thing I have two witnesses." Giselle had had enough of the concerned citizens and motioned for Tierney and Charley to walk in through the mudroom. She used the front door, and a stormy-eyed Stephanie met her there.

"Who the hell was that?" Stephanie, who rarely cursed, was livid. "Were they after Tierney?"

"Yes. And me, it felt like." Giselle shook her head. What a blessing that Manon Belmont was coming to the house today. Normally, she didn't feel comfortable using her friend's connections, yet she was perfectly willing to do so again within just a few days, to keep the Walters couple and Daphne away from Tierney and Stephanie.

Twenty minutes later, a sweet-smelling, clean Charley bounded through the house, taking command of the still-covered love seat by the window in the music room. Giselle sat at the piano, going over her music sheets and the lyrics Tierney had been working on one last time. Today was a big day, as their meeting with Chicory Ariose had been moved up. Some of her clients' concerts had been postponed, and since she was flexible, Giselle had worked around the clock the last four days to accommodate them.

Rubbing her neck, she closed her eyes and moaned at how stiff she was. Then she grew even more rigid when gentle hands warmed her aching muscles. As Giselle opened her eyes, she gazed up at Tierney, who, despite the gentle smile on her lips, looked very tense around her eyes.

"May I give you a massage?" Tierney moved her hands and applied increasing pressure.

"Sh-sure." Giselle couldn't keep her eyes open. As she squeezed them closed, Tierney's strong fingers pressed against her trapezius. They hurt, but mostly they felt wonderful. So close behind her, Tierney smelled even better, a mix of soap and light body splash or lotion. Giselle inhaled greedily, grateful Tierney's hands were already so much better.

"This good?" Tierney gently pinched the skin surrounding the hard muscles. "Try to relax more, or this might really hurt."

"You're doing…fine." Giselle had thought she would get used to Tierney's proximity and touches. They'd shared a bed, very chastely, since the accident. Giselle hadn't asked Tierney to stay with her during the night, nor had Tierney questioned the arrangement. They usually fell asleep after politely telling each other good night, only to wake up and find that their bodies had found each other while they slept.

Now, Tierney bent and whispered in her ear, breaking Giselle out of her reverie. "Are you truly okay after going toe-to-toe with those self-proclaimed pillars of the community?"

"I really should be the one asking. They targeted you."

"Only because I live here. When I talked to Leanne in town, both when I arrived here and when I walked her dog, she radiated jealousy and greed. You're connected, you work with famous people, and you keep turning down their attempts to 'help you.' They only want to get a foot in the door. If their first plan had worked, I bet they thought I'd be so grateful to them I'd spill everything that goes on behind said door. Which I would never do."

Tierney was certainly perceptive. Ever since she'd started working for Giselle, not counting all the drama that wasn't really Tierney's fault, Giselle had never had to resort to endless bouts of discussion to explain herself. Tierney simply knew what to do, and she *got* Giselle.

Reaching around Giselle's shoulders and down toward her collarbones, Tierney massaged firmly, finding knots Giselle had no idea she had. The fact she was so close to her breasts made Giselle draw a new, long breath. "Tierney…"

"Shh." Tierney alternated between firm strokes and caresses. "We're going to be working all afternoon, and that means hours at the piano for you. Your muscles need to be loose and rested."

"Oh, God." Giselle's stomach clenched, and that alone sent moisture down between her thighs. "You're playing dirty, Tierney."

"I'm not." A faint yet so obvious laughter lived in Tierney's voice. "I just want to take care of you, if you'll let me."

"That sounds pretty one-sided." Giselle studied her perfect, blunt nails.

"You think so?" Tierney slid her hands up and down Giselle's arms, finding uncharted territory when her fingers found a way in under the short sleeve of Giselle's shirt. "Who took care of me when I was injured? Who went against her entire being, driving the car through rush-hour traffic, to get to me?" Tierney grasped Giselle's shoulders and made her pivot on the piano stool. She cupped Giselle's cheeks, looking into her eyes, her gaze serious. "Sometimes I feel I take such liberties when I touch you, since you're so damn beautiful and way out of my league. I'm not a very selfless person, that much is clear, since I can't keep my hands off you." Tierney colored faintly. "So, there it is."

"It is?" Giselle stood, pulling Tierney into her arms. "Do I give you any signals that I don't like for you to touch me?"

"Well, no, perhaps not, but—"

"Or do I tell you to move out of my bed?" Giselle pushed her fingers into the auburn masses of hair and tugged very gently to expose Tierney's neck. She pressed her lips behind the soft shell of Tierney's ear and had to force herself not to suck the blood to the pale skin. She'd never given anyone a hickey, and this wasn't the time to start.

"No. Oh, please don't do that. I know we're new. I mean together. We're so very new and, I suppose, unconventional, but I don't care. All

I do care about is you—and Stephanie." Trembling, Tierney rested her face against Giselle's shoulder. "And I really want to be there for you. If it can be only as your assistant, so be it. If it's more…" She gazed up again. "I can't think of anything that could make me happier."

"You really don't know me," Giselle said mildly. She ran her hand over Tierney's unruly hair. "You've seen bit and pieces. I'm not easy to deal with most days of the week, and then there's my, um, disability."

Tierney shook her head. "If you think the latter would have anything to do with how I feel, you're selling me short. And yourself. You have phobias and anxiety. Perhaps you don't know, since you don't exactly get out much," Tierney said and winked, "but it's not uncommon. Granted, not everyone suffers from panic attacks, but I also think you've proved to yourself that you can overcome them, little by little. After all, you did drive in broad daylight into East Quay."

Tugging gently at Tierney's hair, Giselle scowled. "That was because my fear of losing you usurped my other fears."

"Exactly." Tierney's smile was equal parts sweet and infuriating. "You had other things to focus on. The possibility of me dying won over your agoraphobia."

"Tierney!" Horrified, Giselle tugged even harder on the wild red hair. "Don't jinx anything."

"And you're superstitious too. You're such a find." Tierney laughed irreverently, only to then grow serious. "I think it's true though. You can will the anxiety to lessen, if not to go away instantly. I suppose it's a process, but you've shown it's possible."

Tierney was right. "You're not saying anything my former therapist didn't try to convince me of." She didn't want to talk about her anxiety anymore and dipped her head for another kiss.

Tierney moaned. "I just want to hold you."

"I second that." Giselle pushed her warm hands under the back of Tierney's T-shirt. Silky, warm skin created small bonfires throughout her system. Giselle gently caressed the small of Tierney's back.

"Oh, fu—" Tierney clipped the word off and pressed her mouth against Giselle's. Parting her lips, she teased the inside of Giselle's, tempting her to reciprocate. Giselle couldn't have resisted Tierney if she'd wanted to. And, oh Lord, she didn't want to. In fact, resisting was the last thing on her mind. She opened her mouth and met Tierney's tongue with her own.

"Tierney, angel..." Giselle whispered and then deepened the kiss further, reveling in the taste of Tierney's lips and mouth while groaning out loud.

Tierney echoed the groan, clinging to Giselle and wrapping a leg around her hip. "Yes, like that..."

Voices came from the foyer, and Giselle slowly let go of Tierney's lips and took half a step back. "I think it's Chicory Ariose."

"All four of them?" Tierney smoothed her hair back and then did the same with Giselle's. "There. Better."

"Thank you." Giselle straightened, taking a deep breath. Tierney had never looked more radiant, but they had work to do, and she had to regroup. "You ready?"

"As I'll ever be." Tierney crinkled her nose, causing tenderness to erupt like a volcano in Giselle's chest.

Giselle let go of Tierney's waist and ran her fingers along her jawline. "All right. Let's go meet them."

CHAPTER TWENTY-FIVE

"Tierney!" Mike exclaimed when she saw them. "How are you doing? And how are you, Giselle? What a week you've had. Vivian and I could hardly believe what happened just after Tierney and I saw each other with the dogs."

"Tell me how she looks," Vivian said and took Mike's arm.

"Tierney looks fine, just a few, barely visible bruises," Mike said reassuringly. "Tierney," Mike said, and motioned behind her and Vivian. Two other women hung their coats in the small closet. "I know you recognize these two, but this is Manon Belmont. She plays the keyboard." She pointed to an elegant woman with chocolate-brown hair in a low, full bun. "And that's Eryn Goddard, our illustrious journalist and guitarist. Prefers electric guitars." Eryn was slightly taller than Manon, her red hair a darker, more coppery tone than Tierney's own.

"A fellow redhead," Eryn said merrily and strode up to Tierney, pulling her in for a hug. "I'm sorry if I'm too forward, but after talking with Mike, I feel I know you somewhat."

"No problem." Tierney murmured, feeling a little shell-shocked.

"Nice to meet you, Tierney." Manon extended a hand but also kissed Tierney's cheek. "And where's the young lady I helped liberate from the Brodys?"

"Here, ma'am." A shy voice from the kitchen revealed Stephanie's presence. Her eyes were huge and stayed glued to the celebrities. She took a few, slow steps toward Manon. "My name's Stephanie. Thank you for helping me catch a break from the system."

"Oh, sweetheart, that was the least I could do. I've dedicated a sizable portion of my life to helping young people." Manon placed her arm around Stephanie's shoulders. "I think I hear the second car."

Giselle walked over to the front door and opened it. "Yes. Here they are." She gazed back at Stephanie. "You may have to hold onto something, Stephanie."

"What? I mean, why?"

"Welcome," Giselle said, and motioned for two more women to step inside.

Tierney stared, but that was nothing compared to Stephanie's response. The young girl gave a muted whimper, and then her knees gave in. "Noelle Laurent?" she whispered.

"That's right," Manon said, and held Stephanie tighter. "Don't forget to breathe."

"Oh, God," the other woman who'd just joined them said, snorting. "I think you've done it again, darling." She motioned for Noelle to look over at Stephanie.

"Whoops." Noelle grinned, but not without kindness. The world-famous pop star took a few long strides toward Stephanie. "Hey, no fainting. I hear you're a genuine fan." She winked and tossed her long white-and-black hair back over her shoulder.

"I am," Stephanie said, tears clinging to her eyelashes. "I know all your songs by heart. I used to have a poster of you above my bed, but someone painted all over it with Sharpies."

"I see. Not a nice thing to do, but we can get you a new one if you like. Perhaps one with you and me together? What do you think, Helena?" Noelle asked her wife.

"Not a problem," Helena Forsythe, media mogul and well-known business tycoon, said. "In fact, we have a lot to offer young women like you, if you're interested."

Tierney's chest constricted when she saw how Stephanie covered her mouth with a trembling hand. Noelle merely smiled and kissed Stephanie's cheek.

"Helena and I agree that it's important to provide young people with the resources they need to make it in the entertainment business, if that's what they dream about. We wouldn't mind a test pilot for the start of our joint foundation." Noelle winked at Steph, whose shocked expression was memorable.

After the final introductions were made, it was Tierney's turn to be on the receiving end of Noelle's total attention. "I hear you're the lyrics guru around here." She hooked her arm around Tierney's. "And I also heard about your ordeal earlier this week. I'm glad you came out on top, so to speak." She squeezed Tierney's arm gently. "And now you have to sing all the lyrics to date for me. If I'm going to make the best of them, together with Vivian, I want to hear what the lyricist had in mind. Someone like you could easily be considered for our foundation as well. Rich kids have their parents' resources, but we think people from all walks of life and all socioeconomic backgrounds deserve a fair shot as well."

Tierney couldn't speak for the next few moments. The idea of Noelle seeming so impressed with her lyrics, which she herself thought might be amateurish, and talking about something that sounded like a grant made the floor move beneath her feet.

"Yikes. Please tell me you won't faint. I really have to work on my approach." Noelle made a funny face. "You must be used to people adoring your texts by now."

"Not really," Tierney managed to say. "I've never shown them to anyone except Giselle. Her music is what brought the new ones out. She's the talented one, as I'm sure you know."

"Giselle is a genius, but she doesn't take to writing lyrics." Noelle blew Giselle a kiss. "The two of you seem to be a match made in heaven, if you ask me."

"Geez, Noelle. Now you've made them both crimson," Mike said, chuckling. "Why don't we sit down somewhere in case someone else has a response like they have?"

"Good idea." Eryn pulled a Roland keyboard from its casing. "Can I plug this in the usual socket in the music room, Giselle?"

"Absolutely." She put her arm around Tierney as they walked to the music room.

Looking back, Tierney saw Stephanie still back in the foyer, looking forlorn. She nudged Giselle and motioned at the uncertain girl with her head.

"Stephanie?" Giselle said. "Why don't you pour us some juice and water and then join us? You may have to bring one more chair for yourself, okay?"

Brightening, Stephanie did her usual thumbs-up. She hurried toward the kitchen, and soon Tierney heard the clinking of glasses and the fridge being opened.

"Thanks," Tierney whispered to Giselle, quickly raising her hand to her lips and kissing it.

"We can't have her sit all alone when the rest of us are diving headlong into the music. That'd be cruel."

"If you only knew how many people Steph and I've met who just don't give a damn about what we want or how we feel."

"I guess I don't, but knowing you and Stephanie, I can understand how devastating that would be." Giselle pushed some wild tresses from Tierney's face.

"Not all were that bad, but a few were, and it leaves a mark."

"Yes." Giselle moved toward the music room. "It does."

Later in the evening, after they had worked diligently at the songs Chicory Ariose and Noelle liked the most, they all sat down to dinner. Noelle couldn't stop gushing over Tierney's voice and her way with words. Giselle enjoyed witnessing Tierney blush because of all the praise. She doubted Tierney had been on the receiving end of such comments before, but she certainly deserved them.

After their dinner, they retired to the living-room area with their wineglasses, except Eryn, who'd settled for mineral water. This wasn't normally the case, but Eryn was most likely the designated driver back to East Quay.

"Mineral water?" Mike now said, clearly noticing the same thing regarding Eryn's choice of beverage.

"Well. Yes." Eryn smiled at Manon, looking flustered and happy. "Now?"

"Why not?" Manon scooted closer on the couch.

"We're pregnant." Eryn placed a hand protectively on her stomach.

The silence was short and infused with all kinds of emotions. Giselle could see how this announcement affected her friends, and Manon had to wipe away some errant tears.

"When?" Mike asked.

"I'm in the beginning of week eighteen." Eryn beamed.

"Yet you're so slender," Manon said. "Just a little rounder around your belly."

"Do you know what gender yet?" Vivian asked. "Or do you want to be surprised?"

Manon and Eryn exchanged glances, and Giselle could tell they knew.

"It's a boy, and he already has a name. Jack Belmont Goddard. Jack, after Manon's brother." Eryn smiled broadly. "We're so happy."

"And now we're happy too!" Vivian raised her glass. "Congratulations, Eryn, Manon. When do I start campaigning for godmotherhood?"

Eryn and Manon started laughing. "Now, that will be a surprise! You have to wait and see, Vivian."

"Ah, you're so cruel." Laughing in her vivacious, typical way, Vivian squeezed Mike's hand.

Later, the visitors who lived in East Quay drove off, promising to be back early the next day for one more session in the music room. Helena and Noelle withdrew to the guesthouse. Giselle watched Tierney and Stephanie go outside to exercise Charley, who had been on her own most of the day.

After walking into the bathroom, Giselle drew a bath, her back aching from sitting at the piano most of the day. Normally she took lots of micro breaks, but today had been about showing off their material for their clients and friends. Stretching, she moaned and then climbed into the oval bathtub. She hadn't had to do much else to the house when she moved in, but she had had the kitchen, mudroom, and bathrooms gutted and redone completely.

Sinking just below the thick, smooth layer of bath bubbles, Giselle closed her eyes. "Oh, my God," she whispered, and every cell in her body seemed to relax at once. The women had been so impressed and thrilled about her music, especially most of Tierney's lyrics. Not having to involve an external lyricist seemed to suit them. And it had warmed Giselle when she saw how Tierney was tossed between being excited and embarrassed. She obviously wasn't used to abundant praise, and when it came from such successful artists, it had to be overwhelming. Giselle had never seen the rather aloof and always business-centered

Helena warm up so quickly to virtual strangers, which was what Tierney and Stephanie essentially were.

"Eh? Giselle?" Tierney said from the bedroom. "I—shall I, I mean, do you, eh, would you rather I sleep in the guest room?"

Giselle sat up, soapy water streaming down her breasts. "What? Why do you ask?" She thought fast. Why this question again? Then she realized. "You mean, because of Helena and Noelle?"

"Yeah."

"Only if you're uncomfortable. I—" She meant to say she wanted Tierney next to her, but if that wasn't what Tierney truly wanted, it might create an awkwardness detrimental to their relationship, both professional and personal. Still, she couldn't let Tierney think she didn't care either way. "I really like for you to share my bed." There. Ambiguous enough but still not too casual. She hoped.

"All right." Tierney sounded relieved, unless Giselle read too much into her words. "I'll use the bathroom there again."

"Good." Giselle sank back into her previous position in the bath, with bubbles all the way to her chin. She remained there for another fifteen minutes, but when her skin began to wrinkle severely, she stood and rinsed off the suds. Letting the self-cleaning bathtub do its thing, she brushed her teeth and put on her aqua nightgown. The satin caressed her skin, and she placed her robe loosely around her shoulders.

The bedroom was almost dark, with only the night light and the lamp on her side of the bed still on. Tierney was already in bed, curled up on her side. As Giselle climbed into bed, she could smell the shower oil on Tierney's skin and the fresh scent of her long hair.

"You smell good," Giselle said, not giving herself time to self-edit.

"You should know. They're your shower products." Tierney pulled the duvet closer. "Wow. It's been a long day."

"It certainly has. Do you need any help with your bandages? You haven't said anything."

"I'm bandage-free as of today." Peering up at Giselle, Tierney grinned. "Can you take a look at that bruise I had on the small of my back? It feels better, but still."

"Sure." Switching on the lamp again, Giselle watched Tierney pull the duvet down and tug at her old T-shirt. "Turn around," Giselle said, short of breath. Tierney's skin was so smooth it gleamed in the light from the lamp. At the small of Tierney's back, Giselle could see a bruise that was now in its yellow-green stage. "You're quite colorful. Does it hurt when I touch it?" Giselle pressed gently with her fingertips.

"Ah. A little bit, but not at all as bad as those first two days." Tierney pivoted so fast, Giselle's fingertips ended up below her bellybutton. "Oh."

Staring down at Tierney, Giselle blinked slowly. "Yes. Oh, indeed."

"Maybe, um, we should go to sleep?"

"Probably," Giselle said, but her body suggested that she explore more of Tierney's body under her deplorable T-shirt.

"Or?"

"Or I can make sure you're not black or blue anywhere else?" Groaning at her cheesy line, Giselle wanted to take it back. To her surprise, Tierney began to tremble.

"Giselle..." Tierney spoke with husky breathlessness.

"Angel..." Giselle pulled Tierney close. "Tell me if this isn't what you want. I don't seem to be able to keep my eyes, or hands, off you. I know we haven't known each other for very long, but I still feel like I've wanted you for ages." Giselle knew her actions were way out of character, but she had to taste Tierney, touch her, and give her pleasure, if she allowed it.

"Damn. You're so beautiful. So fucking hot. I wouldn't be able to resist you if I tried." Arching, Tierney wrapped her arms around Giselle's neck. "I want you so much. And I have, almost since that first time I saw you."

Giselle felt Tierney push the spaghetti straps of her nightgown down. Not feeling as vulnerable as she'd feared when fantasizing about this moment, Giselle moaned out loud. Tierney caressed her upper chest, letting her thumbs follow the gentle curve of her breasts above the nightgown.

"May I take your T-shirt off?" Giselle murmured as she played with the hem of the threadbare garment. "Hmm?"

"Let me." With quick fingers, Tierney pulled off the T-shirt and was now naked from the waist up. She wore sleep boxers, and Giselle couldn't wait to remove them. It had been so long since she'd been this close to anyone, and even then, her desire had never flooded her system like this. It was like someone had poured champagne into her bloodstream and it had gone directly between her legs. Moving restlessly, Giselle needed anchoring. She pressed her lips against Tierney's and slipped her tongue into her mouth, not asking for permission, but also with all the tenderness she could muster.

Tierney held her closer, raising one leg up along Giselle's thigh, wrapping it around her hip. Now they were as close as it was possible without removing their last pieces of clothing. Giselle's hands moved as of their own volition and found Tierney's firm, small breasts. She cupped them, rolled them, and eventually pinched the diamond-hard nipples

Finally, not satisfied with just using her hands, she bent and took the closest one in her mouth. Licking it fiercely, she let go of it, nuzzled it, blew a stream of cool air on it, and quit only when Tierney growled in exasperation and shoved her fingers into Giselle's hair.

"Don't tease," Tierney said, hissing the last word as Giselle bit the dark-red nipple lightly.

Glad the lamp was still switched on, Giselle furtively glanced at every hill and valley that made up Tierney's body. Yes, she was slender, too slender, after not having enough to eat sometimes, but she was also curvaceous where it mattered. Especially the seductive curve of her hips turned Giselle on even more.

"I want to taste you everywhere." Giselle tugged at the elastic band at the top of Tierney's boxers. "May I?"

"Yes. Off." Raising her hips, Tierney wriggled as Giselle removed the last piece of her clothing.

"Your turn?" Half sitting, Tierney pulled up the nightgown from below and pushed it down from above, efficiently creating a satin band around her waist. "Oh, God. You're stunning. So sexy I'm going to self-combust. I need to touch you. Devour you." Tierney pushed Giselle onto her back.

Tierney looked greedily at the blond, sparse tuft of hair between Giselle's thighs. After she pushed the silken legs apart, she nuzzled the warm, damp folds. Allowing her tongue access, she licked along the wet, seeping opening between Giselle's labia. Then she parted the folds

with her fingers, flattened her tongue, and massaged the entire area. Not wanting this to end too soon, she kissed a trail up to the slightly fuller breasts, and mimicking Giselle's technique, she showed the hard nipples all the attention Giselle had done to hers. It seemed like a good plan, since Giselle buried her heels into the mattress and arched beneath her.

"You're making me…I mean…so close…" Trembling, but not in that pre-panic-attack way, Giselle held Tierney's head gently between her hands. "Your hand."

"How? Show me?" Tierney looked up at Giselle. "Show me how you like it."

"Like this." Giselle let go of Tierney's head, and holding her right hand, she maneuvered it in the way she clearly wanted it to be. Tierney entered Giselle with two fingers and circled her clit with her thumb. After half a minute of this, Tierney bent and took the clit between her lips again. Licking it fiercely, she insistently nudged Giselle toward her orgasm. When slight flutters began against Tierney's fingertips, she curled her fingers up and locked her lips around Giselle's clit, flicking the tip of her tongue against the hard ridge of nerves, over and over.

Crying out, Giselle then whimpered, over and over, as the convulsions traveled through her system. "Oh, God. Oh, Jesus. Damn." Giselle clung to Tierney and pulled her up. "Tierney, my angel. I can never get enough of you. I can't." She buried her face in Tierney's hair. "Soon. Your turn soon." She was still out of breath but still strong as she tugged Tierney onto her shoulder. "Now, angel, what would you like me to do?"

CHAPTER TWENTY-SIX

Giselle looked expectantly down at Tierney, whose eyes were huge in her narrow face. Her eyes, so large, so pale, seemed to read her easily, which wasn't always a good thing, but for the most part her understanding made Giselle feel safe.

"Show me. What do you like? I'm a bit rusty, you know. I need directions." Smiling fondly, Giselle held Tierney closer. "Don't be shy."

"I'm not. Not really." Tierney bit her lower lip. "I just don't want to embarrass you."

"Really? Such naughty desires, angel?" Grinning now, Giselle felt so free to express herself that it baffled her.

"Not naughty. Well, I don't suppose so." Tierney wormed her way in under Giselle. "I'd like it if you'd kind of give me orders." She blushed, and Giselle was able to see even that subtle reaction.

"Orders, hmm?" Giselle thought fast. Taking hold of Tierney's wrists, she pushed them up against the cast-iron-and-wood headboard. "Hold onto the bars and don't let go. Not until I tell you it's okay. If I do something you don't want, or don't like, just take your arms down and let me know. All right?"

"Yes, All right." Obviously turned on now, Tierney slurred her words again. "Yes." She gripped the bars so tight, the bed squeaked. Parting her legs, she made Giselle feel welcome to fulfill her desires and make her reach the climax Giselle had just experienced.

As she pressed open-mouth kisses on every square inch of Tierney's torso, she moved up to her face, giving her deep, long kisses as if they had all the time in the world. Tierney yanked at the headboard bars, perhaps wanting to hold Giselle.

"In a minute," Giselle promised her. "Just hold on. She slipped her hand down between Tierney's legs and found such wetness, she nearly wept from happiness. "How?" she murmured against Tierney's stomach.

"Inside. Like I did with you." Tierney pulled her legs up and let them fall to the sides. "Now, please, please, please."

The scent of shower oil, bath bubbles, and sex permeated the air when Giselle pushed her middle- and ring-finger into Tierney, who cried out sharply before she turned her head and bit the pillow.

"Giselle," she said, moaning. "Giselle. Oh, God."

"Like this, like you did?" Giselle searched and found the small patch of rougher texture inside Tierney. Massaging it firmly, knowing how amazing that sensation felt, Giselle looked unwaveringly at Tierney, not wanting to miss a millisecond of her climax.

"Giselle!" Arching, Tierney then convulsed as she contracted around Giselle's fingers. Sweat poured from her as Tierney kept coming, even after Giselle removed her fingers.

"Tierney. You're amazing." Loosening the tight fists that gripped the bars by massaging them gently, Giselle pulled Tierney into a fierce embrace. "I can't get enough of you. I just have to hold you like this and feel your chest move when you breathe, and your heart beat against mine."

"Same here," Tierney whispered. "I came so hard. Unbelievable."

"Me too." Giselle pulled at the duvet as the sweat on her skin began to cool her too much. "Only with you."

"Yes. Only with you."

They lay in silence, Giselle reveling in the sound of Tierney's breath and heartbeat until sleep began to claim her. "Sleep well, angel," she murmured. "I have you."

"Mm. Same here," Tierney said again, then chuckled. "So happy."

Smiling against the top of Tierney's head, Giselle closed her eyes and knew that very few things had ever felt this right.

❖

Not sure why she woke up with her heart thundering painfully, Giselle sat up in bed, trembling. Distant voices from her dream kept shouting at her, but the words were garbled and made no sense. Closing her eyes, she tried to remember as she pulled the covers up to her chin.

"Why can't you just be normal?" a stern voice had said in her dream. It sounded familiar, and she thought it belonged to a former friend from her Juilliard days. The young woman, whose name eluded her, looked at her in dismay, or was it exasperation, and repeated the words with added contempt. "We always have to jump through hoops for you. It can never be easy, can it? It's always 'poor little Giselle who is afraid of her own fucking shadow.' And then the teachers, who know nada about it, think you're the best thing since they landed on the moon."

Holding her hand over her stampeding heart, Giselle couldn't stop the old memories from her late teens and early twenties flood through her like a mudslide. "No," she whispered. She had fallen asleep feeling so blessed, so happy, and now—reality came hurtling in for its usual check.

Another person, a teacher, had once shaken his head sorrowfully and claimed that it was a pity someone with her extraordinary talent would never be able to have a proper career, unless she settled for studio work and having someone act as a front in public. It didn't take a genius to understand that he was underhandedly offering to be that front and bask in the glory of her talent.

What would her phobias and limitations do to Tierney's life if Giselle allowed herself to be selfish? Tierney was as loyal as they came, and she would stick by Giselle, defend her, care for her, *assist* her. Then one day, the young woman would wake up, realize she wasn't young anymore and that she missed all the fantastic opportunities she could have had. Same thing went for Stephanie. Giselle could tell the girl liked her, looked up to her as well as Tierney, and it wasn't rocket science to figure out that Stephanie would like to remain with them. What if Giselle inadvertently turned her into yet another caregiver or assistant? Stephanie would feel she owed Giselle and Tierney everything for "saving her."

Glancing over at the sleeping woman next to her, she nearly wept at the thought of losing her, but how could she justify tying Tierney down, when she was just starting to spread her wings? A small, insistent voice claimed that it was entirely possible Tierney was in love with her, that it would break the young woman's heart if Giselle turned her away. She refused to listen to the voice, suspecting it was her own subconscious trying to persuade her to be selfish.

Giselle got up from the warm bed, donned her bathrobe, and tied the belt so hard it hurt. After padding down to the kitchen, she made some chamomile tea and sat on one of the bar stools at the counter. She ran an index finger along the hot rim of her mug. She had to make a decision, and it would be the hardest one she'd ever made.

CHAPTER TWENTY-SEVEN

After another four hours of working together, Tierney realized that the love she'd been so certain she and Giselle had shared last night wasn't enough. Perhaps it never was. Giselle refused to look at her, and most important, she didn't speak up when Helena Forsyth laid out her amazing plans. These plans would effectively take Tierney away from East Quay. From Giselle.

If only Giselle would object, just once, then Tierney would know what they shared was important and real. But now, Giselle, appearing so strong and unyielding, seemed distant and aloof, acting as if whatever Tierney decided didn't affect her.

Tierney was walking on proverbial eggshells. She stood in the music room, surrounded by Helena, Noelle, and the Chicory Ariose members. Looking so rigid she might shatter, Giselle sat by the piano, and Stephanie had climbed up into the wide window seat, hugging her knees close. Could the others tell how tense the entire situation was?

Tierney tried to fathom what had changed since last night. Yes, Giselle wasn't easy to understand, but Tierney had thought she did get her and her way of responding better than most. Something was off, and Tierney was beginning to fear the outcome. Was it because of the sealed records that she had yet to discuss with Giselle? Had that been the last straw somehow? Had Leanne, her cop husband, and Daphne managed to plant a seed of mistrust despite how contemptible Giselle found the trio? All these questions and negative thoughts whirled through Tierney's head, creating enough turbulence to make it almost impossible to keep up with the business part of Helena's proposal.

"I think it's a marvelous opportunity for you," Helena said, smiling broadly. "As a debut singer-songwriter, to be working with not only established artists like Chicory Ariose and Noelle Laurent is practically unheard of. It's a chance of a lifetime, if you ask me." She looked around the room, clearly looking for consensus. The others merely nodded but refrained from speaking.

"I know it is. It's a wonderful way to kick-start a career," Tierney said while she focused only on Giselle. "Would I keep working with Giselle?"

"Certainly. Mainly at a distance, though, as we'd like you to gain as much experience as possible in order to determine your stage presence, your personal way of expressing yourself, and so on." Helena had pulled her tablet from her briefcase and tapped the screen. "Luckily, we have internet these days, which facilitates long-distance collaboration. I would suggest that you and Giselle find a schedule that works for you and get to know each other properly as colleagues, rather than employer and employee."

"Helena," Noelle said, her voice a low warning.

"Yes?" Oblivious of her wife's tone, Helena gazed up, only to return her focus to her tablet.

"I think Tierney and Giselle can figure such things out themselves." Noelle looked apologetically at Tierney. Without makeup and wearing her hair in a simple braid, she looked like a woman Tierney could have met and befriended anywhere—certainly not like the mega-star she was to the masses.

For Tierney, Helena's matter-of-fact words cut deeper with each syllable. "Yes. We'll figure it out." But how could they do it without killing Tierney with the agony of missing the most important person in her life? "Giselle?"

"You'll never find a better path to a fantastic career in the music industry." Giselle nodded regally. "As for working together, I think our vastly unique styles may have clicked for Chicory Ariose, but I miss composing instrumental pieces of a classical nature. Yet with Helena's backing, you'll find a lot of musicians grateful for your lyrics. Being on the road will suit you perfectly, don't you think? Isn't that how you prefer to live?"

It was awful to hear Giselle talk about her as if they hardly knew each other. Intellectually, Tierney knew Giselle's defense mechanisms were in full swing, but these thoughts had to originate from somewhere. This could be what Giselle had felt all along, despite their passion and budding romance. If only the six women hadn't arrived before she and Giselle had had time to find their footing and establish how they viewed their relationship.

As it were, Giselle was in damage-control mode, pushing Tierney toward a future she assumed Tierney had always dreamed of. Pulling away, allowing her own fear to dictate her retreat, Tierney didn't exactly help keep them on track. This was her method of operation, how she'd always coped. When things became unbearable, or close to it, she left. She found a new town, a place where nobody knew her or of her past. She'd learned it was the best way to survive—better to take control, lay claim to the wheel, and do all the steering before someone else ran you into the ground.

Giselle played a few soft chords. "This is the last song we worked on before you came," she said to their visitors. "Tierney named it 'Haunted.'" As she carefully raised her gaze to Tierney, a faint trace of what had existed there during their night of all-overshadowing lovemaking flickered in Giselle's eyes. "Sing it for them?"

"But they already have several to choose from," Tierney said, helpless. "Haunted" was far too personal. "And it's not quite ready."

"I'd love to hear this one, no matter if we will perform it or if you keep it for yourself." Noelle spoke gently, placing a soft hand on Tierney's arm. "If you're up for it."

Admitting defeat, Tierney stood by Giselle's side. "All right." God, she was doomed. "Can I borrow that acoustic guitar?" she asked, pointing at the guitar sitting in its stand in a corner.

"Here you go." Mike handed her the guitar, looking a little apprehensive. "You okay?" she mouthed to Tierney.

Giselle played the intro, the ballad fitting the theme that love was reduced to a flickering, dying light. Tierney placed the guitar with the back of it against her thighs. Striking the strings in a slow, reverberating rhythm with one hand, she drummed her fingers against the wood with the other. The sound was suggestive and echoed how Giselle had played the intro a second time.

Your name on my lips
Like a kiss of hunger and passion
Yet I cannot reach you
I sit by the window
Stare at the candles
Refusing to need you

Tierney swallowed as Giselle played the beautiful melody, heading toward the chorus. Then she picked up the pace, hitting the strings harder.

Images of you
And your voice
They taunt me
Kisses turn to ghosts
And our caresses
Will haunt me

When Tierney finished singing, her voice raspy from withheld emotions, she lowered her hands that instantly began to tremble. She saw several of the women in the room wiping away tears and rubbing goose bumps on their arms.

"Tierney, my darling," Vivian whispered. "Where have you been hiding?"

On the road for the most part, Tierney thought. Ever since she was on her own, she'd lived day to day, walking, riding trains without tickets, and hitchhiking. If the others knew this, she didn't think they'd see her the same way, no matter how open-minded they were. " I've been around. And honestly, I'm sure thousands of singer-songwriters write better than I do. I suppose it's just a matter of one's vantage point."

"And also, it's a matter of how quick, and brilliant, a lyricist can be," Giselle said. "I mean, it's one thing to keep at it for weeks, even months, but Tierney has a way of listening once or twice to a melody and then feeling which topic and words suit it best."

The praise was not unexpected. Giselle had been taken by Tierney's texts from day one. If only Tierney had been important enough for Giselle to dare to take a chance on her. Was it truly only her defense mechanism that made Giselle pull back? Or were other variables involved that Tierney was blind to? Something entirely to do with Giselle and not with her at all? It might well be that Tierney was selfish enough to think it had anything to do with her.

"I want to try harmonizing some of the song," Vivian said. "I think I managed to retain the words of the chorus, but do forgive me in advance for screwing up the rest."

"No problem," Tierney managed to say. She began singing, and Vivian joined her. She placed her harmony one minor third below Tierney's, her mezzo-soprano reverberating like a moody cello. Their voices wove around each other, sparred, and even if Tierney sang with Vivian, she couldn't take her eyes off Giselle.

A small hand found Tierney's, and she jerked but then realized Stephanie had moved to stand next to her. Her eyes were dark with emotions, and she held onto Tierney's hand with both of hers. When the song rang out, Stephanie didn't let go. She kept clinging to Tierney, and that was when Tierney heard the unmistakable sound of a sob from Giselle.

"I think we need another break," Giselle said huskily. "Or I do, at least." She rose, and only then did Tierney realize how fast and shallow Giselle's breathing was.

"Oh, dear," Vivian said when Giselle had left the music room. "Is she all right?"

"Not sure," Mike murmured. "Tierney? Something amiss that we're unaware of?"

"I—I have no idea," Tierney lied. Of course Giselle had to feel the impact of their wild emotional journey that had lasted several days. What was more, Tierney feared for the worst, given the pale, haggard look on Giselle's face when she fled.

Giselle gasped for air, but precious little seemed to find its way to her lungs. Her heart was hammering painfully, thrashing against her ribs as if trying to cast off its moorings. Cold sweat gathered at the nape of her neck, between her breasts, and in the small of her back. Clinging to the sink in her en suite bathroom, she groaned when she sank to her knees. The heated floor tiles did little to help her regain some warmth. Her blouse stuck to her body, and so did her hair, which seemed glued to the back of her neck.

If only her distress had been caused by the love she felt for the wondrous, talented woman who so blatantly cared for her. That alone could have torn down her defenses and made Giselle believe it could work. But so many things worked against them, and as Giselle tried to fathom how it had all come down to the single hardest decision she'd ever made—it was the way it was. She had to let Tierney go. Having endured so much in her life, she deserved this chance at a career in order to wash away the past, the sealed records, and her reputation for being a troubled kid, betrayed by the system.

Sighing deeply and with such force, it made her cough, Giselle began to sob. She kept herself quiet by pressing her knuckles into her mouth and biting down so hard she was afraid she'd broken her skin as she tasted iron. She refused to get sick, even if her stomach rolled and she was beginning to sweat. A panic attack was just around the corner, and she was certain it would hit her relentlessly in a few moments.

A knock on the door made her wince.

"Giselle?"

Of course. Trust Tierney to realize something was very wrong. "I'll be…right back. Soon." Her teeth clattered, and Giselle clenched her jaws to keep her reaction from being obvious.

"Can I come in?" Tierney sounded concerned. "Please, Giselle?"

"I said I'll be right back…for heaven's sake!" Growling, Giselle tried to stop the treacherous tears from falling. "Go back to the others." To Giselle's dismay and fury, the door, which she hadn't had time to lock, opened a few inches. She managed to clamor to her feet.

"I'm sorry, but I can't. I can't leave you alone to deal with something that's my fault." Tierney stood in the doorway, looking only marginally better than Giselle.

"How arrogant of you," Giselle said, running the faucet. She rinsed her hands in warm water, trying to restore the feeling in her fingertips, knowing she wouldn't be able to keep playing if she didn't.

"I don't mean to sound arrogant. I still think that performing that song with Vivian and you was too much. Too much and too hard. I wrote when I was really, really vulnerable."

Gasping for air again, hating how weak this situation made her feel, Giselle flinched when Tierney's arms came around her. "Do. Not. Touch me." Her staccato words sounded fiercer than intended.

Tierney whimpered and held on. "Please don't push me away. I can't bear it."

"Tierney, stop being so dramatic. This is about your life and what can happen to you now that you have Helena Forsythe's undivided attention. You're going to leave. I won't have you here to hold me, or *assist* me, like before. I must get used…get used to being on my own and fending for myself." Surprised that she could get as many words out, Giselle pushed Tierney's hands away. If Tierney held her much longer, her resolve would wither, and she might even sink low enough to beg Tierney to stay.

It wasn't a matter of pride. She was being selfless. Tierney had a bright future in her grasp. Going on tour with Chicory Ariose, learning from the best, was such an opportunity, and Tierney deserved it. She refused to hold her back. Not now. Not ever. "You've been a good assistant while I needed one. If it makes this decision easier and clearer for you, I'm firing you. I no longer have any need for your services, Tierney."

Giselle could tell that her stark words hit home, but she had to be strong and allow Tierney this opportunity. If she told Tierney she wanted nothing more than for her to stay, she knew the warmhearted, unselfish young woman would give up her future in a heartbeat and do so. She would forever be the kid who never had a true home, who had a sealed record following her, and who lived her life as her lover's damn assistant.

Shudders and tears created a picture of total shock on Tierney's face. Her pale eyes looked even more colorless than before. "You don't mean that." Tierney drew her breath in, utter little jagged sobs. "You *can't* mean that."

"I do. Earlier, when you were walking Charley with Stephanie, I learned of Helena's sudden, fantastic plans for you. Then, I talked to Manon. She had several suggestions how to go about this. When Chicory Ariose leaves, Manon has agreed to take you and Stephanie with her. Manon will call Stephanie's social worker and let her know that Stephanie will stay with you at her and Eryn's place until her new foster home is ready for her." Wondering if the searing pain in her abdomen was like the suffering that ulcers caused, Giselle splashed some water on her face, then dried her tears along with the droplets.

"You have it all figured out, don't you?" Tierney spat, her eyes igniting like fireworks as her fury grew into a blaze. "You don't ask me what I really want. What I *really* want. You certainly don't ask Steph. You and your friends decide for us and expect us to just obey, no questions asked. What the hell? You're acting as if we're fucking marionettes. Well, I don't see how I could ever live with someone who shows such blatant disregard for other people's feelings just because they're so damn afraid. Perhaps you're doing us a favor after all." Gripping the doorframe with both hands, Tierney stared at Giselle, the sting of her gaze hitting its target when Giselle's heart began to bleed. "If they ask about me, tell them I'm packing. I'll help Steph gather her few belongings as well. Surely you know you're breaking her heart. When it comes to mine, it's already shattered, so it really can't get much worse, but Steph deserves better."

Giselle used to know very little of shattered or broken hearts, since she had never truly put her own on the line. It was different now. Where her heart used to be was now a cold, empty cavity. She didn't second-guess herself very often. Now, as she watched Tierney walk away from her, she feared she might have made the worst mistake of her life. That said, she would have to live with it, as she saw no other way forward. Tierney would have a brilliant future, and one day she might even look back and thank Giselle for it.

But that wouldn't be enough to heal what had just fractured into millions of shards inside Giselle.

CHAPTER TWENTY-EIGHT

Tierney?" Manon walked into the room that had been Tierney's for the last month. Much like at Giselle's house, she shared a bathroom with Steph, who stayed in a room that mirrored her own.

"Yes?" Tierney sat with her back against the headboard, looking up from the small keyboard where she was trying to play the melody that plagued her.

"This can't go on, sweetheart." Manon pulled up a chair and sat down next to the bed.

"What do you mean?" Tierney pulled up her knees and laced her fingers on top of them.

"You're miserable, and Stephanie is even worse off. Surely you've noticed that?" Manon stroked Tierney's cold hands.

Tierney was aware that Steph seemed to have lost her appetite and remained in her room most of the time. Whenever someone tried to encourage her and discuss her next foster home, Steph shut down and refused to engage. "Yeah," Tierney said now and tipped her head back, hoping her ever-flowing tears would run back into their ducts.

"It's useless to cast blame and try to figure out who's responsible for what's going on, as it's nobody's fault. But I'm certain that only you can do something about it." Manon moved and sat down next to Tierney. "You're the strong one in this equation, no matter what you think."

"I'm not! I'm not. I wouldn't know where to start." Tierney allowed Manon to hug her only because she trusted this woman and she was desperate. Tierney trembled in Manon's soothing embrace.

"All right," Manon said quietly. "Let me ask a few questions. Do you miss Giselle?"

Appalled, Tierney lifted her head to face Manon. "Of course I do. Every second of every fucking day." She winced. "Sorry."

Manon didn't seem to mind the curse word. "Do you agree that Giselle is all alone because her fears have shut us all out?"

"All of us? You mean she doesn't even talk to you?" Shocked, Tierney stared at Manon, who slowly shook her head, her eyes sad.

"Not even Vivian. We've tried calling, and sometimes she picks up, but she hangs up after ten seconds, max. Only when I ask about the dog and the cat does she reply, very briefly."

"Steph misses Charley desperately. I never realized how firmly they'd bonded, even if I knew they were always together at Giselle's," Tierney said. "I imagine the dog is mourning too."

"Giselle has problems getting her to eat." Manon sighed.

"And when it comes to a retriever, that's a huge deal."

"So I've heard. Next question. If you thought you could reach Giselle by telling her how you really feel about her, would you do that?"

"Sh-she fired me. She said she didn't need me, that I would love being back on the road, just like before. Giselle doesn't get it. She'll never get it." Weeping silently, Tierney wiped at her cheeks.

"Still, if you thought perhaps there was the smallest of chances for you to make Giselle see how much you miss her, and that you love her very deeply, would you be brave enough to try?" Studying Tierney, Manon exuded nothing but kindness. "I know what I'm talking about. I hurt Eryn when we fell in love. I was so sure it was a mistake that I fled. A friend of mine talked to me like I'm talking to you right now. I know you didn't hurt Giselle. It's the opposite in this case. But if I dared to bare my heart and soul to Eryn that time, I think you can do it too. You're much stronger and braver than I was."

"You mean I should put everything on the line, risk her breaking my heart all over again?" Raising her chin, Tierney challenged Manon. She should have known Manon wouldn't budge. This woman was so regal and collected, Tierney found it impossible not to want to please her.

"And how is that different from how you're feeling now? And how Stephanie is feeling? I'm sure you can imagine Giselle pacing the rooms all alone, unable to even step outside."

"Unable? How…?" Paling, Tierney gaped. "You've had someone drive by and check things out, haven't you?" She meant the statement as an accusation, but instead a budding hope ignited in Tierney's chest. "You haven't abandoned her…like I have." The last three words came out in a broken whisper.

"You haven't abandoned her." Manon shook her gently. "You've been licking your wounds, as I'm sure Giselle had to be damn harsh to get you to leave. She's talked herself into believing she's being selfish for wanting you, and now she's thinking only of your bright future in the music industry. She had to fight hard to get where she is, which is quite different from her original hopes and dreams. No wonder she wants the best for you. She thinks this type of chance is what you really want above all else and that you'll resent her forever if she shows how much she cares for you. And for young Steph, for that matter."

Tenderness erupted, and Tierney freed herself and stood. "That stubborn…woman!" She shook her head. "I already knew what she was up to, but my own insecurities and, I suppose, my experiences drowned it out." She pulled on her sneakers. "Do you think it's too late?"

"No." One word, spoken with utter surety.

"Then may I borrow a car? I'll bring it back as soon as I can."

Manon got up and hugged her. "Take Eryn's little car. And don't rush."

Tierney's heart made what had to be described as a quadruple somersault. "I won't. Wish me luck."

"That, and be sure you remember how stubborn *you* are, sweetheart."

Running toward the stairs, Tierney thought of Steph and turned around, hurrying into her room. The girl was sitting on the bed, much like Tierney had been only moments ago. She had a book on her lap but was merely looking out the window.

"Hey, kiddo. I'm going to try to talk some sense into Giselle. Wish me luck."

"You are? You really are?" Blinking, Steph rose to her knees. "Yes. Oh, yes. I hope you can convince her that she needs you. I mean us!" Steph pushed her shoulders back. "Good luck. Or should I say, break a leg?"

"Are you kidding? I nearly did that when I crashed into that car! Let's settle for good luck." To her relief, Steph smiled. Over by the door, Tierney waved, and then she ran down the stairs and grabbed the car keys Eryn held out to her without a word.

Reminding herself to not drive like a car thief, Tierney headed out of East Quay, toward Giselle's house. She couldn't disappoint Steph, Manon, or herself. She refused to let herself fail.

CHAPTER TWENTY-NINE

The music room, which was normally Giselle's refuge, felt empty. Was the thermostat working correctly? It seemed freezing cold in there. Rubbing her arms, she walked over to the regulator on the wall, checking the temperature. When she read the numbers and realized it was set to the usual seventy-two degrees, she knew something was wrong with her, not the heating system. Giselle was cold from the inside and out.

Sitting down at the piano, she slowly opened the lid. She remained still, merely staring at the keys, her eyes burning. Something touched her leg, and she flinched before she realized it was Charley, who sat down by her side, placing her head on her lap.

"You miss her too, right? Both of them, even."

Charley gave a muted "moff" and nudged her hand. Giselle scratched behind Charley's ears.

"I know, girl. I know." So. This was what a thoroughly broken heart felt like. Giselle shook her head. She'd always thought the worst thing that could happen was having more anxiety attacks in public and thus seeing the repulsion and pity in people's eyes. That was nothing compared to this. Her home, her *life*, without Tierney, and of course, without Stephanie, was so empty that it chilled her to the core.

She played a few lackluster chords, listening for something to inspire her. Nothing. They were just chords, nothing that sparked her muse or made her become electrified about composing. If she couldn't work in tandem with Tierney, what was the use? The joy of creation was gone. How had her originality become so tied in with Tierney's presence and efforts?

Giselle glanced down at her dog. If she felt the loss of her inspiration, Charley was mourning Tierney and, even more so, Stephanie. "I'm so sorry, Charley. Perhaps I never should have employed her. If I hadn't, you and I wouldn't have suffered so much."

Giselle closed the lid again and rested her arms against it. Burying her face in the sleeves of her cardigan, she wept. She couldn't control her pain and cried for the young woman she would perhaps never see again. Even if she did, Tierney would have the life she deserved and find success all on her own. She should have more of a life than being stuck in the East Quay countryside with someone who was a burden.

"Giselle?"

Sobbing, Giselle was certain her distraught mind had conjured up the sound of Tierney's voice. Only when a gentle hand ran through her hair and cupped the back of her neck did she realize she wasn't alone. Looking up, she blinked through the tears that blurred her vision. Tierney stood there, a worried frown on her face. "Giselle?"

"Angel..." Giselle whispered. "What—what are you doing here?" Why was she here? If she'd come for something she'd forgotten, why couldn't she just have sent for it? Did she have to return, only to leave and cut Giselle's heart into a million pieces again?

"I'm here to ask you something," Tierney said, crouching next to the piano stool and holding on to Giselle's knees. She looked nervous but determined to get whatever it was off her chest. "I just want you to hear me out, okay?"

Giselle didn't want to listen to anything at all. She wanted to hide under the covers in her bed, or at least she would have if it wasn't for the memory of their lovemaking that permeated it. "Can I stop you?" she whispered.

Tierney winced. "Of course you can. You can show me the door. I hope you'll hear me out, though, and then if you still want me to leave, I'll go, and that's...that."

And if she didn't want Tierney to leave, did this mean she might stay? Chastising herself for allowing such a thought to surface, Giselle nodded. "Go ahead."

"Ah. Okay." Glancing at the love seat, Tierney pointed. "Can we sit over there? The floor's not very comfortable."

Getting up, Giselle disregarded the fact that Tierney was still crouching and sat down on the couch. Tierney rose effortlessly and joined her. "Well. This isn't easy for me. I'm really nervous."

"Whatever for?" Giselle raised a deliberate eyebrow.

"You look kind of intimidating right now, but here goes." Tierney cleared her throat. "I never should've allowed you to chase me away."

Whatever Giselle might have guessed, this was definitely not how she had thought Tierney would have initiated her talk. "Go on," Giselle said matter-of-factly.

"I never should have fallen for the reasons you invented, like when you claimed you would be fine on your own and that you needed to restore your privacy." Her lips tense and pale, Tierney pressed her palms together. "It hurt so badly, but I told myself you really must think I'd overstayed my welcome. After all, I bullied my way into your life, didn't I? When you and Manon seemed to have figured everything out for me, and for Steph, I didn't think I had any option but to leave. It's been a month. Steph and I miss you—and Charley—so much, we haven't stopped crying."

Stephanie in tears? The mere thought was like a knife stabbing her heart. Where was this conversation leading? Giselle took her eyes off the window and returned her gaze to Tierney. Tears balanced at the tips of her eyelashes, and her hands were tight fists inside her sweater sleeves.

"Yes?" Giselle shifted, uneasy at the pain so evident on Tierney's face.

"As soon as we left, I knew I should have fought more. I should have cornered you and have you say to my face that the night we made love meant nothing. I guess I'm so used to living a nomadic life that it never dawned on me that I might, just might, have played right into your hands. That I was all too ready to believe you, when I should've taken a step back and read between the lines. Manon talked to me today and showed me how wrong I've been—and if I've been wrong, chances are that you have too. I had to make sure."

Straightening her back, Giselle smoothed down her low ponytail. "Make sure what exactly?"

"You called me 'angel,' and we made such amazing love. For being the first time for us together, it was damn miraculous. I know how I feel, and I'm ready to tell you even if you don't reciprocate. I'd rather you know even if you don't feel the same way."

As Giselle waited breathlessly for what Tierney had to say, a miniscule flame of hope erupted just beneath her breastbone. Adjusting the bottom hem of the cardigan, she shifted again. She couldn't even encourage Tierney to start talking, only watch her with dry, aching eyes.

Tierney drew a deep breath. "I love you, Giselle. I love you with all my heart, and I think of you day and night. I have endured a month of hellish days, and the nights have been even worse. Stephanie feels the same way." Coughing, probably against the tears streaming down her face and most likely running down her throat, Tierney sobbed quietly. "If there's even the slightest way you can see yourself giving me a chance—oh!"

Giselle didn't realize that she'd tugged Tierney into her arms until she held her close and buried her face in the wild, wavy red hair. "Tierney, oh, my angel. Tierney." Gasping for air, Giselle trembled as Tierney wrapped her arms around her neck. "Yes. Like that. Don't let go. Don't ever let go. And don't let me make you leave again."

"I won't," Tierney said, crying again. "I won't. I belong with you. You see that too, right?" A fraction of insecurity still lingered in Tierney's voice.

"I do. You belong here with me, or wherever we are, we need to be together, because I love you so very much." Giselle spoke so fast, she was tripping over the syllables. "I thought I was doing the right thing by setting you free. You're used to being on the road, a free spirit, and the idea of tying you down seemed so selfish. I'm never going to be like you. I just can't. I'll be a hindrance, and I feared you might resent me for that one day. I still fear that, but my love for you is so strong, I'm hoping it will compensate—"

"I don't need compensation!" Tierney kissed Giselle hard on the lips. "I need only you. My days without you, well, let's say, I don't want to relive them anytime soon. I saw you everywhere. Even with my eyes closed. And, oh God, in my dreams…I kept trying to find you, but the nightmares kept suggesting you were dead or with someone else. You can imagine how upset I was when I woke up."

"I've had similar dreams. Nightmares." Giselle kissed Tierney, more softly, and ran her hands over her body as far as she could reach. "Does this mean you're home to stay?"

"I am." Tierney beamed through her lingering tears. "And, if you want, Manon says she can make sure we can provide a foster home for Steph." She seemed to hold her breath for a few moments while looking at Giselle. "Giselle?"

"You're certain about that? Is that what Stephanie wants?"

"Are you kidding?" Now Tierney smiled broadly, her best, authentic smile that made Giselle return it without hesitation. "Stephanie will be so thrilled, she'll be impossible to live with for the first weeks."

"I can endure that." Coughing, Giselle took Tierney's hands in hers. "I do love you, so very much." She grew serious. "If you change your mind—"

"You won't lose me, because I'm dying to come home. I love it here, but most of all, I can't imagine my life without you in it. I just can't. We're unbeatable together. Personally, and professionally, I think you and I will have a great life together. Can you imagine working on music side by side? And raising Stephanie? And these two?" Tierney pointed at Charley and Mister, who sat at their feet at attention.

"I can. I can. Can you abide having a lover, or partner, who won't always be able to function in public?" This was always her worst fear.

"Yes. As long as we're together, we can work around such things. They don't scare or deter me." Tierney held one of Giselle's hands against her face. "You should know just one more thing though."

"Yes?" Giselle caressed Tierney's wild hair. She could tell Tierney was apprehensive.

"The juvenile records."

"I don't care about those." Giselle kissed Tierney's lips lightly.

"You need to know either way." Tierney buried her face against Giselle for a moment before straightening her back. "My friend Dina and I shoplifted a lot when we were seventeen and lived at the same group home in a suburb of Chicago." Tierney sighed. "I ended up there because the authorities had mistakenly assumed that the distant relative I had there would be interested in raising me the last two years before I became of age. As it turned out, the aunt was not my aunt by blood, but she had once been married to an uncle of mine in the eighties. He was dead and she wasn't interested." Tierney winced. "I'm not proud of what we did, but we were really hungry. So were the younger kids at the group home. We stole bread, some ham and cheese, and milk, repeatedly, over a period of five months. And chocolate." Tierney sighed. "Lollipops for the youngest. And, because we were stupid, some glossy magazines about famous people we recognized from TV. The store manager who finally caught us didn't want to press charges, but the owner had a strict zero-tolerance policy when it came to shoplifters." Tierney wiped at her eyes. "I confessed to it all, even to what we had stolen at the other stores, and so did Dina. We offered to work the debt off by cleaning, but the store owner was convinced that foster kids like us needed jail time to learn the error of our ways. As it was, we got suspended sentences since the judge took pity on us after the court heard about the situation at the group home. She was the one who arranged for the CPS to move us to another group home, which was better. Cleaner. And we got enough food. So, you see? I had an intense, if short, career as a thief."

"You were a starving child trying to survive." Giselle kissed Tierney slowly. "That's the only part I need to understand. If you can forgive yourself for that, I'll make myself do something I used to loathe. I'll go back into therapy. Perhaps this time it'll work since I'm more motivated. I've always wondered why I have these panic attacks and the agoraphobia. I may never know, but perhaps I can find better tools to deal with them."

"You'll do great. I know you will." Tierney flung her arms around Giselle's neck again. "God, I love you, Giselle."

"And I love you, my angel."

As they sat there on the love seat, holding onto each other, Giselle tried to understand how a day that had started in utter despair could turn into unimaginable happiness within a few moments. "I have a few suggestions," Giselle said softly.

"Mm?" Tierney looked at her with such adoration, Giselle's cheeks grew hot.

"Yes. I want you all to myself today, and, oh God, tonight. But tomorrow morning, we need to go bring Stephanie home."

New, fat tears ran down Tierney's face. "When you put your mind to it, you have the best ideas. I totally agree, but let's call her and Manon and let them know. I don't want Steph to wonder a second longer than necessary."

"Agreed." Pulling her cellphone from her pocket, she held it up to Tierney. "Should I call her, or you?"

"You," Tierney said, and snuggled closer.

Giselle dialed Manon's number, and soon she had a squealing, laughing, crying Stephanie proclaiming her undying love and happiness for her and Tierney. When they hung up, she wrapped her arms firmly around Tierney, knowing she'd never been this happy. Listening to Tierney quietly sing the song with the lyrics that spoke of how she loved Giselle, she closed her eyes and gave herself over to the miracle that was the woman she loved.

EPILOGUE

Eight months later

Stephanie looked down at her outfit—black slacks, a blue shirt, and a dark-blue cardigan. She'd never thought she'd dress in this kind of preppy style—or afford clothes of this quality. Her ankle boots were super cool, and she'd caught Tierney casting envious glances at them, which thrilled her to no end.

Over the last months, she'd visited the two homes in Providence where her former foster siblings had been placed. Watching them be well fed, loved, and cared for had settled something deep within her. In theory, she'd always known that most foster homes were decent, loving places where kids grew up feeling safe, going to school, and accepted as members of the family. The Brodys and some of the other ones Stephanie had endured didn't represent most foster homes in the US. She had started yet another group on Facebook, where not only foster kids had access, but so did the foster parents who selflessly gave of themselves and their resources. It had grown into a vast, loving community, which Stephanie hoped would instill hope among the kids that hadn't had the same luck as she had. The group also worked on a project to encourage people to sign up to be foster parents. Two of the ones who already had were Paul and John, the men who had helped Tierney when she was injured in her accident. The last Stephanie had heard, they planned to open their home to a four-year-old boy and an eleven-year-old girl.

Realizing that someone had entered the impressive, if also a little intimidating, office where she sat with Tierney, Giselle, Manon, and her social worker, Mrs. Crain, Stephanie went rigid as everyone stood, including Charley. The latter was present as Giselle's service dog. After Tierney and Stephanie had trained the retriever for six months, she'd passed the service-dog test without a single glitch. Giselle found she could go places she never thought she'd dare to, knowing she was safe with Charley by her side. The dog would alert her if she felt her owner starting to display symptoms leading to a panic attack. Charley's mere presence seemed to stave off most of those attacks as well.

Stephanie stood on unsteady legs. The system had screwed her over enough times that she expected hurdles and obstacles at every turn. This time was no exception. All this might be too good to be true after all.

"Hello, Stephanie," a middle-aged woman wearing a black robe said and sat down behind the dark wooden desk. "I'm Judge Alicia Donovan. I believe this is a big day for you."

"Yes, Your Honor," Stephanie said, her voice husky with emotions.

"I can tell you're nervous, but you don't have to be. Everything is already decided, and the only one who can change the outcome is you." Judge Donovan smiled reassuringly. "I have one important question, and I want you to answer me with complete truthfulness. All right?"

"Yes, Your Honor." Stephanie heard herself repeat her words from earlier, sounding like a parrot.

"Giselle and Tierney Bonnaire wish to adopt you, which means you will be their daughter forever. In the eyes of the law this makes you their heir, and their child, forever. They will be required by law to provide for you and be responsible for you until you come of age. As your adoptive parents, they will make medical decisions for you as well. Naturally, I'm certain they will discuss most things with you ahead of time since you're a young lady, not a small child. But you will be their child the same way as if one of them had given birth to you. Do you understand this point?"

"I do, Your Honor."

"Excellent." Judge Donovan smiled warmly. "Do you wish to be adopted by Giselle and Tierney Bonnaire? To learn from them and be their child in every way possible, legally and emotionally?"

"Oh, yes. I do!" Stephanie took Giselle's and Tierney's hands in hers. "Your Honor," she added belatedly.

"Very good. Now I just need some signatures, and then the three of you can be on your way. Congratulations, Mrs. and Mrs. Bonnaire. You are adding a wonderful young lady to your family."

"We know, Your Honor," Giselle said. "We truly are the lucky ones."

"I think the three of you, or four," the judge added after looking at Charley, "are well suited to form a strong family unit. I wish you the very best."

They thanked Judge Donovan and left her office. After walking through the corridors, they stepped out into the beautiful spring weather. East Quay showed its best side, the air fresh and new leaves adorning trees and bushes. Stephanie hugged her mothers, uncertain how she would ever be able to repay them for giving her a true family. But as she looked into their respective smiling faces, it dawned on her that she didn't have to repay them at all.

That was what being a family unit was all about.

About the Author

Gun Brooke, author of more than twenty novels, resides in Sweden, surrounded by a loving family and two affectionate dogs. When she isn't writing her novels for Bold Strokes Books, she works on her art, and crafts, whenever possible—certain that practice pays off. Gun loves creating cover art for her own books and others using digital art software.

Web site http://www.gbrooke-fiction.com
Facebook: http://www.facebook.com/gunbach
Twitter : http://twitter.com/redheadgrrl1960
Tumblr :http://gunbrooke.tumblr.com/

Books Available from Bold Strokes Books

Alias by Cari Hunter. A car crash leaves a woman with no memory and no identity. Together with Detective Bronwen Pryce, she fights to uncover a truth that might just kill them both. (978-1-63555-221-8)

Death in Time by Robyn Nyx. Working in the past is hell on your future. (978-1-63555-053-5)

Hers to Protect by Nicole Disney. High school sweethearts Kaia and Adrienne will have to see past their differences and survive the vengeance of a brutal gang if they want to be together. (978-1-63555-229-4)

Of Echoes Born by 'Nathan Burgoine. A collection of queer fantasy short stories set in Canada from Lambda Literary Award finalist 'Nathan Burgoine. (978-1-63555-096-2)

Perfect Little Worlds by Clifford Mae Henderson. Lucy can't hold the secret any longer. Twenty-six years ago, her sister did the unthinkable. (978-1-63555-164-8)

Room Service by Fiona Riley. Interior designer Olivia likes stability, but when work brings footloose Savannah into her world and into a new city every month, Olivia must decide if what makes her comfortable is what makes her happy. (978-1-63555-120-4)

Sparks Like Ours by Melissa Brayden. Professional surfers Gia Malone and Elle Britton can't deny their chemistry on and off the beach. But only one can win... (978-1-63555-016-0)

Take My Hand by Missouri Vaun. River Hemsworth arrives in Georgia intent on escaping quickly, but when she crashes her Mercedes into the Clip 'n Curl, sexy Clay Cahill ends up rescuing more than her car. (978-1-63555-104-4)

The Last Time I Saw Her by Kathleen Knowles. Lane Hudson only has twelve days to win back Alison's heart. That is if she can gather the courage to try. (978-1-63555-067-2)

Wayworn Lovers by Gun Brooke. Will agoraphobic composer Giselle Bonnaire and Tierney Edwards, a wandering soul who can't remain in one place for long, trust in the passionate love destiny hands them? (978-1-62639-995-2)

Breakthrough by Kris Bryant. Falling for a sexy ranger is one thing, but is the possibility of love worth giving up the career Kennedy Wells has always dreamed of? (978-1-63555-179-2)

Certain Requirements by Elinor Zimmerman. Phoenix has always kept her love of kinky submission strictly behind the bedroom door and inside the bounds of romantic relationships, until she meets Kris Andersen. (978-1-63555-195-2)

Dark Euphoria by Ronica Black. When a high-profile case drops in Detective Maria Diaz's lap, she forges ahead only to discover this case, and her main suspect, aren't like any other. (978-1-63555-141-9)

Fore Play by Julie Cannon. Executive Leigh Marshall falls hard for Peyton Broader, her golf pro…and an ex-con. Will she risk sabotaging her career for love? (978-1-63555-102-0)

Love Came Calling by CA Popovich. Can a romantic looking for a long-term, committed relationship and a jaded cynic too busy for love conquer life's struggles and find their way to what matters most? (978-1-63555-205-8)

Outside the Law by Carsen Taite. Former sweethearts Tanner Cohen and Sydney Braswell must work together on a federal task force to see justice served, but will they choose to embrace their second chance at love? (978-1-63555-039-9)

The Princess Deception by Nell Stark. When journalist Missy Duke realizes Prince Sebastian is really his twin sister Viola in disguise, she plays along, but when sparks flare between them, will the double deception doom their fairy-tale romance? (978-1-62639-979-2)

The Smell of Rain by Cameron MacElvee. Reyha Arslan, a wise and elegant woman with a tragic past, shows Chrys that there's still beauty to embrace and reason to hope despite the world's cruelty. (978-1-63555-166-2)

The Talebearer by Sheri Lewis Wohl. Liz's visions show her the faces of the lost and the killers who took their lives. As one by one, the murdered are found, a stranger works to stop Liz before the serial killer is brought to justice. (978-1-635550-126-6)

White Wings Weeping by Lesley Davis. The world is full of discord and hatred, but how much of it is just human nature when an evil with sinister intent is invading people's hearts? (978-1-63555-191-4)

A Call Away by KC Richardson. Can a businesswoman from a big city find the answers she's looking for, and possibly love, on a small-town farm? (978-1-63555-025-2)

Berlin Hungers by Justine Saracen. Can the love between an RAF woman and the wife of a Luftwaffe pilot, former enemies, survive in besieged Berlin during the aftermath of World War II? (978-1-63555-116-7)

Blend by Georgia Beers. Lindsay and Piper are like night and day. Working together won't be easy, but not falling in love might prove the hardest job of all. (978-1-63555-189-1)

Hunger for You by Jenny Frame. Principe of an ancient vampire clan Byron Debrek must save her one true love from falling into the hands of her enemies and into the middle of a vampire war. (978-1-63555-168-6)

Mercy by Michelle Larkin. FBI Special Agent Mercy Parker and psychic ex-profiler Piper Vasey learn to love again as they race to stop a man with supernatural gifts who's bent on annihilating humankind. (978-1-63555-202-7)

Pride and Porters by Charlotte Greene. Will pride and prejudice prevent these modern-day lovers from living happily ever after? (978-1-63555-158-7)

Rocks and Stars by Sam Ledel. Kyle's struggle to own who she is and what she really wants may end up landing her on the bench and without the woman of her dreams. (978-1-63555-156-3)

The Boss of Her: Office Romance Novellas by Julie Cannon, Aurora Rey, and M. Ullrich. Going to work never felt so good. Three office romance novellas from talented writers Julie Cannon, Aurora Rey, and M. Ullrich. (978-1-63555-145-7)

The Deep End by Ellie Hart. When family ties become entangled in murder and deception, it's time to find a way out... (978-1-63555-288-1)

A Country Girl's Heart by Dena Blake. When Kat Jackson gets a second chance at love, following her heart will prove the hardest decision of all. (978-1-63555-134-1)

Dangerous Waters by Radclyffe. Life, death, and war on the home front. Two women join forces against a powerful opponent, nature itself. (978-1-63555-233-1)

Fury's Death by Brey Willows. When all we hold sacred fails, who will be there to save us? (978-1-63555-063-4)

It's Not a Date by Heather Blackmore. Kade's desire to keep things with Jen on a professional level is in Jen's best interest. Yet what's in Kade's best interest...is Jen. (978-1-63555-149-5)

Killer Winter by Kay Bigelow. Just when she thought things could get no worse, homicide Lieutenant Leah Samuels learns the woman she loves has betrayed her in devastating ways. (978-1-63555-177-8)

Score by MJ Williamz. Will an addiction to pain pills destroy Ronda's chance with the woman she loves or will she come out on top and score a happily ever after? (978-1-62639-807-8)

Spring's Wake by Aurora Rey. When wanderer Willa Lange falls for Provincetown B&B owner Nora Calhoun, will past hurts and a fifteen-year age gap keep them from finding love? (978-1-63555-035-1)

The Northwoods by Jane Hoppen. When Evelyn Bauer, disguised as her dead husband, George, travels to a Northwoods logging camp to work, she and the camp cook Sarah Bell forge a friendship fraught with both tenderness and turmoil. (978-1-63555-143-3)

Truth or Dare by C. Spencer. For a group of six lesbian friends, life changes course after one long snow-filled weekend. (978-1-63555-148-8)

A Heart to Call Home by Jeannie Levig. When Jessie Weldon returns to her hometown after thirty years, can she and her childhood crush Dakota Scott heal the tragic past that links them? (978-1-63555-059-7)

Children of the Healer by Barbara Ann Wright. Life becomes desperate for ex-soldier Cordelia Ross when the indigenous aliens of her planet are drawn into a civil war and old enemies linger in the shadows. Book Three of the Godfall Series. (978-1-63555-031-3)

Hearts Like Hers by Melissa Brayden. Coffee shop owner Autumn Primm is ready to cut loose and live a little, but is the baggage that comes with out-of-towner Kate Carpenter too heavy for anything long term? (978-1-63555-014-6)

Love at Cooper's Creek by Missouri Vaun. Shaw Daily flees corporate life to find solace in the rural Blue Ridge Mountains, but escapism eludes her when her attentions are captured by small town beauty Kate Elkins. (978-1-62639-960-0)

Somewhere Over Lorain Road by Bud Gundy. Over forty years after murder allegations shattered the Esker family, can Don Esker find the true killer and clear his dying father's name? (978-1-63555-124-2)

Twice in a Lifetime by PJ Trebelhorn. Detective Callie Burke can't deny the growing attraction to her late friend's widow, Taylor Fletcher, who also happens to own the bar where Callie's sister works. (978-1-63555-033-7)

Undiscovered Affinity by Jane Hardee. Will a no strings attached affair be enough to break Olivia's control and convince Cardic that love does exist? (978-1-63555-061-0)